Alfred Hitchcock's
DARING DETECTIVES

Alfred Hitchcock's

DARING
DETECTIVES

Illustrations by Arthur Shilstone

RANDOM HOUSE New York

The editor wishes to thank the following, for permission to reprint:

Brandt & Brandt for "The Day the Children Vanished" by Hugh Pentecost, first published in This Week Magazine. Copyright © 1958 by Hugh Pentecost.

The author's estate and the agents for the estate of Cornell Woolrich, Scott Meredith Literary Agency, Inc. for "Through A Dead Man's Eye," Copyright 1939, renewed 1967, by Cornell Woolrich.

Dodd, Mead & Company and Hughes Massie Limited for "The Disappearance of Mr. Davenheim" from *Poirot Investigates* by Agatha Christie. Copyright 1925 by Dodd, Mead & Company, Inc. Copyright renewed 1953 by Agatha Christie Mallowan.

Jennifer Palmer and the agents for the estate of Stuart Palmer, Scott Meredith Literary Agency, Inc. for "Green Ice," by Stuart Palmer, Copyright 1941 by Stuart Palmer; Copyright © renewed 1969 by Jennifer Palmer.

Paul R. Reynolds, Inc. for "The Grave Grass Quivers," Copyright 1931 by MacKinlay Kantor.

Collins-Knowlton-Wing, Inc. for "The Case of the Irate Witness," by Erle Stanley Gardner, Copyright © 1953 by Erle Stanley Gardner.

August Derleth for "The Adventure of the Grice-Paterson Curse," Copyright © 1956 by Star Editions, Inc. for *The Pursuit Detective Story Magazine,* November 1956.

Michael Gilbert, Harper & Row, and Curtis Brown Ltd. for "The Headmaster" from *Game Without Rules* by Michael Gilbert. Copyright © 1962 by Michael Gilbert. First published in the United States in Ellery Queen's Mystery Magazine under the title "Melodrama in Three Acts."

The author and the author's agents, Scott Meredith Literary Agency, Inc. for "The Adventure of the Seven Black Cats," by Ellery Queen. Copyright 1933, 1934, by Ellery Queen; Copyright renewed 1961.

Leslie Charteris for "The Wicked Cousin" from *The Happy Highwayman,* Copyright 1932 by Leslie Charteris.

David Higham Associates, Ltd. for "The Footprint in the Sky" from *The Department of Queer Complaints* by John Dickson Carr, Copyright 1940 by William Morrow & Company.

The editor gratefully acknowledges the invaluable assistance of Robert Arthur in the preparation of this volume.

If you're not in too much of a hurry—

Welcome, young readers! Those of you who have joined me before in these cozy collections of chills and suspense know that in earlier volumes I have explored various unusual fields to bring you exciting and absorbing stories.

In the past I have delved into the world of ghosts, haunts and apparitions of various types and differing degrees of spookiness. I have taken you into the shadowy world of the spies and counterspies who are so much a part of our life today. I have picked out my favorite spellbinders in sheer suspense to share with you. We have, in short, adventured into strange and colorful places together.

This time, though, we stand firmly on the side of the law. This is a collection of some of my favorite detective stories. In it we shall peer over the shoulders of many of fiction's finest detectives, to track down the malefactor and set wrong to right. We will pick up clues, solve tantalizing mysteries, and unravel riddles that seem impenetrable.

Ellery Queen is here, and Hercule Poirot of the little gray cells. Perry Mason is with us. The Saint puts in an appearance, a Robin Hood of crime impudently joining his more law-abiding companions. Hildegarde Withers, the spinster schoolma'rm who appeared in countless motion pictures, demonstrates her detective ability. Such masters of mystery as Cornell Woolrich, John Dickson Carr, Hugh Pentecost, and Michael Gilbert lend us their talents.

MacKinlay Kantor, famous for his serious novels, appears with us in one of his rare detective stories. And last, but not least, as a special treat I am including a detective who may seem oddly familiar to you, though the name is strange. Who exactly is Solar Pons, of "The Adventure of the Grice-Paterson Curse," and his companion, Dr. Parker? Surely they can't be—— No, no, they are not the Great Detective and his medical friend in disguise. They are instead two characters created with humble and admiring care by August Derleth to carry on a tradition known and loved by every reader of detective stories.

I believe you will find this group of stories as exciting, as engrossing, as any I have brought you. Now the game's a-foot and the chase is on! Turn the page and we'll be on our way.

ALFRED HITCHCOCK

Contents

Alfred Hitchcock's

DARING DETECTIVES

HUGH PENTECOST

The Day the Children Vanished

On a bright, clear winter's afternoon the nine children in the town of Clayton who traveled each day to the Regional School in Lakeview disappeared from the face of the earth, along with the bus in which they traveled and its driver, as completely as if they had been sucked up into outer space by some monstrous interplanetary vacuum cleaner.

Actually, in the time of hysteria which followed the disappearance, this theory was put forward by some distraught citizen of Clayton, and not a few people, completely stumped for an explanation, gave consideration to it.

There was, of course, nothing interplanetary or supernatural about the disappearance of nine children, one adult, and a special-bodied station wagon which was used as a school bus. It was the result of callous human villainy. But, because there was no possible explanation for it, it assumed all the aspects of black magic in the minds of tortured parents and a bewildered citizenry.

Clayton is seven miles from Lakeview. Clayton is a rapidly growing quarry town. Lakeview, considerably larger and with a long history of planning for growth, recently built a new school. It was agreed between the boards of education of the two towns that nine

children living at the east end of Clayton should be sent to the Lakeview School where there was adequate space and teaching staff. It was to be just a temporary expedient.

Since there were only nine children, they did not send one of the big, forty-eight-passenger school buses to get them. A nine-passenger station wagon was acquired, properly painted and marked as a school bus, and Jerry Mahoney, a mechanic in the East Clayton Garage, was hired to make the two trips each day with the children.

Jerry Mahoney was well liked and respected. He had been a mechanic in the Air Force during his tour of duty in the armed services. He was a wizard with engines. He was engaged to be married to Elizabeth Deering, who worked in the Clayton Bank and was one of Clayton's choice picks. They were both nice people, responsible people.

The disappearance of the station wagon, the nine children and Jerry Mahoney took place on a two-mile stretch of road where disappearance was impossible. It was called the "dugway," and it wound along the side of the lake. Heavy wire guard rails protected the road from the lake for the full two miles. There was not a gap in it anywhere.

The ground on the other side of the road rose abruptly upward into thousands of acres of mountain woodlands, so thickly grown that not even a tractor could have made its way up any part of it except for a few yards of deserted road that led to an abandoned quarry. Even over this old road nothing could have passed without leaving a trail of torn brush and broken saplings.

At the Lakeview end of the dugway was a filling station owned by old Jake Nugent. On the afternoon of the disappearance the bus, with Jerry Mahoney at the wheel and his carload of kids laughing and shouting at each other, stopped at old man Nugent's. Jerry Mahoney had brought the old man a special delivery letter from the post office, thus saving the RFD driver from making a special trip. Jerry and old Jake exchanged greetings, the old man signed the receipt for his letter—which was from his son in Chicago asking for a loan of fifty dollars—and Jerry drove off into the dugway with his cargo of kids.

At the Clayton end of the dugway was Joe Gorman's Diner, and one of the children in Jerry's bus was Peter Gorman, Joe's son. The Diner was Jerry's first stop coming out of the dugway with his cargo of kids.

It was four-thirty in the afternoon when Joe Gorman realized that the bus was nearly three-quarters of an hour late. Worried,

he called the school in Lakeview and was told by Miss Bromfield, the principal, that the bus had left on schedule.

"He may have had a flat, or something," Miss Bromfield suggested.

This was one of seven calls Miss Bromfield was to get in the next half hour, all inquiring about the bus. Nine children; seven families.

Joe Gorman was the first to do anything about it seriously. He called Jake Nugent's filling station to ask about the bus, and old Jake told him it had gone through from his place on schedule. So something had happened to Jerry and his busload of kids in the dugway. Joe got out his jeep and headed through the dugway toward Lakeview. He got all the way to Jake Nugent's without seeing the bus or passing anyone coming the other way.

Jake Nugent was a shrewd old gent, in complete possession of all his faculties. He didn't drink. When he said he had seen the bus—that it had stopped to deliver him his letter—and that he had watched it drive off into the dugway, you had to believe it. Cold sweat broke out on Joe Gorman's face as he listened. The dugway had a tendency to be icy. He had noticed coming over that it hadn't been sanded. Joe hadn't been looking for a major tragedy. But if the bus had skidded, gone through the guard rail . . .

He used Jake's phone to call the Dicklers in Clayton. The Dicklers' two children, Dorothy and Donald, were part of Jerry's load and they were the next stop after Joe's Diner. The Dicklers were already alarmed because their children hadn't appeared.

Joe didn't offer any theories. He was scared, though. He called the trooper barracks in Lakeview and told them about the missing bus. They didn't take it too seriously, but said they'd send a man out.

Joe headed back for Clayton. This time his heart was a lump in his throat. He drove slowly, staring at every inch of the wire guard rails. There was not a break anywhere, not a broken or bent post. The bus simply couldn't have skidded over the embankment into the lake without smashing through the wire guard rail.

Joe Gorman felt better when he came out at his diner at the Clayton end. He felt better, but he felt dizzy. Five minutes later Trooper Teliski came whizzing through from Lakeview and stopped his car.

"What's the gag?" he asked Joe.

Joe tried to light a cigarette and his hands were shaking so badly he couldn't make it. Teliski snapped on his lighter and held it out. Joe dragged smoke deep into his lungs.

"Look," he said. "The bus started through the dugway at the regular time." He told about Jerry's stop at Nugent's. "It never came out this end."

A nerve twitched in Teliski's cheek. "The lake," he said.

Joe shook his head. "I—I thought of that, right off. I just came through ahead of you—looking. Not a break in the guard rail anywhere. Not a scratch. Not a bent post. The bus didn't go into the lake. I'll stake my life on that."

"Then what else?" Teliski asked. "It couldn't go up the mountain."

"I know," Joe said, and the two men stared at each other.

"It's some kind of a joke," Teliski said.

"What kind of a joke? It's no joke to me—or the Dicklers. I talked to them."

"Maybe they had permission to go to a special movie or something," Teliski said.

"Without notifying the parents? Miss Bromfield would have told me, anyway. I talked to her. Listen, Teliski. The bus went into the dugway and it didn't come out. It's not in the dugway now, and it didn't go into the lake."

Teliski was silent for a moment, and then he spoke with a solid attempt at common sense. "It didn't come out this end," he said. "We'll check back on that guard rail, but let's say you're right. It didn't skid into the lake. It couldn't go up the mountain. So where does that leave us?"

"Going nuts!" Joe said.

"It leaves us with only one answer. The station wagon never went into the dugway."

Joe Gorman nodded. "That's logic," he said. "But why would Jake Nugent lie? Jerry's an hour and three-quarters late now. If he didn't go in the dugway, where is he? Where *could* he go? Why hasn't he telephoned if everything is okay?"

A car drove up and stopped. A man got out and came running toward them. It was Karl Dickler, father of two of the missing children. "Thank God you're here, Teliski. What's happened?"

"Some kind of a gag," Teliski said. "We can't figure it out. The bus never came through the dugway."

"But it did!" Karl Dickler said.

"It never came out this end," Joe Gorman said. "I was watching for Pete, naturally."

"But it did come through!" Dickler said. "I passed them myself on the way to Lakeview. They were about half a mile this way from

Jake Nugent's. I saw them! I waved at my own kids!"

The three men stared at each other.

"It never came out this end," Joe Gorman said, in a choked voice.

Dickler swayed and reached out to the trooper to steady himself. "The lake!" he whispered.

But they were not in the lake. Joe Gorman's survey proved accurate; no broken wire, no bent post, not even a scratch . . .

It was nearly dark when the real search began. Troopers, the families of the children, the selectmen, the sheriff and twenty-five or thirty volunteer deputies, a hundred or more school friends of the missing children.

The lake was definitely out. Not only was the guard rail intact, but the lake was frozen over with about an inch of ice. There wasn't a break in the smooth surface of the ice anywhere along the two miles of shore bordering the dugway.

Men and women and children swarmed through the woods on the other side of the road, knowing all the time it was useless. The road was called the "dugway" because it had been dug out of the side of the mountain. There was a gravel bank about seven feet high running almost unbrokenly along that side of the road. There was the one old abandoned trail leading to the quarry. It was clear, after walking the first ten yards of it, that no car had come that way. It couldn't.

A hundred phone calls were made to surrounding towns and villages. No one had seen the station wagon, the children or Jerry Mahoney. The impossible had to be faced.

The bus had gone into the dugway and it hadn't come out. It hadn't skidded into the lake and it hadn't climbed the impenetrable brush of the mountain. It was just gone! Vanished into thin air! . . .

Everyone was deeply concerned for and sympathetic with the Dicklers, and Joe Gorman, and the Williamses, the Trents, the Ishams, the Nortons, and the Jennings, parents of the missing children. Nobody thought much about Jerry Mahoney's family, or his girl.

It wasn't reasonable, but as the evening wore on and not one speck of evidence was found or one reasonable theory advanced, people began to talk about Jerry Mahoney. He was the driver. The bus had to have been driven somewhere. It couldn't navigate without Jerry Mahoney at the wheel. Jerry was the only adult involved. However it had been worked—this disappearance—Jerry must have had a hand in it.

It didn't matter that, until an hour ago, Jerry had been respected, trusted, liked. Their children were gone and Jerry had taken them somewhere. Why? Ransom. They would all get ransom letters in the morning, they said. A mass kidnaping. Jerry had the kids somewhere. There weren't any rich kids in Clayton so he was going to demand ransom from all seven families.

So Jerry Mahoney became a villain because there was no one else to suspect. Nobody stopped to think that Jerry's father and Jerry's girl might be as anxious about his absence as the others were about the missing children.

At nine-thirty Sergeant Mason and Trooper Teliski of the State Police, George Peabody, the sheriff, and a dozen men of the community including Joe Gorman and Karl Dickler stormed into the living room of Jerry Mahoney's house where an old man with silvery white hair sat in an overstuffed armchair with Elizabeth Deering, Jerry's fiancée, huddled on the floor beside him, her face buried on his knees, weeping.

The old man wore a rather sharply cut gray flannel suit, a bright scarlet vest with brass buttons and a green necktie that must have been designed for a St. Patrick's Day parade. As he stroked the girl's blond hair, the light from the lamp reflected glittering shafts from a square-cut diamond in a heavy gold setting he wore on his little finger. He looked up at Sergeant Mason and his small army of followers, and his blue eyes stopped twinkling as he saw the stern look on the Sergeant's face.

"All right, Pat," Sergeant Mason said. "What's Jerry done with those kids?" Pat Mahoney's pale blue eyes met the Sergeant's stare steadily. Then crinkles of mirth appeared at the corners of his eyes and mouth.

"I'd like to ask you something before I try to answer that," Pat Mahoney said.

"Well?"

"Have you stopped beating your wife, Sergeant?" Pat Mahoney asked. His cackle of laughter was the only sound in the room . . .

There are those who are old enough to remember the days when Mahoney and Faye were listed about fourth on a bill of eight star acts all around the Keith-Orpheum vaudeville circuit. Pat Mahoney was an Irish comic with dancing feet, and Nora Faye—Mrs. Mahoney to you—could match him at dancing and had the soprano voice of an angel.

Like so many people in show business, Pat was a blusterer, a boaster, a name dropper, but with it all a solid professional who would practice for hours a day to perfect a new routine, never missed an entrance in forty years, and up to the day young Jerry was born in a cheap hotel in Grand Rapids, Michigan, had given away half what he earned to deadbeats and hopeless failures.

The diamond ring he wore today had been in and out of a hundred hock shops. It had been the basis of his and Nora's security for more years than he liked to remember.

If you were left alone with Pat for more than five minutes, he went back to the old days—to the people he had idolized, like Sophie Tucker, and Smith and Dale, and Williams and Wolfus, and Joe Jackson. He'd known them all, played on the same bills with them all. "But," he would tell you, and a strange radiance would come into the pale blue eyes, "the greatest of them all was Nora Faye—Mrs. Mahoney to you."

Once he was started on his Nora, there was no way of stopping Pat Mahoney. He told of her talents as a singer and dancer, but in the end it was a saga of endless patience, of kindness and understanding, of love for a fat-headed, vain little Irish comic, of tenderness as a mother, and finally of clear-eyed courage in the face of stark tragedy.

Mahoney and Faye had never played the Palace, the Broadway goal of all vaudevillians. Pat had worked on a dozen acts that would crack the ice and finally he'd made it.

"We'd come out in cowboy suits, all covered with jewels, and jeweled guns, and jeweled boots, and we'd do a little soft shoe routine, and then suddenly all the lights would go out and only the jewels would show—they were made special for that—and we'd go into a fast routine, pulling the guns, and twirling and juggling them, and the roof would fall in! Oh, we tried it out of town, and our agent finally got us the booking at the Palace we'd always dreamed of."

There'd be a long silence then, and Pat would take a gaudy handkerchief from his hip pocket and blow his nose with a kind of angry violence. "I can show you the costumes still. They're packed away in a trunk in the attic. Just the way we wore them—me and Nora—the last time we ever played. Atlantic City it was. And she came off after the act with the cheers still ringing in our ears, and down she went on the floor of the dressing room, writhing in pain.

"Then she told me. It had been getting worse for months. She didn't want me to know. The doctor had told her straight out. She'd only a few months she could count on. She'd never said a word to me—working toward the Palace—knowing I'd dreamed of it. And only three weeks after that—she left us. Me and Jerry—she left us.

We were standing by her bed when she left—and the last words she spoke were to Jerry. 'Take care of Pat,' she says to him. 'He'll be helpless without someone to take care of him.' And then she smiled at me, and all the years were in that smile."

And then, wherever he happened to be when he told the story, Pat Mahoney would wipe the back of his hand across his eyes and say: "If you'll excuse me, I think I'll be going home. . . ."

Nobody laughed when Pat pulled the old courtroom wheeze about "have you stopped beating your wife" on Sergeant Mason. Pat looked past the Sergeant at Trooper Teliski, and Joe Gorman, and Karl Dickler, and Mr. and Mrs. Jennings, whose two daughters were in the missing bus, and George Peabody, the fat, wheezing sheriff.

"The question I asked you, Sergeant," he said, "makes just as much sense as the one you asked me. You asked me what Nora's boy has done with those kids. There's no answer to that question. Do I hear you saying, 'I know what you must be feeling, Pat Mahoney, and you, Elizabeth Deering? And is there anything we can do for you in this hour of your terrible anxiety?' I don't hear you saying that, Sergeant."

"I'm sorry, Pat," Mason said. "Those kids are missing. Jerry had to take them somewhere."

"No!" Liz Deering cried. "You all know Jerry better than that!"

They didn't, it seemed, but they could be forgiven. You can't confront people with the inexplicable without frightening them and throwing them off balance. You can't endanger their children and expect a sane reaction. They muttered angrily, and old Pat saw the tortured faces of Joe Gorman and Karl Dickler and the swollen red eyes of Mrs. Jennings.

"Has he talked in any way queerly to you, Pat?" Mason asked. "Has he acted normal of late?"

"Nora's boy is the most normal boy you ever met," Pat Mahoney said. "You know that, Sergeant. Why, you've known him since he was a child."

Mrs. Jennings screamed out: "He'd protect his son. Naturally he'd protect his son. But he's stolen our children!"

"The Pied Piper rides again," Pat Mahoney said.

"Make him talk!" Mrs. Jennings cried, and the crowd around her muttered louder.

"When did you last see Jerry, Pat?"

"Breakfast," Pat said. "He has his lunch at Joe Gorman's Diner."

The corner of his mouth twitched. "He should have been home for dinner long ago."

"Did he have a need for money?" Mason asked.

"Money? He was a man respected—until now—wasn't he? He was a man with a fine girl in love with him, wasn't he? What need would he have for money?"

"Make him answer sensibly!" Mrs. Jennings pleaded in a despairing voice.

Joe Gorman stepped forward. "Pat, maybe Jerry got sick all of a sudden. It's happened to men who saw action overseas. Maybe you saw signs of something and wouldn't want to tell of it. But my Pete was on that bus, and Karl's two, and Mrs. Jennings' two. We're nowhere, Pat—so if you can tell us anything! Our kids were on that bus!"

Pat Mahoney's eyes, as he listened to Joe Gorman, filled with pain. "My kid is on that bus, too, Joe," he said.

They all stared at him, some with hatred. And then, in the distance, they heard the wail of a siren. The troopers' car was coming from Lakeview.

"Maybe it's news!" someone shouted.

"News!"

And they all went stumbling out of the house to meet the approaching car—all but Elizabeth Deering, who stayed behind, clinging to the old man.

"I don't understand it," she said, her voice shaken. "They think he's harmed their children, Pat! Why? Why would they think he'd do such a thing? Why?"

Old Pat's eyes had a faraway look in them. "Did I ever tell you about The Great Thurston?" he asked. "Greatest magic act I ever saw."

"Pat!" Elizabeth said, her eyes widening in horror.

"First time I ever caught his act was in Sioux City," Pat said. "He came out in a flowing cape, and a silk hat, and he . . ."

Dear God, he's losing his reason, Elizabeth Deering told herself. Let the news be good! Let them be found safe!

Outside the siren drew close.

The police car with its wailing siren carried news, but it was not the sort the people of Clayton were hoping to hear.

It was reassuring to know that within a few hours of the tragedy the entire area was alerted, that the moment daylight came a fleet of army helicopters would cover the area for hundreds of miles

around, that a five-state alarm was out for the missing station wagon
and its passengers, and that the Attorney General had sent the best
man on his staff to direct and coördinate the search.

Top officials, viewing the case coldly and untouched by the
hysteria of personal involvement, had a theory. Of course there had
to be a rational explanation of the disappearance of the bus, and
Clyde Haviland, tall, stoop-shouldered, scholarly looking investigator from the Attorney General's office, was ordered to produce
that explanation as soon as possible upon his arrival in Clayton.
But beyond that, officials had no doubt as to the reason for the disappearance: this was a mass kidnaping; something novel in the
annals of crime.

Since none of the families involved had means, Haviland and
his superiors were convinced the next move in this strange charade
would be a demand on the whole community to pay ransom for the
children. The FBI was alerted to be ready to act the moment there
was any indication of involvement across state lines.

While mothers wept and the menfolk grumbled angrily that
Jerry Mahoney, the driver, was at the bottom of this, officialdom
worked calmly and efficiently. The Air Force turned over its complete data on Technical Sergeant Jerry Mahoney to the FBI. Men
who had known Jerry in the service were waked from their sleep
or pulled out of restaurants or theaters to be questioned. Had he
ever said anything that would indicate he might move into a world
of violence? Did his medical history contain any record of mental
illness?

Sitting at a desk in the town hall, Clyde Haviland reported on
some of this to George Peabody, the sheriff, the town's three selectmen, Sergeant Mason and a couple of other troopers. Haviland,
carefully polishing his shell-rimmed glasses, was a quiet, reassuring
sort of man. He had a fine reputation in the state. He was not an
unfamiliar figure to people in Clayton because he had solved a
particularly brutal murder in the neighboring town of Johnsville,
and his investigation had brought him in and out of Clayton for
several weeks.

"So far," he said, with a faint smile, "the report on Jerry Mahoney is quite extraordinary."

"In what way?" Sergeant Mason asked, eager for the scent of
blood.

"Model citizen," Haviland said. "No one has a bad word for
him. No bad temper. Never held grudges. Never chiseled. Saves
his money. His savings account in the Clayton bank would surprise

some of you. On the face of it, this is the last person in the world to suspect."

"There has to be a first time for everything," Karl Dickler said. He was a selectman as well as one of the bereaved parents.

"It's going down toward zero tonight," George Peabody, the sheriff, said, glumly. "If those kids are out anywhere——"

"They're a long way from here by now, if you ask me," Sergeant Mason said.

Haviland looked at him, his eyes unblinking behind the lenses of his glasses. "Except that they never came out of the dugway."

"Nobody saw them," Mason said. "But they're not there so they did come out."

"They didn't come out," Joe Gorman said. "I was watching for them from the window of my diner at this end."

"That was the three seconds you were getting something out of the icebox in your pantry," Mason said.

"And I suppose everyone else along Main Street had his head in a closet at just that time!" Joe Gorman said.

"Or someone reached down out of the heavens and snatched that station wagon up into space," Haviland said. He was looking at Peabody's pudgy face as he spoke, and something he saw there made him add quickly: "I'm kidding, of course."

Peabody laughed nervously. "It's the only good explanation we've had so far."

Karl Dickler put his hand up to his cheek. There was a nerve there that had started to twitch, regularly as the tick of a clock. "I like Jerry. I'd give the same kind of report on him you've been getting, Mr. Haviland. But you can't pass up the facts. I'd have said he'd defend those kids with his life. But did he? And the old man— his father. He won't answer questions directly. There's something queer about him. Mr. Haviland, my kids are—out there, some- where!" He waved toward the frost-coated window panes.

"Every highway within two hundred miles of here is being patrolled, Mr. Dickler," Haviland said. "If they'd driven straight away from here in daylight—granting Mason is right and every- body was in a closet when the station wagon went through town— they'd have been seen a hundred times after they left Clayton. There isn't one report of anyone having seen the station wagon with the school-bus markings." Haviland paused to light a cigarette. His tapering fingers were nicotine stained.

"If you'd ever investigated a crime, Mr. Dickler, you'd know we usually are swamped with calls from people who think they've seen the wanted man. A bus—a busload of kids. Somebody *had* to see it! But there isn't even a crackpot report. If there was some place he could have stayed under cover—and don't tell me, I know there isn't—and started moving after dark, he might get some distance. But alarms are out everywhere. He couldn't travel five miles now without being trapped."

"We've told ourselves all these things for hours!" Dickler said, pinching savagely at his twitching cheek. "What are you going to *do*, Haviland?"

"Unless we're all wrong," Haviland said, "we're going to hear from the kidnapers soon. Tonight—or maybe in the morning—by mail, or phone or in some unexpected way. But we'll hear. They'll demand money. What other purpose can there be? Once we hear, we'll have to start to play it by ear. That's the way those cases are."

"Meanwhile you just sit here and wait!" Dickler said, a kind of despair rising in his voice. "What am I going to say to my wife?"

"I think all the parents of the children should go home. You may be the one the kidnapers contact. It may be your child they put on the phone to convince you the kids are safe," Haviland said. "As soon as it's daylight——"

"You think the kids *are* safe?" Dickler cried out.

Haviland stared at the distraught father for a minute. Then he spoke, gently. "What kind of assurance could I give you, Mr. Dickler? Even if I tried, you wouldn't believe me. People who play this kind of game are without feelings, not rational. When you fight them, you have to walk quietly. If you scare them, God knows what to expect. That's why I urge you all to go home and wait." He dropped his cigarette on the floor and heeled it out. "And pray," he said . . .

Elizabeth Deering, Jerry Mahoney's girl, was sick with anxiety. Jerry was foremost in her mind; Jerry, missing with the children; Jerry, worse than that, suspected by his friends. But on top of that was old Pat Mahoney.

He hadn't made the slightest sense since the angry crowd had left his house. He had talked on endlessly about the old days in vaudeville. He seemed obsessed with the memory of the first time he had seen The Great Thurston in Sioux City. He remembered card tricks, and sawing the lady in half, and his wife Nora's childish delight in being completely bewildered. He seemed to remember everything he had seen the great man do.

Elizabeth tried, but she could not bring Pat back to the present. The tragedy seemed to have tipped him right out of the world of reason. She was partly relieved when she heard firm steps on the front porch. The other part of her, when she saw Sergeant Mason and the tall stranger, was the fear that they had news—bad news about Jerry.

Mason was less aggressive than he had been on his first visit. He introduced Haviland and said they wanted to talk to Pat. Elizabeth took them back into the living room where old Pat still sat in the overstuffed armchair.

Mason introduced Haviland. "Mr. Haviland is a special investigator from the Attorney General's office, Pat."

Pat's eyes brightened. "Say, you're the fellow that solved that murder over in Johnsville, aren't you?" he said. "Smart piece of work."

"Thanks," Haviland said. He looked at Pat, astonished at his gaudy vest and tie and the glittering diamond on his finger. He had been prepared for Pat, but not adequately.

"Sit down," Pat said. "Maybe Liz would make us some coffee if we asked her pretty."

Mason nodded to Liz, who went out into the kitchen. He followed her to tell her there was no news. Haviland sat down on the couch next to Pat, stretched out his long legs and offered Pat a cigarette.

"Don't smoke," Pat said. "Never really liked anything but cigars. Nora hated the smell of 'em. So what was I to do? You go to vaudeville in the old days, Mr. Haviland?"

"When I was a kid," Haviland said, lighting a cigarette. "I never had the pleasure of seeing you, though, Mr. Mahoney."

"Call me Pat," Pat said. "Everyone does. I was nothing, Mr. Haviland. Just a third-rate song-and-dance man. But Nora—well, if you ever saw my Nora . . ."

Haviland waited for him to go on, but Pat seemed lost in his precious memories.

"You must be very worried about your son, Pat," he said.

For a fractional moment the mask of pleasant incompetence seemed to be stripped from Pat's face. "Wouldn't you be?" he asked, harshly. Then, almost instantly, the mask was fitted back into place, and old Pat gave his cackling laugh. "You got theories, Mr. Haviland? How're you going to handle this case?"

"I think," Haviland said, conversationally, "the children and your son have been kidnaped. I think we'll hear from the kidnapers soon. I think, in all probability, the whole town will be asked to get up a large ransom."

Pat nodded. "I'll chip in this diamond ring," he said. "It's got

Jerry out of trouble more than once."

Haviland's eyes narrowed. "He's been in trouble before?"

"His main trouble was his Pop," Pat said. "Sometimes there wasn't enough to eat. But we could always raise eating money on this ring." He turned his bright, laughing eyes directly on Haviland. "You figured out how the bus disappeared?"

"No," Haviland said.

"Of course it doesn't really matter, does it?" Pat said.

"Well, if we knew——" Haviland said.

"It wouldn't really matter," Pat said. "It's what's going to happen now that matters."

"You mean the demand for money?"

"If that's what's going to happen," Pat said. The cackling laugh suddenly grated on Haviland's nerves. The old joker did know something!

"You have a different theory, Pat?" Haviland asked, keeping his exasperation out of his voice.

"You ever see The Great Thurston on the Keith-Orpheum circuit?" Pat asked.

"I'm afraid not," Haviland said.

"Greatest magic act I ever saw," Pat said. "Better than Houdini. Better than anyone. I first saw him in Sioux City——"

"About the case here, Pat," Haviland interrupted. "You have a theory?"

"I got no theory," Pat said. "But I know what's going to happen."

Haviland leaned forward. "What's going to happen?"

"One of two things," Pat said. "Everybody in this town is going to be looking for that station wagon in the lake, where they know it isn't and they're going to be looking for it in the woods, where they know it isn't. That's one thing that may happen. The other thing is, they buy this theory of yours, Mr. Haviland—and it's a good theory, mind you—and they all stay home and wait to hear something. There's one same result from both things, isn't there?"

"Same result?"

"Sure. Nobody in Clayton goes to work. The quarries don't operate. The small businesses will shut down. People will be looking and people will be waiting . . ."

"So?"

"So what good will that do anyone?" Pat asked.

Haviland ground out his cigarette in an ash tray. "It won't do anyone any good. The quarry owners will lose some money. The small businesses will lose some money."

"Not much point in it, is there?" Pat said, grinning.

Haviland rose. He'd had about enough. Mason and Elizabeth were coming back from the kitchen with coffee. "There isn't much point to anything you're saying, Mr. Mahoney."

Pat's eyes twinkled. "You said you never saw The Great Thurston, didn't you?"

"I never saw him," Haviland said.

"Well, we'll see. If they're supposed to stay home and wait, they'll stay home and wait. If they're supposed to be out searching, they'll be out searching. Ah, coffee! Smells real good. Pull up a chair, Sergeant. By the way, Mr. Haviland, I'll make you a bet," Pat said.

"I'm not a betting man," Haviland said.

"Oh, just a manner-of-speaking bet," Pat said. "I'll make you a bet that tomorrow morning they'll be out searching. I'll make you a bet that even if you order them to stay home and wait, they'll be out searching."

"Look here, Pat, if you know something . . ."

A dreamy look came into Pat's eyes. "Nora was so taken with The Great Thurston that time in Sioux City I went around to see him afterwards. I thought maybe he'd show me how to do a few simple tricks. I pretended it was for Nora, but really I thought we might use 'em in our act. He wouldn't tell me anything—that is, not about any of his tricks. But he told me the whole principle of his business."

"Sugar?" Elizabeth asked Haviland. Poor old man, she thought.

"The principle is," Pat said, "to make your audience think only what you want them to think, and see only what you want them to see." Pat's eyes brightened. "Which reminds me, there's something I'd like to have you see, Mr. Haviland."

Haviland gulped his coffee. Somehow he felt mesmerized by the old man. Pat was at the foot of the stairs, beckoning. Haviland followed.

Elizabeth looked at Mason and there were tears in her eyes. "It's thrown him completely off base," she said. "You know what he's going to show Mr. Haviland?" Sergeant Mason shook his head.

"A cowboy suit!" Elizabeth said, and dropped down on the couch, crying softly. "He's going to show him a cowboy suit."

And she was right. Haviland found himself in the attic, his head bowed to keep from bumping into the sloping beams. Old Pat had opened a wardrobe trunk and, with the gesture of a waiter taking the silver lid off a tomato surprise, revealed two cowboy suits, one hanging neatly on each side of the trunk—Nora's and his. Chaps, shirt, vest, boots, Stetsons, and gun belts—all studded with stage jewelry.

". . . and when the lights went out," Pat was saying, "all you could see was these gewgaws, sparkling. And we'd take out the guns . . ." And suddenly Pat had the two jeweled six-shooters in his hands, twirling and spinning them. "In the old days I could draw these guns and twirl 'em into position faster than Jesse James!"

The spell was broken for Haviland. The old guy was cuckoo. "I enjoyed seeing them, Mr. Mahoney," he said. "But now, I'm afraid I've got to get back . . ."

As soon as dawn broke, Haviland had Sergeant Mason and Sheriff George Peabody take him out to the scene of the disappearance. Everyone else was at home, waiting to hear from the kidnapers. It had been a terrible night for the whole town, a night filled with forebodings and dark imaginings. Haviland covered every inch of the two-mile stretch of the dugway. You couldn't get away from the facts. There was no way for it to have happened—but it had happened.

About eight-thirty he was back in Clayton in Joe's Diner, stamping his feet to warm them and waiting eagerly for eggs and toast to go with his steaming cup of black coffee. All the parents had been checked. There'd been no phone calls, no notes slipped under doors, nothing in the early-morning mail.

Haviland never got his breakfast. Trooper Teliski came charging into the diner just as Joe Gorman was taking the eggs off the grill. Teliski, a healthy young man, was white as parchment, and the words came out of him in a kind of choking sob. "We've found 'em," he said. "Or at least we know where they are. Helicopters spotted 'em. I just finished passing the word in town."

Joe Gorman dropped the plate of eggs on the floor behind the counter. Haviland spun around on his counter stool. Just looking at Teliski made the hair rise on the back of his neck.

"The old quarry off the dugway," Teliski said, and gulped for air. "No sign of the bus. It didn't drive up there. But the kids." Teliski steadied himself on the counter. "Schoolbooks," he said. "A couple of coats—lying on the edge of the quarry. And in the quarry—more of the same. A red beret belonging to one of the kids——"

"Peter!" Joe Gorman cried out.

Haviland headed for the door. The main street of Clayton was frightening to see. People ran out of houses, screaming at one another, heading crazily toward the dugway. Those who went for their cars scattered the people in front of them. There was no order—only blind panic.

Haviland stood on the curb outside the diner, ice in his veins. He looked down the street to where old Pat Mahoney lived, just in time to see a wildly weeping woman pick up a stone and throw it through the front window of Pat's house.

"Come on—what's the matter with you?" Teliski shouted from behind the wheel of the State Police car.

Haviland stood where he was, frozen, staring at the broken window of Pat Mahoney's house. The abandoned quarry, he knew, was sixty feet deep, full to within six feet of the top with icy water fed in by constantly bubbling springs.

A fire engine roared past. They were going to try to pump out the quarry. It would be like bailing out the Atlantic Ocean with a tea cup.

"Haviland!" Teliski called desperately.

Haviland still stared at Pat Mahoney's house. A cackling old voice rang his ears. "I'll make you a bet, Mr. Haviland. I'll make you a bet that even if you order them to stay at home and wait, they'll be out searching."

Rage such as he had never known flooded the ice out of Haviland's veins. So Pat had known! The old codger had known *last night!*

Haviland had never witnessed anything like the scene at the quarry.

The old road, long since overgrown, which ran about 200 yards in from the dugway to the quarry, had been trampled down as if by a herd of buffalo.

Within three-quarters of an hour of the news reaching town, it seemed as if everyone from Clayton and half the population of Lakeview had arrived at the quarry's edge.

One of the very first army helicopters which had taken to the air at dawn had spotted the clothes and books at the edge of the abandoned stone pit.

The pilot had dropped down close enough to identify the strange objects and radioed immediately to State Police. The stampede had followed.

Haviland was trained to be objective in the face of tragedy, but he found himself torn to pieces by what he saw. Women crowded forward, screaming, trying to examine the articles of clothing and books. Maybe not all the children were in this icy grave. It was only the hope of desperation. No one really believed it. It seemed, as Trooper Teliski had said, to be the work of a maniac.

Haviland collected as many facts about the quarry as he could from a shaken Sheriff Peabody.

"Marble's always been Clayton's business," Peabody said. "Half the big buildings in New York have got their marble out of Clayton quarries. This was one of the first quarries opened up by the Clayton Marble Company nearly sixty years ago. When they started up new ones, this one was abandoned."

In spite of the cold, Peabody was sweating. He wiped the sleeve of his plaid hunting shirt across his face. "Sixty feet down, and sheer walls," he said. "They took the blocks out at ten-foot levels, so there is a little ledge about every ten feet going down. A kid couldn't climb out of it if it was empty."

Haviland glanced over at the fire engine which had started to pump water from the quarry. "Not much use in that," he said.

"The springs are feeding it faster than they can pump it out," Peabody said. "There's no use telling them. They got to feel they're doing something." The fat sheriff's mouth set in a grim slit. "Why would Jerry Mahoney do a thing like this? *Why?* I guess you can only say the old man is a little crazy, and the son has gone off his rocker too."

"There are some things that don't fit," Haviland said. He noticed his own hands weren't steady as he lit a cigarette. The hysterical shrieking of one of the women near the edge of the quarry grated on his nerves. "Where is the station wagon?"

"He must have driven up here and—and done what he did to the kids," Peabody said. "Then waited till after dark to make a get-away."

"But you searched this part of the woods before dark last night," Haviland said.

"We missed it somehow, that's all," Peabody said, stubbornly.

"A nine-passenger station wagon is pretty hard to miss," Haviland said.

"So we missed it," Peabody said. "God knows how, but we missed it." He shook his head. "I suppose the only thing that'll work here is grappling hooks. They're sending a crane over from one of the active quarries. Take an hour or more to get it here. Nobody'll leave here till the hooks have scraped the bottom of that place and they've brought up the kids."

Unless, Haviland thought to himself, the lynching spirit gets into

them. He was thinking of an old man in a red vest and a green necktie and a diamond twinkling on his little finger. He was thinking of a broken window pane—and of the way he'd seen mobs act before in his time.

Someone gripped the sleeve of Haviland's coat and he looked down into the horror-struck face of Elizabeth Deering, Jerry Mahoney's girl.

"It's true then," she whispered. She swayed on her feet, holding tight to Haviland for support.

"It's true they found some things belonging to the kids," he said. "That's all that's true at the moment, Miss Deering." He was a little astonished by his own words. He realized that, instinctively, he was not believing everything that he saw in front of him. "This whole area was searched last night before dark." he said. "No one found any schoolbooks or coats or berets then. No one saw the station wagon."

"What's the use of talking that way?" Peabody said. His eyes were narrowed, staring at Liz Deering. "I don't want to believe what I see either, Mr. Haviland. But I got to." The next words came out of the fat man with a bitterness that stung like a whiplash. "Maybe you're the only one in Clayton that's lucky, Liz. You found out he was a homicidal maniac in time—before you got married to him."

"Please, George!" the girl cried. "How can you believe——"

"What can anyone believe but that?" Peabody said, and turned away.

Liz Deering clung to Haviland, sobbing. The tall man stared over her head at the hundreds of people grouped around the quarry's edge. He was reminded of a mine disaster he had seen once in Pennsylvania: a whole town waiting at the head of the mine shaft for the dead to be brought to the surface.

"Let's get out of here," he said to Liz Deering, with sudden energy . . .

Clayton was a dead town. Stores were closed. Joe's Diner was closed. The railroad station agent was on the job, handling dozens of telegrams that were coming in from friends and relatives of the parents of the missing children. The two girls in the telephone office, across the street from the bank, were at their posts.

Old Mr. Granger, a teller in the bank, and one of the stenographers were all of the bank staff that had stayed on the job. Old Mr. Granger was preparing the payroll for the Clayton Marble Company. He didn't know whether the truck from the company's offices with the two guards would show up for the money or not.

Nothing else was working on schedule today. Even the hotel down the street had shut up shop. One or two salesmen had driven into town, heard the news, and gone off down the dugway toward the scene of the tragedy. A few very old people tottered in and out the front doors of houses, looking anxiously down Main Street toward the dugway. Even the clinic was closed. The town's doctors and nurses had all gone to the scene of the disaster.

Down the street a piece of newspaper had been taped over the hole in Pat Mahoney's front window. Pat Mahoney sat in the big overstuffed armchair in his living room. He rocked slowly back and forth, staring at an open scrapbook spread across his knees. A big black headline from a show-business paper was pasted across the top.

MAHONEY AND FAYE
BOFFO BUFFALO

Under it were pictures of Pat and Nora in their jeweled cowboy suits, their six-shooters drawn, pointing straight at the camera. There was a description of the act, the dance in the dark with only the jewels showing and the six-shooters spouting flame. "Most original number of its kind seen in years," a Buffalo critic had written. "The ever popular Mahoney and Faye have added something to their familiar routines that should please theater audiences from coast to coast. We are not surprised to hear that they have been booked into the Palace."

Pat closed the scrapbook and put it down on the floor beside him. From the inside pocket of his jacket he took a wallet. It bulged with papers and cards. He was an honorary Elk, honorary police chief of Wichita in 1927, a Friar, a Lamb.

Carefully protected by an isinglass guard were some snapshots. They were faded now, but anyone could see they were pictures of Nora with little Jerry at various stages of his growth. There was Jerry at six months, Jerry at a year, Jerry at four years. And Nora, smiling gently at her son. The love seemed to shine right out of the pictures, Pat thought.

Pat replaced the pictures and put the wallet back in his pocket. He got up from his chair and moved toward the stairway. People who knew him would have been surprised. No one had ever seen Pat when his movements weren't brisk and youthful. He could still go into a tap routine at the drop of a hat, and he always gave the impression that he was on the verge of doing so. Now he moved slowly, almost painfully—a tired old man, with no need to hide it from anyone. There was no one to hide it from; Jerry was missing, Liz was gone.

He climbed to the second floor and turned to the attic door. He opened it, switched on the lights, and climbed up to the area under the eaves. There he opened the wardrobe trunk he'd shown to Haviland. From the left side he took out the cowboy outfit—the chaps, the boots, the vest and shirt and Stetson hat, and the gun belt with the two jeweled six-shooters. Slowly he carried them down to his bedroom on the second floor. There Pat Mahoney proceeded to get into costume.

He stood, at last, in front of the full-length mirror on the back of the bathroom door. The high-heeled boots made him a couple of inches taller than usual. The Stetson was set on his head at a rakish angle. The jeweled chaps and vest glittered in the sunlight from the window. Suddenly old Pat jumped into a flat-footed stance, and the guns were out of the holsters, spinning dizzily and then pointed straight at the mirror.

"Get 'em up, you lily-livered rats!" old Pat shouted. A bejeweled gunman stared back at him fiercely from the mirror.

Then, slowly, he turned away to a silver picture frame on his bureau. Nora, as a very young girl, looked out at him with her gentle smile.

"It'll be all right, honey," Pat said. "You'll see. It'll be another boffo, honey. Don't you worry about your boy. Don't you ever worry about him while I'm around. You'll see."

It was a terrible day for Clayton, but Gertrude Naylor, the chief operator in the telephone office, said afterward that perhaps the worst moment for her was when she spotted old Pat Mahoney walking down the main street—right in the middle of the street—dressed in that crazy cowboy outfit. He walked slowly, looking from right to left, staying right on the white line that divided the street.

"I'd seen it a hundred times before in the movies," Gertrude Naylor said, afterward. "A cowboy, walking down the street of a deserted town, waiting for his enemy to appear—waiting for the moment to draw his guns. Old Pat's hands floated just above those crazy guns in his holster, and he kept rubbing the tips of his fingers against his thumb. I showed him to Millie, and we started to laugh, and then, somehow, it seemed about the most awful thing of all. Jerry Mahoney had murdered those kids and here was his old man, gone nutty as a fruitcake."

Old Mr. Granger, in the bank, had much the same reaction when the aged, bejeweled gun toter walked up to the teller's window.

"Good morning, Mr. Granger," Pat said, cheerfully.

Mr. Granger moistened his pale lips. "Good morning, Pat."

"You're not too busy this morning, I see," Pat said.

"N-no," Mr. Granger said. The killer's father—dressed up like a kid for the circus. He's ready for a padded cell, Mr. Granger thought.

"Since you're not so busy," Pat said, "I'd like to have a look at the detailed statement of my account for the last three months." As he spoke, he turned and leaned against the counter, staring out through the plate-glass bank window at the street. His hands stayed near the guns, and he kept rubbing his fingertips against the ball of his thumb.

"You get a statement each month, Pat," Mr. Granger said.

"Just the same, I'd like to see the detailed statement for the last three months," Pat said.

"I had to humor him, I thought," Mr. Granger said later. "So I went back in the vault to get his records out of the files. Well, I was just inside the vault door when he spoke again, in the most natural way. 'If I were you, Mr. Granger,' he said, 'I'd close that vault door, and I'd stay inside, and I'd set off all the alarms I could lay my hands on. You're about to be stuck up, Mr. Granger.'

"Well, I thought it was part of his craziness," Mr. Granger said, later. "I thought he meant *he* was going to stick up the bank. I thought that was why he'd got all dressed up in that cowboy outfit. Gone back to his childhood, I thought. I was scared, because I figured he was crazy. So I *did* close the vault door. And I *did* set off the alarm, only it didn't work. I didn't know then all the electric wires into the bank had been cut."

Gertrude and Millie, the telephone operators, had a box seat for the rest of it. They saw the black sedan draw up in front of the bank and they saw the four men in dark suits and hats get out of it and start up the steps of the bank. Two of them were carrying small suitcases and two of them were carrying guns.

Then suddenly the bank doors burst open and an ancient cowboy appeared, hands poised over his guns. He did a curious little jig step that brought him out in a solid square stance. The four men were so astonished at the sight of him they seemed to freeze.

"Stick 'em up, you lily-livered rats!" old Pat shouted. The guns were out of the holsters, twirling. Suddenly they belched flame, straight at the bandits.

The four men dived for safety, like men plunging off the deck of a sinking ship. One of them made the corner of the bank building.

Two of them got to the safe side of the car. The fourth, trying to scramble back into the car, was caught in the line of fire.

"I shot over your heads that first time!" Pat shouted. "Move another inch and I'll blow you all to kingdom come!" The guns twirled again and then suddenly aimed steadily at the exposed bandit. "All right, come forward and throw your guns down," Pat ordered.

The man in the direct line of fire obeyed at once. His gun bounced on the pavement a few feet from Pat and he raised his arms slowly. Pat inched his way toward the discarded gun.

The other men didn't move. And then Gertrude and Millie saw the one who had gotten around the corner of the bank slowly raise his gun and take deliberate aim at Pat. She and Millie both screamed, and it made old Pat jerk his head around. In that instant there was a roar of gunfire.

Old Pat went down, clutching at his shoulder. But so did the bandit who'd shot him and so did one of the men behind the car. Then Gertrude and Millie saw the tall figure of Mr. Haviland come around the corner of the hotel next door, a smoking gun in his hand. He must have spoken very quietly because Gertrude and Millie couldn't hear him, but whatever he said made the other bandits give up. Then they saw Liz Deering running across the street to where old Pat lay, blood dripping through the fingers that clutched at his shoulder . . .

Trooper Teliski's car went racing through the dugway at breakneck speed, siren shrieking. As he came to the turn-in to the old quarry, his tires screamed and he skidded in and up the rugged path, car bounding over stones, ripping through brush. Suddenly just ahead of him on the path loomed the crane from the new quarry, inching up the road on a caterpillar tractor. Trooper Teliski sprang out of his car and ran past the crane, shouting at the tractor driver as he ran.

"Never mind with that!" Teliski shouted. Stumbling and gasping for breath, he raced out into the clearing where hundreds of people waited in a grief-stricken silence for the grappling for bodies to begin.

"Everybody!" Teliski shouted. "Everybody! Listen!" He was half laughing, half strangling for breath. "Your kids aren't there! They're safe. They're all safe—the kids, Jerry Mahoney, everyone! They aren't here. They'll be home before you will! Your kids——" And then he fell forward on his face, sucking in the damp, loam-scented air.

Twenty minutes later Clayton was a mad house. People running, people driving, people hanging onto the running boards of cars and clinging to bumpers. And in the middle of the town, right opposite the bank, was a station wagon with a yellow school bus sign on its roof, and children were spilling out of it, waving and shouting at their parents, who laughed and wept. And a handsome young Irishman with bright blue eyes was locked in a tight embrace with Elizabeth Deering . . .

Haviland's fingers shook slightly as he lit a cigarette. Not yet noon and he was on his third pack.

"You can't see him yet," he said to Jerry Mahoney. "The doctor's with him. In a few minutes."

"I still don't get it," Jerry said. "People thought *I* had harmed those kids?"

"You don't know what it's been like here," Liz Deering said, clinging tightly to his arm.

Jerry Mahoney turned and saw the newspaper taped over the broken front window, and his face hardened. "Try and tell me, plain and simple, about Pop," he said.

Haviland shook his head, smiling like a man still dazed. "Your Pop is an amazing man, Mr. Mahoney," he said. "His mind works in its own peculiar ways . . . The disappearance of the bus affected him differently from some others. He saw it as a magic trick, and he thought of it as magic trick—or, rather, as *part* of a magic trick. He said it to me and I wouldn't listen. He said it is a magician's job to get you to think what he wants you to think and see what he wants you to see. The disappearance of the children, the ghastly faking of their death in the quarry—it meant one thing to your Pop, Mr. Mahoney. Someone wanted all the people in Clayton to be out of town. Why?

"There was only one good reason that remarkable Pop of yours could think of. The quarry payroll. Nearly a hundred thousand dollars in cash, and not a soul in town to protect it. Everyone would be looking for the children, and all the bandits had to do was walk in the bank and take the money. No cops, no nothing to interfere with them."

"But why didn't Pop tell you his idea?" Jerry asked.

"You still don't know what it was like here, Mr. Mahoney," Haviland said. "People thought you had done something to those kids; they imagined your Pop knew something about it. If he'd told his story, even to me, I think I'd have thought he was either touched in the head or covering up. So he kept still—although he did throw me a couple of hints. And suddenly, he was, to all intents and purposes, alone in the town. So he went upstairs, got dressed in those cowboy clothes and went, calm as you please, to the bank to meet the bandits he knew must be coming. And they came."

"But why the cowboy suit?" Liz Deering asked.

"A strange and wonderful mind," Haviland said. "He thought the sight of him would be screwy enough to throw the bandits a little off balance. He thought if he started blasting away with his guns they might panic. They almost did."

"What I don't understand," Liz said, "is how, when he fired straight at them, he never hit anybody!"

"Those were stage guns—prop guns," Jerry said. "They only fire blanks."

Haviland nodded. "He thought he could get them to drop their own guns and then he'd have a real weapon and have the drop on them. It almost worked. But the one man who'd ducked around the corner of the building got in a clean shot at him. Fortunately, I arrived at exactly the same minute, and I had them all from behind."

"But how did you happen to turn up?" Jerry asked.

"I couldn't get your father out of my mind," Haviland said. "He seemed to know what was going to happen. He said they'd be searching for the kids, whether I told them to wait at home or not. Suddenly I had to know why he'd said that."

"Thank God," Jerry said. "I gather you got them to tell you where we were?"

Haviland nodded. "I'm still not dead clear how it worked, Jerry."

"It was as simple as pie à la mode," Jerry said. "I was about a half mile into the dugway on the home trip with the kids. We'd just passed Karl Dickler headed the other way when a big trailer truck loomed up ahead of me on the road. It was stopped, and a couple of guys were standing around the tail end of it.

"Broken down, I thought. I pulled up. All of a sudden guns were pointed at me and the kids. They didn't talk much. They just said to do as I was told. They opened the back of the big truck and rolled out a ramp. Then I was ordered to drive the station wagon right up into the body of the truck. I might have tried to make a break for it except for the kids. I drove up into the truck, they closed up the rear end, and that was that. They drove off with us—right through the main street of town here!"

Haviland shook his head. "An old trick used hundreds of times back in bootleg days. And I never thought of it!"

"Not ten minutes later," Jerry went on, "they pulled into that big deserted barn on the Haskell place. We've been shut up there ever since. They were real decent to the kids—hot dogs, ice cream cones, soda.

"So we just waited there, not knowing why, but nobody hurt, and the kids not as scared as you might think," Jerry laughed. "Oh, we came out of the dugway all right—and right by everybody in town. But nobody saw us."

The doctor appeared in the doorway. "You can see him for a minute now, Jerry," he said. "I had to give him a pretty strong sedative. Dug the bullet out of his shoulder and it hurt a bit. He's pretty sleepy —but he'll do better if he sees you, I think. Don't stay too long, though."

Jerry bounded up the stairs and into the bedroom where Pat Mahoney lay, his face very pale, his eyes half closed. Jerry knelt by the bed.

"Pop," he whispered. "You crazy old galoot!"

Pat opened his eyes. "You okay, Jerry?"

"Okay, Pop."

"And the kids?"

"Fine. Not a hair of their heads touched." Jerry reached out and covered Pat's hand with his. "Now look here, Two-Gun Mahoney . . ."

Pat grinned at him. "It was a boffo, Jerry. A real boffo."

"It sure was," Jerry said. He started to speak, but he saw that Pat was looking past him at the silver picture frame on the dresser.

"I told you it'd be all right, honey," Pat whispered. "I told you not to worry about your boy while I was around to take care of him." Then he grinned at Jerry, and his eyes closed and he was asleep.

Jerry tiptoed out of the room to find his own girl.

CORNELL WOOLRICH

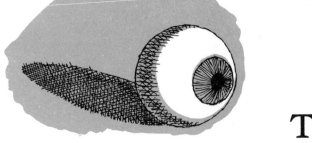

Through a Dead Man's Eye

The idea in swapping is to start out with nothing much and run it up to something. I started out with a buckle without a tongue and a carved peach pit, that day, and swapped it to a kid named Miller for a harmonica that somebody had stepped on. Then I swapped that to another kid for a penknife with one blade missing. By an hour after dark, I had run my original capital up to a baseball with its outside cover worn off, so I figured I'd put in a pretty good afternoon. Of course, I should have been indoors long before then, but swapping takes time and makes you cover a lot of ground.

I was just in the middle of a deal with the Scanlon kid, when I saw my old man coming. He was still a block away, but he was walking fast like when he's sore, and it's hard to use good business judgment when you're being rushed like that. I guess that's why I let Scanlon high-pressure me into swapping for a piece of junk like he had. It was just somebody's old cast-off glass eye, that he must have picked up off some ash heap.

"You got a nerve!" I squalled. But I looked over my shoulder and I saw Trouble coming up fast, so I didn't have much time to be choosy.

Scanlon knew he had me. "Yes or no?" he insisted.

"All right, here goes," I growled, and I passed him the peeled baseball, and he passed me the glass eye.

That was about all I had time for before Trouble finally caught up with me. I got swung around in the direction in which I live, by the back of the neck, and I started to move over the ground fast—but only about fifty percent under my own speed. I didn't mind that, only people's Old Men always have to make such long speeches about everything. I don't know why.

"Haven't I got troubles enough of my own," he said, "without having to go on scouting expeditions looking for you all over the neighborhood every time I get home? Your mother's been hanging out the window calling you for hours. What time d'ye think it is, anyway?" And all that kind of stuff. I got it for five solid blocks, all the way back to our house, but I just kept thinking about how I got swindled just now, so I got out of having to hear most of it.

I'd never seen him so grouchy before. At least not since that time I busted the candy-store window. Most times when he had to come after me like this, he'd take a lick at the bat himself, if we were playing baseball for instance, and then wink at me and only pretend to bawl me out in front of Ma when we got back. He said he could remember when he was twelve himself, and that shows how good he was, because twenty-three years is a pretty long time to remember, let me tell you. But tonight it was the McCoy. Only I could tell it wasn't me he was sore at so much, it was something else entirely.

By the time we got through supper my mother noticed it too. "Frank," she said after a while, "what's eating you? There's something troubling you, and you can't fool me."

He was drawing lines on the tablecloth with the back of his fork. "I've been demoted," he said.

Like a fool I had to butt in right then, otherwise I could have listened to some more. "What's demoted mean, Pop?" I said. "Is it like when you're put back in school? How can they do that to you, Pop?"

Ma said, "Frankie, you go inside and do your homework!"

Just before I closed the door I heard her say, kind of scared, "You haven't been put back into blues, Frank, have you?"

"No," he said, "but it might just as well have been that."

When they came out after a while they both looked kind of downhearted. They forgot I was in there or else didn't notice me reading *Black Mask* behind my geography book. She said, "I guess now we'll have to move out of here."

"Yeah, there's a big difference in the salary."

I pricked up my ears at that. I didn't want to have to move away from here, especially since I was marbles champion of the block.

"What hurts most about it," he said, "is I know they couldn't find a thing against me on my record. I'm like a burnt sacrifice, the captain practically admitted as much. Whenever the Commissioner gets these brain waves about injecting more efficiency into the division, somebody has to be made the goat. He calls that getting rid of the deadwood. If you haven't cracked six cases in a row single-handed, you're deadwood."

"Well," she said, "maybe it'll blow over and they'll reinstate you after a while."

"No," he said, "the only thing that'll save me is a break of some kind, a chance to make a big killing. Once the order goes through, I won't even be on Homicide any more. What chance'll I have then, running in lush-workers and dips? What I need is a flashy, hard-to-crack murder case."

Gee, I thought, I wish I knew where there was one, so I could tell him about it. What chance did a kid like me have of knowing where there was a murder case—at least that no one else knew about and he could have all to himself? I didn't even know how to begin to look for one, except behind billboards and in vacant lots and places, and I knew there wouldn't be any there. Once in a while you found a dead cat, that was all.

Next morning I waited until Ma was out of the room, and I asked him, "Pop, how does somebody know when a murder case has happened?"

He wasn't paying much attention. "Well, they find the body, naturally."

"But suppose the body's been hidden some place where nobody knows about it, then how do they know there was a murder case?"

"Well, if somebody's been missing, hasn't been seen around for some time, that's what first starts them looking."

"But suppose no one even tells 'em somebody's missing, because nobody noticed it yet, *then* how would they know where to look?"

"They wouldn't, they'd have to have some kind of a clue first. A clue is some little thing, any little thing, that don't seem to belong where it's found. It's tough to explain, Frankie; that's the best I can do. It could be some little thing belonging to someone, but the person it belongs to isn't around; then you wonder why he isn't, and what it's doing where you found it instead of where it ought to be."

Just then Ma came back in again, so he said, "You quit bothering your head about that stuff, and stick to your school work. That last report you brought back wasn't so hot, you know." And then he said, more to himself than to me, "One flop in the family is enough."

Gee, it made me feel bad to hear him say that. Ma must have heard him, too. I saw her rest her hand on his shoulder, and kind of push down hard, without saying anything.

I looked the Scanlon kid up after school that afternoon, to ask him about that eye I'd traded off him the night before. It was about the only thing I had in the way of a clue and I couldn't help wondering. . . .

I took it out and looked it over, and I said, "Scanny, d'you suppose anyone ever *used* this? I mean, really wore it in his puss?"

"I dunno," he said. "I guess somebody musta when it was new; that's what they're made for."

"Well, then, why'd he quit using it, why'd he throw it away?"

"I guess he got a new one, that's why he didn't want the old one no more."

"Naw," I said, "because once you've got one of these, you don't need another, except only if it cracks or breaks or something." And we could both see this wasn't cracked or chipped or anything. "A guy can't see through one of these even when it's new; he just wears it so people won't know his own is missing," I explained. "So why should he change it for a new one, if it's still good?"

He scratched his head without being able to answer. And the more I thought about it, the more excited I started to get.

"D'you suppose something *happened* to the guy that used to own it?" I whispered. I really meant did he suppose the guy that used to own it had been murdered, but I didn't tell him that because I was afraid he'd laugh at me. Anyway, I couldn't figure out why anybody would want to swipe a man's glass eye, even if they did murder him, and then throw it away.

I remembered what my old man had said that morning. A clue is any little thing that don't seem to belong where it's found. If this wasn't a clue, then what was? Maybe I could help him. Find out about somebody being murdered, that nobody else even knew about yet, and tell him about it, and then he could get re—whatever that word was I'd heard him and her use.

But before I could find out who it belonged to, I had to find out where it came from first. I said, "Whereabouts did you find it, Scan?"

"I didn't find it," he said. "Who tole you I found it? I swapped it off a guy, just like you swapped it off me."

"Who was he?"

"How do I know? I never seen him before. Some kid that lives on the other side of the gas works, down in the tough part of town."

"Let's go over there, try and find him. I want to ask him where *he* got it."

"Come on," he said, "I bet I can show him to you easy. He was a little bit of a runt. He was no good at swapping, either. I cleaned him just like I cleaned you. That's why he had to go inside his father's store and bring out this peeper. He didn't have anything else left."

I got sort of disappointed. Maybe this wasn't the right kind of a clue after all. "Oh, does his father sell them kind of glims in his store?"

"Naw, he presses pants."

I got kind of relieved again. Maybe it still was a useful clue.

When we got over there on the other side of the gas works, Scanny said, "Here's where I swapped him. I don't know just where his father's store is, but it must be around here some place, because it didn't take him a minute to go back for that glim." He went as far as the corner and looked down the next street, and then he said, "I see him! There he is!" And he stretched his mouth wide and let out a pip of a whistle.

A minute later a dark, undersized kid came around the corner. The minute he saw Scanlon he started to argue with him. "You gotta gimme that thing back I took out of the shop yesterday. My father walloped me for picking it up off the ironing board. He says maybe the customer'll come back and ask fer it, and what'll he tell him?"

"Where'd it come from?" I butted in. I tried to sound tough like I imagined my old man did when he questioned suspects.

"I should know. It came out of one of the suits that was brought in to be cleaned."

"From the pocket?"

"Naw. It was sticking in one of the cuffs on the bottom of his pants. They were wide open and needed basting."

"In the *cuff!*" Scanlon piped up. "Gee, that's a funny place to go around carrying a glass eye in!"

"He didn't know it was down there," I said impatiently. "It musta bounced in without his knowing it, and he brought the suit over to be pressed, and it stayed in there the whole time."

"Aw, how could that happen?"

"Sure it could happen. Once my father dropped a quarter, and he never heard it hit the floor; he looked all over for it and couldn't find it. Then when he was taking his pants off that night, it fell out of the cuff. He carried it around with him all day long and never knew it."

Even the tailor's kid backed me up in this. "Sure," he said, "that could happen. Sometimes a thing rolls around to the back where the cuff is tacked up, and the stitching holds it in. People have different ways of taking their pants off; I've watched it in my father's shop when they're getting a fitting. If they pull them off by the bottom, like most do, that turns them upside down, and if something was caught in the cuff it falls out again. But if they just let them fall down flat by their feet and step out of them, it might still stay in, like this did." He was a smart kid all right, even if his old man was just a tailor and not a detective. I had to hand it to him.

I thought to myself: The only way a thing like that could fall into a man's trouser cuff without him seeing it would be from low down, like if the owner was lying flat on the floor around his feet and he was bending over him shaking him or something. That made it seem like maybe I *could* dig up a murder in this and help my old man after all. But I had to find out where that eye came from.

I said to the tailor's kid, "Do you think this guy'll come back, that left the suit?" If he'd really murdered someone, maybe he wouldn't. But then if he wasn't coming back, he didn't have to leave the suit to be cleaned in the first place, so that showed he probably was.

"My father promised it for him by tonight," he said.

I wondered if there was any blood on it. I guessed not, or the guy wouldn't have left it with a tailor. Maybe it was some other kind of a murder, where there wasn't any blood spilled. I said, "Can we come in and look at it?"

Again his shoulder went way up. "It's just a suit," he said. "Didn't you ever see a suit before? All right, come in if you gotta look at it."

We went around the corner and into his father's shop. It was a little dinky place, down in the basement like most of them are. His father was a short little guy, not much taller than me and Scanlon. He was raising a lot of steam from running a hot iron over something.

"This is it, here," the kid said, and he picked up the sleeve of a gray suit hanging there on a rack with two or three others. The cuff had a little scrap of paper pinned to it: "Paulsen—75¢."

"Don't any address go with it?" I said.

"When it's called for and delivered, an address. When it's brought in and left to be picked up, no address, just the name."

His father noticed us handling the suit just then and he got sore all of a sudden and came running at us waving his hands, with the hot iron still left in one. He probably wasn't going to hit us with it, he just forgot to put it down, but it was no time to wait and find out. He hollered, "Keep your hands off those cleaning jobs, you hear me? What you want here? Outside!"

When we quit running, outside the door, and he turned back and went in again, I said to Sammy, that was this kid's name, "You want these five immies I got with me?"

He looked them over. They weren't as good as some of my others, but they were probably better than he was used to. "Why should I say no?" he said.

"All right, then here's what you gotta do. When the customer that left that suit comes in to get it, you tip us off. We'll be waiting down at the corner."

"What do you want from him?" he asked.

"This feller's father is a—" Scanlon started to say. I just kicked him in time, so he'd shut up.

"We're just playing a game," I changed it to. I was afraid if we told him, he'd tell his father the first thing, and then his father would probably tell the customer.

"Some game!" he said disgustedly. "All right, when he comes I'll tell you."

He went back inside the shop and we hung around there waiting by the corner. This was about half-past four. At half-past six it was all dark, and we were still waiting there. Scanlon kept wanting to give up and go home. "All right, no one's keeping you here," I told him. "You go home. I'm staying until that guy shows up. I don't care if it takes all night. You can't expect a civilian to show as much forty-tude as a police officer."

"You're not a police officer," he grumbled.

"My father is, so that makes me practic'ly as good as one." I had him there, so he shut up and stuck around.

The thing was, I had to go home for supper sooner or later. I couldn't just stay out and keep watch, or I'd get the tar bawled out of me. And I knew he had to, too.

"Look," I said, "you stay here and keep watching for Sammy's signal. I'll beat it back and get my mother to feed me fast. Then I'll come back here again and relieve you, and you can go back to your house and eat. That way we'll be sure of not missing him if he shows up."

"Will they let you out at night during school?" he asked.

"No, but I'll slip out without them knowing it. If the man calls for his suit before I get back, follow him wherever he goes, and then come back and meet me here and tell me where it is."

I ran all the way back to our house, and I told Ma I had to eat right away. She said, "What's your hurry?"

I explained. "Well, we got an awful important exam coming up tomorrow and I gotta study hard tonight."

She looked at me kind of suspicious and even felt my forehead to see if I was running a temperature. "You're actually *worried* about an exam?" she said. "Well, you may as well eat now. Your poor father's way out at the ends of the earth; he won't be home until all hours."

I could hardly wait until I got through but then I always eat fast so she didn't notice much difference. Then I grabbed up my books for a bluff and said, "I'm going to study upstairs in my room, it's quieter."

As soon as I got up there I locked the door and then I opened the window and got down to the ground easy by way of that old tree. I'd done it plenty of times before. I ran all the way back to where Scan was waiting.

"He didn't come yet," he said.

"All right, now it's your turn," I told him. Parents are an awful handicap when you're working on a case. I mean, a detective shouldn't have to run home to meals right in the middle of something important. "Come back as soon as you get through," I warned him, "if you want to be in on this."

But he didn't. I found out later he got caught trying to sneak out.

Well, I waited and I waited and I waited, until it was almost ten o'clock. It looked like he wasn't coming for that suit any more tonight, but as long as there was still a light showing in Sammy's father's shop I wasn't going to give up. Once a cop came strolling by and looked me over, like he wondered what a kid my age was doing standing so still by himself on a corner, and I just about curled up and died, but all he said was, "Whaddye say, son?" and went on his way.

While I was standing there hoping the cop wouldn't come back, Sammy, the tailor's kid, suddenly came up to me in the dark when I least expected it. "What's the matter with you, didn't you see me calling you with my hand?" he said. "That guy just come in for his suit."

I saw someone come up the steps out of the shop just then, with a folded suit slung over his arm; he turned and went up the street the other way.

"That's him. Now gimme the marbles you said."

I spilled them into his hand with my eyes on the guy's back. Even from the back he didn't look like a guy to monkey around with. "Did your old man say anything to him about the eye that popped out of his cuff?" I asked Sammy.

"Did he ask us? So why should we tell him? In my father's business anything that ain't missed, we don't know nothing about."

"Then I guess I'll just keep that old glass eye."

The guy was pretty far down the street by now, so I started after him without waiting to hear any more. I was kind of scared, because now there was a grownup in it, not just kids any more. I was wishing Scan had come back, so I'd have him along with me. But then I thought maybe it was better he hadn't. The man might notice two kids following him quicker than he would just one.

He kept on going, until we were clear over in a part of town I'd never been in before. He was hard to keep up with, he walked fast and he had longer legs than me. Sometimes I'd think I'd lost him, but the suit over his arm always helped me pick him up again. I think without it I would have lost him sure.

Some of the streets had only about one light on them every two blocks, and between lights they were as black as the dickens. I didn't like the kind of people that seemed to live around here either. One time I nearly bumped into a funny thin man hugging a doorway and wiping his hand under his nose like he had a cold.

I couldn't figure out why, if he lived this far away from Sammy's father's shop, the man with the suit had to come all this way over just to leave it to be cleaned. There must have been other tailors that were nearer. I guess he did it so he'd be sure the tailor wouldn't know who he was or where he lived. That looked like he had something to be careful about, didn't it?

Finally the lights got a little better again, and it was a good thing they did; by that time I was all winded, and my left shoe was starting to develop a bad squeak. I could tell ahead of time he was going to look back, by the way he slowed up a little and his shoulders started to turn around. I ducked down quick behind an ashcan standing on the sidewalk. A grownup couldn't have hidden behind it, but it hid me all over.

I counted ten and then I peeked around it. He was on his way again, so I stood up and kept going myself. He must have stopped and looked back like that because he was getting close to where he lived and he wanted to make sure no one was after him. But, just the same, I wasn't ready for him when he suddenly turned into a doorway and disappeared. I was nearly a block behind him, and I ran like anything to get down there on time, because I couldn't tell from where I'd been just which one of them it was. There were three or four of them that were alike.

The entrances had inside doors, and whichever one he'd just opened had finished closing already, and I couldn't sneak in the hall and listen to hear if the stairs were creaking under him or not. There were names under the letter boxes, but I didn't have any matches and there were no lights outside the doors, so I couldn't tell what they were.

Another thing, if he went that far out of his way to have a suit cleaned, he wouldn't give his right name on that little scrap of paper that was pinned to the sleeve.

Suddenly I got a bright idea. If he lived in the back of the house it wouldn't work, but maybe he had a room in the front. I backed up all the way across to the other side of the street and stood watching to see if any window would light up. Sure enough one did a minute or two later, a dinky one way up on the top floor of the middle house. I knew that must be his because no one else had gone in there just now.

Right while I was standing there he came to the window and looked down, and caught me staring square up at him with my head way back. This was one time I couldn't move quick enough to get out of sight. He stared down at me hard, without moving. I got the funniest creepy feeling, like I was looking at a snake or something and couldn't move. Finally I turned my head away as if I hadn't been doing anything, and stuck my hands in my pockets, and shuffled off whistling, as if I didn't know what to do with myself.

Then when I got a little further away, I walked faster and faster, until I'd turned the corner out of sight. I didn't dare look back, but something told me he'd stayed up there at that window the whole time looking after me.

It was pretty late, and this was miles from my own part of town, and I knew I'd better be getting back and put off anything else until tomorrow. At least I'd found out which house he lived in—305 Decatur St. I could come tomorrow with Scanny.

I got back into my room from the outside without any trouble, but Ma sure had a hard time getting me up for school the next morning.

Scanlon and I got together the minute of three, and we left our books in our school lockers and started out right from there, without bothering to go home first. I told him what I'd found out. Then I said, "We'll find out this guy's name first, and then we'll find out if there's anyone living around there who has a glass eye, and who hasn't been seen lately."

"Who'll we ask?"

"Who do you ask when you want to find out anything? The janitor."

"But suppose he don't want to tell us? Some people don't like to answer questions asked by kids."

I chopped my hand at his arm and said, "I just thought of a swell way! Wait'll we get there. I'll show you."

When we got there I took him across the street first and showed him the window. "That's it, up there on the top floor of the middle house."

We went over and started looking under the letter boxes in the vestibule for his name. I don't think we would have found it so easy, it was hard to tell just which name went with which flat, only I happened to notice one that was a lot like the one he left his suit under at the tailor's: Petersen. "That must be it," I told Scanny. "He just changed the first part of it."

"What do we do now?" he said.

I pushed the bell that said Janitor. "Now watch," I said, "how I get it out of him."

He was a cranky old codger. "What you boys want?" he barked.

I said, "We been sent over with a message for somebody that lives in this house, but we forgot the name. He's got a glass eye."

He growled, "There's nobody here got a glass eye!"

"Maybe we got the wrong number. Is there anybody around here in the whole neighborhood got a glass eye?"

"Nobody! Now get out of here. I got vurk to do!"

We drifted back to the corner and hung around there feeling kind of disappointed. "It didn't get us nothing," I said. "If no one in his house has one, and if no one in the neighborhood has one, where'd he get it from?"

Scanlon was beginning to lose interest. "Aw, this ain't fun no more," he said. "Let's go back and dig up a game of—"

"This isn't any game," I told him severely. "I'm doing this to help my old man. You go back if you want to. I'm going to keep at it. He says what every good detective has to have is preservance."

"What's 'at, some kind of a jam?" he started to ask, but all of a sudden I saw something and jumped out of sight around the corner.

"Here's that guy now!" I whispered. "He just came out of the house."

We got down in back of a stoop. There were plenty of people all around us, but nobody paid any attention to us. They thought we were just kids playing a game, I guess.

A minute later this Petersen got to the corner and stood there. I peeked up and got a good look at his face. It was just a face, it didn't look any different from anybody else's. I'd thought until now maybe a murderer ought to have a special kind of a face, but I'd never asked my old man about that, so I wasn't sure. Maybe they didn't, or maybe this guy wasn't a murderer after all, and I was just wasting a lot of good ball time prowling around after him.

He looked around a lot, like he wanted to make sure nobody was noticing him, and then he finally stepped down off the curb, crossed over, and kept going straight along Decatur Street.

"Let's follow him, see where he goes," I said. "I think he saw me last night from the window, and he might remember me, so here's how we better do it. You follow him, and then I'll follow you. I'll stay way back where he can't see me, and just keep you in sight."

We tried that for a while, but all of a sudden I saw Scanlon just standing there waiting for me ahead. "What'd you give up for?" I said when I got to him. "Now you lost him."

"No, I didn't. He just went in there to get somep'n to eat. You can see him sitting in there."

He was sitting in a place with a big glass front, and he was facing our way, so we had to get down low under it and just stick the tops of our heads up. We waited a long time. Finally I said. "He oughta be through by now," and I took another look. He was still just sitting there, with that same one cup still in front of him. "He ain't eating," I told Scanlon, "he's just killing time."

"What do you suppose he's waiting for?"

"Maybe he's waiting for it to get dark." I looked around, and it pretty nearly was already. "Maybe he's going some place that he don't want to go while it's still light, so no one can see him."

Scanlon started to scuff his feet around on the sidewalk like he was getting restless. "I gotta get back soon or I'll catch it," he said. "I'm in Dutch already for trying to sneak out last night."

"Yeah, and then when you do go back," I told him bitterly, "you'll get kept in again like last night. You're a heck of a guy to have for a partner!"

"No, tonight I can make it," he promised. "It's Thursday, and Ma wants to try for a new set of dishes at the movies."

"All right, get back here fast as you can. And while you're there, here's what you do. Call up my house and tell my mother I'm stay-ing for supper at your house. If she asks why, tell her we both got so

much studying to do we decided to do it together. That way I won't
have to leave here. This guy can't sit in there forever, and I want to
find out where he goes when he does come out. If I'm not here when
you come back, wait for me right here, where it says 'Joe's Coffee
Spot'."

He beat it for home fast and left me there alone. Just as I thought,
he wasn't gone five minutes when the guy inside came out, so I was
glad one of us had waited. I flattened myself into a doorway and
watched him around the corner of it.

It was good and dark now, like he wanted it to be, I guess, and he
started up the street in the same direction he'd been going before—
away from that room he lived in. I gave him a half a block start, and
then I came out and trailed after him. We were pretty near the edge
of town now, and big openings started to show between houses, then
pretty soon there were more open places than houses, and finally
there weren't any more houses at all, just lots, and then fields, and
further ahead some trees.

The street still kept on, though, and once in a while a car would
come whizzing by, coming in from the country. He would turn his
face the other way each time one did, I noticed, like he didn't want
them to get a look at him.

That was one of the main things that kept me going after him. He
hadn't been acting right ever since I first started following him the
night before away from the tailor shop. He was too watchful and
careful, and he was always looking around too much, like he was
afraid of someone doing just what I was doing. People don't walk
that way unless they've done something they shouldn't.

I couldn't stay up on the road out here, because there was no one
else on it but him and me and he would have seen me easy. But there
were a lot of weeds and things growing alongside of it, and I got off
into them and kept going with my back bent even with the tops of
them. When they weren't close together I had to make a quick dive
from one clump to the next.

Just before he got to where the trees started in, he kind of slowed
down, like he wasn't going very much further. I looked all around,
but I couldn't see anything, only some kind of old frame house
standing way back off the road. It didn't have any lights and didn't
look like anyone lived in it. It was a spooky kind of a place if there
ever was one, and I sure hoped he wasn't going anywhere near *there*.

But it looked like he was, only he didn't go straight for it. First he
looked both ways, up and down the road, and saw there was no one
around—or thought there wasn't. Then he twisted his head and

listened, to make sure no car was coming just then. Then he took a quick jump that carried him off the road into the darkness. But I could still see him a little, because I knew where he'd gone in.

Then, when he'd gotten over to where this tumbledown house was, he went all around it first, very carefully, like he wanted to make sure there was no one hiding in it waiting to grab him. Luckily there were plenty of weeds and bushes growing all around, and it was easy to get up closer to him.

When he'd gotten back around to the front again, and decided there was no one in it—which I could have told him right from the start just by the looks of it—he finally got ready to go in. It had a crazy kind of a porch with a shed over it, sagging way down in the middle between the two posts that held it. He went in under that, and I could hardly see him any more, it was so dark.

I heard him fiddling around with something that sounded like a lock, and then the door wheezed, and scraped back. There was a white something on the porch and he picked it up and took it in with him.

He left the door open a crack behind him, like he was coming out again soon, so I knew enough not to sneak up on the porch and try to peep in. It would have squeaked under me, anyway. But I moved over a little further in the bushes, where I could get a better line on the door. A weak light came on, not a regular light, but a match that he must have lit there on the other side of the door. But I've got good eyes and it was enough to show me what he was doing. He was picking up a couple of letters that the postman must have shoved under the bottom of the door. He looked at them, and then he seemed to get sore. He rolled them up into a ball with one hand and pitched them way back inside the house. He hadn't even opened them, just looked at the outside.

His match burned out, but he lit another, only this time way back inside some place where I couldn't see him. Then that one went out too, and a minute later the door widened a little and he edged out again as quietly as he'd gone in. He put something down where he'd taken that white thing up from. Then he closed the door real careful after him, looked all around to make sure no one was in sight, and came down off the porch.

I was pretty far out in front of the door, further than I had been when he went in. But I had a big bush to cover me, and I tucked my head down between my knees and made a ball out of myself, to make myself as small as I could, and that was about the sixteenth time he'd missed seeing me. But I forgot about my hand. It was sticking out flat against the ground next to me, to help me balance myself.

He came by so close his pants leg almost brushed my cheek. Just then a car came by along the road, and he stepped quickly back so he wouldn't be seen. His whole heel came down on two of my fingers.

All I could remember was that if I yelled I would be a goner. I don't know how I kept from it. It felt like a butcher's cleaver had chopped the fingers off. My eyes got all full of water, mixed with stars. He stayed on my hand maybe half a minute, but it seemed like an hour. Luckily the car was going fast, and he moved forward again. I managed to hold out without moving until he got out to the road.

Then I rolled over on my face, buried it with both arms, and bawled good and hard, but without making any noise. By the time I got that out of my system, it didn't hurt so much any more.

Then I sat up and thought things over, meanwhile blowing on my fingers to cool them. He'd gone back along the road toward the built-up part of town. I didn't know whether to keep on following him or not. If he was only going back where he came from, there didn't seem to be any sense to it, I knew where that was already. I knew he didn't live here in this house; people don't live in two places at once.

What did he want out here then? What had he come here for? He'd acted kind of sore, the way he looked over those letters and then balled them up and fired them down. Like they weren't what he wanted, like he'd had the trouble of coming all the way out here for nothing. He must be waiting for a letter, a letter that hadn't come yet. I decided to stick around and find out more about this house if I could.

Well, I waited until I couldn't hear him walking along the road any more, then I got up and sneaked up on the porch myself. That thing he had put down outside the door was only an empty milk bottle, like people leave for the milkman to take away with him when he brings the new milk. So that white thing he had picked up at first must have been the same bottle, but with the milk still in it. He must have just taken it in and emptied it out.

What did he want to do a thing like that for? He hadn't been in there long enough to drink it. He just threw it out, and then brought the empty bottle outside again. That showed two things. If the milk-man left milk here, then there was supposed to be somebody living here. But if this guy emptied the bottle out, that showed there wasn't anyone living here any more, but he didn't want the milkman or the mailman or anyone else to find out about it yet.

My heart started to pick up speed, and I got all gooseflesh and

I whispered to myself: "Maybe he murdered the guy that lives here, and nobody's found out about it yet! I bet that's what it is! I bet *this* is where that eye came from!" The only catch was, why did he keep coming back here afterwards, if he did? The only thing I could figure out was he must want some letter that he knew was going to show up here, but it hadn't come yet, and he kept coming back at nights to find out if it had been delivered. And maybe the whole time there was someone dead inside there. . . .

I kept saying to myself, "I'm going in there and see if there is. I can get in there easy, even if the door is locked." But for a long time I didn't move.

Finally I said to myself like this: "It's only a house. What can a house do to you? Just shadows and emptiness can't hurt you. And even if there is somebody lying dead in there, dead people can't move any more. You're not a kid any more you're twelve years and five months old, and besides, your old man needs help. If you go in there you might find out something that'll help him."

I tried the door first, but like I'd thought, it was locked, so I couldn't get in that way. Then I walked slowly all around the outside of the house trying all the windows one after the other. They were up higher than my head, but the clapboards stuck out in lots of places and it was easy to get a toe hold on them and hoist myself up. That wouldn't work either. They were all latched or nailed down tight on the inside.

Finally I figured I might be able to open one of the top-floor windows, so I went around to the front again, spat on my hands, and shinnied up one of the porch posts. There were some old vine stalks twisted around them, so it was pie getting up. It was so old the whole thing shook bad, but I didn't weigh much, so nothing happened.

I started tugging at one of the windows. It was hard to get it started because it hadn't been opened in so long, but I kept at it, and finally it jarred up. The noise kind of scared me, but I swallowed hard and stuck my legs inside and slid into the room. The place smelled stuffy, and cobwebs tickled my face, but I just brushed them off.

I couldn't see much, just the gray where the walls were and the black where the door was. A grownup would have had matches, but I had to use my hands out in front of me to tell where I was going.

I didn't bump into anything much, because I guess the upstairs rooms were all empty and there was nothing to bump into. But the floorboards cracked and grunted under me. I had a narrow escape from falling all the way down the stairs and maybe breaking my neck, because they came sooner than I thought they would. After that I went good and easy, tried out each one with my toe first to make sure it was there before I trusted my whole foot down on it. It took a long time getting down that way, but at least I got down in one piece. Then I started for where I thought the front door was. I wanted to get out.

I don't know what mixed me up, whether there was an extra turn in the stairs that I didn't notice in the dark, or I got my directions balled up by tripping a couple of times over empty boxes and picking myself up again. Anyway I kept groping in what I thought was a straight line out from the foot of the stairs, until I came up against a closed door. I thought it was the front door to the house, of course. I tried it, and it came right open. That should have told me it wasn't, because I'd seen him lock it behind him when he left.

The air was even worse on the other side of it than on my side, all damp and earthy like when you've been burrowing under the ground, and it was darker than ever in front of me, so I knew I wasn't looking out on the porch. Instead of backing up I took an extra step through it, just to make sure what it was, and this time I did fall—and, boy, how I fell! Over and over, all the way down a steep flight of brick steps that hurt like anything every time they hit me.

The only thing that saved me was that at the bottom I landed on something soft. Not real soft like a mattress, but kind of soft and at the same time stiff, if you know what I mean. At first I thought it was a bag of some kind, filled with sawdust.

I was just starting to say to myself, "It's a good thing that was there!" when I put out my hand to brace myself for getting up on my feet again, and all of a sudden I turned to ice all over.

My hand had landed right on top of another hand—like it was waiting there to meet it! It wasn't warm and soft like a hand, it felt more like a stiff leather glove that's been soaked in water, but I knew what it was all right. It went on up into a shoulder, and that went up into a neck, and that ended in a head.

I gave a yell, and jumped about a foot in the air and landed further over on another part of the floor. Then I started scrambling around on my hands and knees to get out of there fast.

I couldn't get at the stairs again without stepping over it at the foot of them, and that kept me there a minute or two longer, until I had time to talk to myself. And I had to talk good and hard, believe me.

"He's murdered, because when dead people die regular they're buried, not left to lie at the bottom of cellar steps. So you see, that Petersen *did* murder someone, just like you been suspecting for two whole days. And instead of being scared to death, you ought to be glad you found him, because now you *can* help your old man just like you wanted to. Nobody knows about this yet, not even the milkman or the mailman, and he can have it all to himself."

That braced me up a lot. I wiped the wet off my forehead, and I pulled my belt over to the fourth notch, which was the last one there was on it. Then I got an idea how I could look at him and make sure he was murdered. I didn't have any matches, but he was a grownup even if he was dead, and he just might have one in—in his pocket.

I started to crawl straight back *toward* him, and when I got there I clenched my teeth together real hard and reached out one hand for about where his pocket ought to be. It shook so, it was no good by itself, but I steadied it by holding it with the other hand, and got it in. Then I had to go around to the other side of him and try that one. He had three matches in there, those long kind. My hand got caught getting it out, and I nearly went crazy for a minute, but I finally pulled the pocket off it with my other hand, and edged back.

Then I scraped one of the matches along the floor. His face was the first thing I saw. It was all wrinkled and dry-like, and it had four black holes in it, one more than it should have. The mouth was a big wide hole, and the nostrils of the nose were two small ones, and then there was another under one eyelid, or at least a sort of a hollow place that was just like a hole. He'd worn a glass eye in that socket, and it was the very one I had in my pocket that very minute. I could see now how he'd come to lose it.

He'd been choked to death with an old web belt, from behind when he wasn't looking. It was still around his neck, so tight and twisted you would have had to cut through it to get it off. It made his other eye, which was a real one, stand out all swollen like it was ready to pop out. And I guess that was what really did happen with the fake one. It got loose and dropped out while he was still struggling down on the floor between the murderer's spread legs, and jumped into his trouser-cuff without him even seeing it. Then, when it was over, he either didn't notice it was missing from the dead man's face, or else thought it had rolled off into a corner and was lying there. Instead it was in the cuff of the suit he had cleaned to make sure it wouldn't have any suspicious dirt or stains on it.

The match was all the way down to my fingertips by now, so I had to blow it out. It had told me all it could. It didn't tell me who the dead old man was, or why that Petersen fellow had killed him.

Or what he was after that made him come back again like that. I crept up the brick cellar steps in the dark, feeling like I could never again be as scared as I had been when I first felt that other hand under mine. I was wrong, wait'll you hear.

I found my way back to the front door without much trouble. The real front door, this time. Then I remembered the two letters I'd seen him crumple and throw away. They might tell me who the dead man was. I had to light one of the two matches I had left to look for them, but the door had no glass in it, just a crack under it, and Petersen must be all the way back in town by now, so I figured it was safe if I didn't keep it lit too long.

I found them right away, and just held the match long enough to smooth them out and read who they were sent to. The dead old man was Thomas Gregory, and that road out there must still be called Decatur Street even this far out, because they said: 1017 Decatur Street. They were just ads. One wanted to know if he wanted to buy a car, the other one wanted to know if he wanted to buy a set of books.

I blew the match out and stuck them up under the lining of my cap. I wanted to take them home and show them to my father, so he'd believe me when I told him I'd found someone murdered way out here. Otherwise he was liable to think I was just making it up.

I found out I couldn't get the door open after all, even from the inside. He'd locked it with Gregory's key and taken that with him. I found another door at the back, but that turned out to be even worse; it had a padlock on it. This Gregory must have been scared of people, or else kind of a crazy hermit, to live all locked up like that, with the windows nailed down and everything. I'd have to go all the way upstairs, climb out, catwalk over that dangerously wobbly porch, and skin down to the ground again.

I'd gotten back about as far as where the stairs started up, and I'd just put my foot on the bottom one, when I heard a scrunch outside. Then someone stepped on the porch! There was a slithering sound by the door, and a minute later a little whistle went *tweet!* I nearly jumped out of my skin. I don't know which of the three scared me most. I think it was that whispering sound under the door. The only reason I stayed where I was and didn't make a break up the stairs was, I could hear steps going away again outside.

I tiptoed to one of the front windows and rubbed a clean spot in the dust and squinted through it. I could see a man walking away from the house back toward the road again. He climbed on a bicycle and rode off. It was only a special delivery mailman.

I waited until he'd rode from sight, then I groped my way back toward the door, and I could see something white sticking through under it, even in the dark. I got down and pinched it between my thumb and finger, but it wouldn't come through; it seemed to have gotten caught. He hadn't shoved it all the way in, and first I thought maybe it was too thick or had gotten snagged on a splinter.

I opened my fingers for a minute to get a tighter grip, and right while I was looking at it, it started getting smaller and smaller, like it was slipping out the other way. I couldn't understand what was making it do that, because there was no tilt to the sill. When there was only about an inch of it left, I grabbed at it quick, and gave it a tug that brought it in again.

Then all of a sudden I let go of it, and stayed there like I was, without moving and with my heart starting to pound like anything. Without hearing a sound, something had told me all at once that there was someone out there on the other side of that door! I was afraid to touch the letter now, but the damage had already been done. That jerk I'd given it was enough to tell him there was someone in here.

Plenty scared, I picked my way back to the window again, as carefully as if I was walking on eggs, to try and see if I could get a side-look at the porch through it. Just as I got to it, one of those things like you see in the movies happened, only this time it wasn't funny. My face came right up against somebody else's. He was trying to look in, while I was trying to look out. Our two faces were right smack up against each other, with just a thin sheet of glass between.

We both jumped together, and he straightened up. He'd been bending down low to look in, and he could tell I was a kid. It was Petersen. I could recognize him even in the faint light out there by the shape of his hat and his pitcher-ears. He must have been waiting around nearby, and had seen the mailman's bike.

We both whisked from the window fast. He jumped for the door and started to stab a key at it. I jumped for the stairs and the only way out there was. Before I could get to them, I went headfirst over an empty packing case. Then I was on them and flashing up them. Just as I cleared the last one, I heard the door swing in below. I might be able to beat him out of the house through the window upstairs, but I didn't give much for my chances of beating him down the road in a straight run. My only hope was to be able to get into those weeds out there ahead of him and then lose myself, and I didn't know how I was going to do it with him right behind me.

I got to the upstairs window just as he got to the bottom step of the stairs. I didn't wait to look, but I think he'd stopped to strike a light so that he could make better time. I straddled the window sill in a big hurry, tearing my pants on a nail as I did. A minute later something much worse happened. Just as I got one foot down on the wooden shed over the porch, and was bringing the other one through the window after me, the two ends went up higher, the middle sank lower, and then the whole business slid to the ground between the two posts that had held it up. Luckily I was still holding onto the window frame with both arms. I pulled myself back just in time and got my leg up on the sill again.

If there'd been a clear space underneath, I would have chanced it and jumped from where I was, although it was a pretty high jump for a kid my size, but the way those jagged ends of splintered wood were sticking up all over, I knew one of them would stab through me sure as anything if I tried it. He'd run back to the door for a minute— I guess at first he thought the whole house was coming down on him—and when he saw that it was just the porch shed, he stuck his head out and around and looked up at me where I was, stranded up there on the window frame.

All he said was, "All right, kid, I've got you now," but he said it in such a calm, quiet way that it scared you more than if he'd cursed.

He went in and started up the stairs again. I ran all around the three sides of the room, looking for a way out, and on the third side I finally found a narrow brick fireplace. I jumped in through that and tried to climb up on the inside. I fell back again to the bottom just as he came into the room. He headed straight over to the fireplace and bent down, and his arm reached in for me and swept back and forth. It missed me the first time, but the second time it got me. There was nothing I could hang onto in there to keep from being pulled out. I came out kicking, and he straightened up and held me by the throat, out where I couldn't reach him with my feet.

He let me swing at his arm with both my fists until I got all tired, and then he said in that same quiet, deadly way, "What're you doing around here, son?"

"Just playin'," I said.

"Don't you think it's a funny place and a funny time of night for a kid your age to be playing?"

What was the use of answering?

He said, "I've seen you before, son. I saw you standing on the street looking up at my window last night. You seem to be crossing

my path a lot lately. What's the idea?" He shook me till my teeth
darn near came out, then he asked me a second time, real slow:
"What's the idea?"

"Nothin'," I drooled. My head lolled all around on my shoulders,
dizzy from the shaking.

"I think there is. Who's your father?"

"Frank Case."

"Who's Frank Case?"

I knew my only chance was not to tell him. I knew if I told him
then he'd never let me get out of here alive. But I couldn't help
telling him, it made me glad to tell him, proud to tell him; I didn't
want any mercy from him. "The best dick in town!" I spit out at
him.

"That's your finish," he said. "So you're a cop's son. Well, a cop's
son is just a future cop. Squash them while they're little. Did your
father teach you how to go out bravely, kid?"

I hated him! My own voice got nearly as husky as if it was changing already, and it wasn't yet. "My father don't have to teach me
that. Just being his kid shows it to me."

He laughed. "Been down to the cellar yet, son?"

I didn't answer.

"Well, we're going down there now."

I hated him so, I didn't even remember to be scared much any
more. You're only scared when there's a chance of not getting hurt,
anyway. When there's no chance of not getting hurt, what's the use
of being scared? "And I'm not coming up again any more, am I?" I
said defiantly while he felt his way down the stairs with me.

"No, you're not coming up again any more. Glad you know it."

I said, "You can kill me like you did him, but I'm not afraid of
you. My pop and every cop in the city'll get even on you, you dirty
murderer, you. You stink!"

We'd gotten down to the first floor by now. It was better than the
basement, anyway. I twisted my head around and got my teeth into
his arm, just below the elbow. I kept it up until they darn near came
together, through his sleeve and skin and muscle. I couldn't even
feel him hitting me, but I know he was, because all of a sudden I
landed flat up against the wall all the way across the room, and my
ears hummed.

I heard him say, "You copper-whelp! If you want it that quick,
here it is!" The white of his shirt showed for a minute, like he'd
pushed back his coat to take out something. Then a long tube of fire
jumped at me, and there was a sound like thunder in the room.

I'd never heard a gun go off before. It makes you kind of excited. It did me, anyway. I knew the wall was pale in back of me and that was bad because I was outlined against it. I dropped down flat on the floor, and started to shunt off sideways over it, keeping my face turned toward him. I knew another of those tubes of light was coming any second, this time pointed right, pointed low.

He heard the slithering sound my body was making across the floor. He must have thought I was hit but still able to move. He said, "You're hard to finish, ain't you, kid? Why ain't you whimpering? Don't it hurt you?" I just kept swimming sideways on the floor. I heard him say:

"Two shots don't make any more noise than one. I'll make sure this time." He took a step forward and one knee dipped a little. I saw his arm come out and point down at me.

I couldn't help shutting my eyes tight for a minute there on the floor. Then I remembered I was a detective's son and I opened them again right away. Not for any murderer was I going to close my eyes.

The tube of light came again, and the thunder, and a lot of splinters jumped up right in front of my face. One of them even caught in my lip and hurt like a needle. I couldn't keep quiet even if I wanted to; the way I hated him made me say, real quiet, like I was a grownup talking to another grownup, not a kid who knew he was going to die in another minute:

"Gee, you're lousy, mister, for a murderer!"

That was all there was time for. All of a sudden there was a sound like someone ploughing through that mass of wreckage outside the door, and the door swung in and hit back against the wall; he hadn't locked it behind him in his hurry to get his hands on me. For a minute there was complete silence—me flat on the floor, him in the shadows.

Then a low voice that I knew by heart whispered, "Don't shoot, fellows, he may have my kid in there with him."

You could make him out against the lighter sky outside, but he had to have light to see by, or I knew Petersen would get him sure. He was just holding his fire because he didn't want to give away where he was. I had one match left in my pocket from the dead man. But a match goes out if you try to throw it through the air. I got it out of my pocket, and I put its tip to the floor and held it there, ready. Then I drew my legs up under me, reared up on them, and ticked the match off as I straightened. I held it way out across the room toward Petersen, with my arm stretched as far as it could reach, as it flamed, and it showed him up in smoky orange from head to foot. "Straight ahead of you, Pop!" I yelled.

Petersen's gun started around toward me fast and angry, to put me and my match both out at once, but there's only one thing that can beat a bullet, and that's another bullet. The doorway thundered, and my pop's bullet hit him so hard in the side of the head that he hicked over sideways like a drunk trying to dance, and went nudging his shoulder all the way down the wall to the floor, still smoky-orange from my match.

I stood there holding it, like the Statue of Liberty, until they had a chance to get over to him and make sure he wouldn't still shoot from where he was lying.

But one of them came straight to me, without bothering about him, and I knew which one it was all right, dark or no dark. He said, "Frankie, are you all right?"

I said, "Sure I'm all right, Pop."

And the funny part of it was, I still was while I was saying it; I was sure I could've gone on all night yet. But all of a sudden when I felt his hands reaching out for me, I felt like I was only twelve years old again and would have to wait a long time yet before I could be a regular detective, and I flopped up against him all loose and went to sleep standing up or something. . . .

When I woke up I was in a car with him and a couple of the others, riding back downtown again. I started to talk the minute my eyes were open, to make sure he hadn't missed any of it, because I wanted to get him re—you know that word.

I said, "Pop, he killed an old guy named Thomas Gregory. He's down—"

"Yeah, we found him, Frankie."

"And, Pop, there's a letter under the front door, which is why he killed him."

"We found that too, Frankie." He took it out of his pocket and showed it to me. It wasn't anything, just an old scrap of pale blue paper.

"It's a certified check for twelve thousand dollars, in payment for a claim he had against a construction company as a result of an accident."

My father explained, almost like I was a grownup instead of a kid, "He was hit in the eye by a steel particle while he was walking past one of their buildings under construction. He had to have the eye taken out. That was five years ago. The suit dragged on ever since, while he turned sour and led a hand-to-mouth existence in that shack out there. They fought him to the last ditch, but the higher court made them pay damages in the end.

"The day the decision was handed down, some of the papers ran little squibs about it, space-fillers down at the bottom of the page like they do. One of these evidently caught Petersen's eye, and he mistakenly thought that meant the check had already come in and the old man had cashed it. He went out there, got himself admitted or forced his way in, probably tortured Greogry first, and when he couldn't get anything out of him, ended up by killing him.

"He was too quick about it. The check didn't come in until tonight, as you saw. He had to keep coming back, watching for it. Once the old man was gone and the check still uncashed, the only thing he could do was take a desperate chance on forging his name to it, and present it for payment, backed up by some credentials taken from Gregory.

"He wasn't very bright or he would have known that he didn't have a chance in a thousand of getting away with anything like that. Banks don't honor checks for that amount when the payee isn't known to them, without doing a little quiet investigating first. But he wanted *something* out of his murder. He'd killed the old man for nothing. . . . But how in the blazes did *you*—"

So then I took out the glass eye and showed it to him, and told him how I traced it back. I saw them give each other looks and shake their heads sort of surprised over it, and one of them said, "Not bad! Not bad at all!"

"Not bad?" snapped my father.

"How'd you know where I was?"

"In the first place," he said, "your mother caught right on that Scanny was lying when he said you were studying over at his house, because in your excitement you kids overlooked the fact that tomorrow's Thanksgiving and there's no school to study for. She sent me over there, I broke Scanny down, and he showed me where this room was you'd followed this fellow Petersen to earlier in the day.

"I broke in, looked it over, and found a couple of those newspaper items about this old man Gregory that he'd taken the trouble to mark off and clip out. I didn't like the looks of that to begin with, and your friend Scanny had already mentioned something about a glass eye. Luckily they gave the recluse's address—which was what had put Petersen onto him, too—and when eleven-thirty came and no sign of you, I rustled up a car and chased out there fast."

We stopped off at Headquarters first, so he could make out his report, and he had me meet some guy with white hair who was his boss, I guess. He clapped my shoulder right where it hurt most from all those falls I'd had, but I didn't let him see that. I saw my father wasn't going to say anything himself, so I piped up: "The whole case is my father's! Now is he going to get re-instituted?"

I saw them wink at each other, and then the man with white hair laughed and said, "I think I can promise that." Then he looked at me and added, "You think a lot of your father, don't you?"

I stood up straight as anything and stuck my chin out and said, "He's the best dick in town!"

AGATHA CHRISTIE

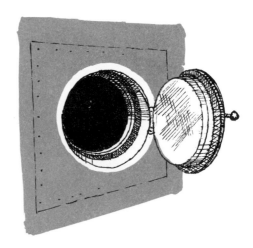

The Disappearance *of* Mr. Davenheim

Poirot and I were expecting our old friend Inspector Japp of Scotland Yard to tea. We were sitting around the tea table awaiting his arrival. Poirot had just finished carefully straightening the cups and saucers which our landlady was in the habit of throwing, rather than placing, on the table. He had also breathed heavily on the metal teapot, and polished it with a silk handkerchief. The kettle was on the boil, and a small enamel saucepan beside it contained some thick, sweet chocolate which was more to Poirot's palate than what he described as "your English poison."

A sharp "rat-tat" sounded below, and a few minutes afterward Japp entered briskly.

"Hope I'm not late," he said as he greeted us. "To tell the truth, I was yarning with Miller, the man who's in charge of the Davenheim case."

I pricked up my ears. For the last three days the papers had been full of the strange disappearance of Mr. Davenheim, senior partner of Davenheim and Salmon, the well-known bankers and financiers.

On Saturday last he had walked out of his house, and had never been seen since. I looked forward to extracting some interesting details from Japp.

"I should have thought," I remarked, "that it would be almost impossible for anyone to 'disappear' nowadays."

Poirot moved a plate of bread and butter the eighth of an inch, and said sharply: "Be exact, my friend. What do you mean by 'disappear'? To which class of disappearance are you referring?"

"Are disappearances classified and labeled, then?" I laughed.

Japp smiled also. Poirot frowned at us both.

"But certainly they are! They fall into three categories: First, and most common, the voluntary disappearance. Second, the much abused 'loss of memory' case—rare, but occasionally genuine. Third, murder, and a more or less successful disposal of the body. Do you refer to all three as impossible of execution?"

"Very nearly so, I should think. You might lose your own memory, but someone would be sure to recognize you—especially in the case of a well-known man like Davenheim. Then 'bodies' can't be made to vanish into thin air. Sooner or later they turn up, concealed in lonely places, or in trunks. Murder will out. In the same way, the absconding clerk, or the domestic defaulter, is bound to be run down in these days of wireless telegraphy. He can be headed off from foreign countries; ports and railway stations are watched; and, as for concealment in this country, his features and appearance will be known to everyone who reads a daily newspaper. He's up against civilization."

"*Mon ami,*" said Poirot, "you make one error. You do not allow for the fact that a man who had decided to make away with another man—or with himself in a figurative sense—might be that rare machine, a man of method. He might bring intelligence, talent, a careful calculation of detail to the task; and then I do not see why he should not be successful in baffling the police force."

"But not *you,* I suppose?" said Japp good-humoredly, winking at me. "He couldn't baffle *you,* eh, Monsieur Poirot?"

Poirot endeavored, with a marked lack of success, to look modest. "Me, also! Why not? It is true that I approach such problems with an exact science, a mathematical precision, which seems, alas, only too rare in the new generation of detectives!"

Japp grinned more widely.

"I don't know," he said. "Miller, the man who's on this case, is a smart chap. You may be very sure he won't overlook a footprint, or a cigar ash, or a crumb even. He's got eyes that see everything."

"So, *mon ami*," said Poirot, "has the London sparrow. But all the same, I should not ask the little brown bird to solve the problem of Mr. Davenheim."

"Come now, monsieur, you're not going to run down the value of details as clues?"

"By no means. These things are all good in their way. The danger is they may assume undue importance. Most details are insignificant; one or two are vital. It is the brain, the little gray cells——" he tapped his forehead——"on which one must rely. The senses mislead. One must seek the truth within—not without."

"You don't mean to say, Monsieur Poirot, that you would undertake to solve a case without moving from your chair, do you?"

"That is exactly what I do mean—granted the facts were placed before me. I regard myself as a consulting specialist."

Japp slapped his knee. "Hanged if I don't take you at your word. Bet you a fiver that you can't lay your hand—or rather tell me where to lay my hand—on Mr. Davenheim, dead or alive, before a week is out."

Poirot considered. "*Eh bien, mon ami,* I accept. *Le sport,* it is the passion of you English. Now—the facts."

"On Saturday last, as is his usual custom, Mr. Davenheim took the 12:40 train from Victoria to Chingside, where his palatial country place, The Cedars, is situated. After lunch, he strolled around the grounds, and gave various directions to the gardeners. Everybody agrees that his manner was absolutely normal and as usual. After tea he put his head into his wife's boudoir, saying that he was going to stroll down to the village and post some letters. He added that he was expecting a Mr. Lowen, on business. If Lowen should come before he himself returned, he was to be shown into the study and asked to wait. Mr. Davenheim then left the house by the front door, passed leisurely down the drive, and out at the gate, and—was never seen again. From that hour, he vanished completely."

"Pretty—very pretty—altogether a charming little problem," murmured Poirot. "Proceed, my good friend."

"About a quarter of an hour later a tall, dark man with a thick black mustache rang the front-door bell, and explained that he had an appointment with Mr. Davenheim. He gave the name of Lowen, and in accordance with the banker's instructions was shown into the study. Nearly an hour passed. Mr. Davenheim did not return. Finally Mr. Lowen rang the bell, and explained that he was unable to wait any longer, as he must catch his train back to town. Mrs. Davenheim apologized for her husband's absence, which seemed

unaccountable, as she knew him to have been expecting the visitor. Mr. Lowen reiterated his regrets and left.

"Well, as everyone knows, Mr. Davenheim did *not* return. Early on Sunday morning the police were communicated with, but could make neither head nor tail of the matter. Mr. Davenheim seemed literally to have vanished into thin air. He had not been to the post office; nor had he been seen passing through the village. At the station they were positive he had not departed by any train. His own motor had not left the garage. If he had hired a car to meet him in some lonely spot, it seems almost certain that by this time, in view of the large reward offered for information, the driver of it would have come forward to tell what he knew. True, there was a small race-meeting at Entfield, five miles away, and if he had walked to that station he might have passed unnoticed in the crowd. But since then his photograph and a full description of him have been circulated in every newspaper, and nobody has been able to give any news of him. We have, of course, received many letters from all over England, but each clue, so far, has ended in disappointment.

"On Monday morning a further sensational discovery came to light. Behind a *portière* in Mr. Davenheim's study stands a safe, and that safe had been broken into and rifled. The windows were fastened securely on the inside, which seems to put an ordinary burglary out of court, unless, of course, an accomplice within the house fastened them again afterwards. On the other hand, Sunday having intervened, and the household being in a state of chaos, it is likely that the burglary was committed on the Saturday, and remained undetected until Monday."

"*Précisément,*" said Poirot dryly. "Well, is he arrested, *ce pauvre M. Lowen?*"

Japp grinned. "Not yet. But he's under pretty close supervision."

Poirot nodded. "What was taken from the safe? Have you any idea?"

"We've been going into that with the junior partner of the firm and Mrs. Davenheim. Apparently there was a considerable amount in bearer bonds, and a very large sum in notes, owing to some large transaction having been just carried through. There was also a small fortune in jewelry. All Mrs. Davenheim's jewels were kept in the safe. The purchasing of them had become a passion with her husband of late years, and hardly a month passed that he did not make her a present of some rare and costly gem."

"Altogether a good haul," said Poirot thoughtfully. "Now, what

about Lowen? Is it known what his business was with Davenheim
that evening?"

"Well, the two men were apparently not on very good terms.
Lowen is a speculator in quite a small way. Nevertheless, he has been
able once or twice to score a *coup* off Davenheim in the market,
though it seems they seldom or never actually met. It was a matter
concerning some South American shares which led the banker to
make his appointment."

"Had Davenheim interests in South America, then?"

"I believe so. Mrs. Davenheim happened to mention that he spent
all last autumn in Buenos Aires."

"Any trouble in his home life? Were the husband and wife on
good terms?"

"I should say his domestic life was quite peaceful and uneventful.
Mrs. Davenheim is a pleasant, rather unintelligent woman. Quite
a nonentity, I think."

"Then we must not look for the solution of the mystery there. Had
he any enemies?"

"He had plenty of financial rivals, and no doubt there are many
people whom he has got the better of who bear him no particular
good will. But there was no one likely to make away with him—and,
if they had, where is the body?"

"Exactly. As Hastings says, bodies have a habit of coming to light
with fatal persistency."

"By the way, one of the gardeners says he saw a figure going
around to the side of the house toward the rose garden. The long
French window of the study opens on to the rose garden, and Mr.
Davenheim frequently entered and left the house that way. But the
man was a good way off, at work on some cucumber frames, and
cannot even say whether it was the figure of his master or not. Also,
he cannot fix the time with any accuracy. It must have been before
six, as the gardeners cease work at that time."

"And Mr. Davenheim left the house?"

"About half-past five or thereabouts."

"What lies beyond the rose garden?"

"A lake."

"With a boathouse?"

"Yes, a couple of punts are kept there. I suppose you're thinking
of suicide, Monsieur Poirot? Well, I don't mind telling you that
Miller's going down tomorrow expressly to see that piece of water
dragged. That's the kind of man he is!"

Poirot smiled faintly, and turned to me. "Hastings, I pray you, hand me that copy of the *Daily Megaphone.* If I remember rightly, there is an unusually clear photograph there of the missing man."

I rose, and found the sheet required. Poirot studied the features attentively.

"H'm!" he murmured. "Wears his hair rather long and wavy, full mustache and pointed beard, bushy eyebrows. Eyes dark?"

"Yes."

"Hair and beard turning gray?"

The detective nodded. "Well, Monsieur Poirot, what have you got to say to it all? Clear as daylight, eh?"

"On the contrary, most obscure."

The Scotland Yard man looked pleased.

"Which gives me great hopes of solving it," finished Poirot placidly.

"Eh?"

"I find it a good sign when a case is obscure. If a thing is clear as daylight—*eh bien,* mistrust it! Someone has made it so."

Japp shook his head almost pityingly. "Well, each to their fancy. But it's not a bad thing to see your way clear ahead."

"I do not see," murmured Poirot. "I shut my eyes—and think."

Japp sighed. "Well, you've got a clear week to think in."

"And you will bring me any fresh developments that arise—the result of the labors of the hard-working and lynx-eyed Inspector Miller, for instance?"

"Certainly. That's in the bargain."

"Seems a shame, doesn't it?" said Japp to me as I accompanied him to the door. "Like robbing a child!"

I could not help agreeing with a smile. I was still smiling as I re-entered the room.

"*Eh bien!*" said Poirot immediately. "You make fun of Papa Poirot, is it not so?" He shook his finger at me. "You do not trust his gray cells? Ah, do not be confused! Let us discuss this little problem— incomplete as yet, I admit, but already showing one or two points of interest."

"The lake!" I said significantly.

"And even more than the lake, the boathouse!"

I looked sidewise at Poirot. He was smiling in his most inscrutable fashion. I felt that, for the moment, it would be quite useless to question him further.

We heard nothing of Japp until the following evening, when he walked in about nine o'clock. I saw at once by his expression that he was bursting with news of some kind.

"*Eh bien,* my friend," remarked Poirot. "All goes well? But do not tell me that you have discovered the body of Mr. Davenheim in your lake, because I shall not believe you."

"We haven't found the body, but we did find his *clothes*—the identical clothes he was wearing that day. What do you say to that?"

"Any other clothes missing from the house?"

"No, his valet is quite positive on that point. The rest of his wardrobe is intact. There's more. We've arrested Lowen. One of the maids, whose business it is to fasten the bedroom windows, declares that she saw Lowen coming *toward* the study through the rose garden about a quarter past six. That would be about ten minutes before he left the house."

"What does he himself say to that?"

"Denied first of all that he had ever left the study. But the maid was positive and he pretended afterward that he had forgotten just stepping out of the window to examine an unusual species of rose. Rather a weak story! And there's fresh evidence against him come to light. Mr. Davenheim always wore a thick gold ring set with a solitaire diamond on the little finger of his right hand. Well, that ring was pawned in London on Saturday night by a man called Billy Kellett! He's already known to the police—did three months last autumn for lifting an old gentleman's watch. It seems he tried to pawn the ring at no less than five different places, succeeded at the last one, got gloriously drunk on the proceeds, assaulted a policeman, and was run in in consequence. I went to Bow Street with Miller and saw him. He's sober enough now, and I don't mind admitting we pretty well frightened the life out of him, hinting he might be charged with murder. This is his yarn, and a very queer one it is.

"He was at Entfield races on Saturday, though I dare say scarfpins was his line of business, rather than betting. Anyway, he had a bad day, and was down on his luck. He was tramping along the road to Chingside, and sat down in a ditch to rest just before he got into the village. A few minutes later he noticed a man coming along the road to the village, 'dark-complexioned gent, with a big mustache, one of them city toffs,' is his description of the man.

"Kellett was half concealed from the road by a heap of stones. Just before he got abreast of him, the man looked quickly up and down the road, and seeing it apparently deserted he took a small object from his pocket and threw it over the hedge. Then he went on toward the station. Now, the object he had thrown over the hedge had fallen with a slight 'chink' which aroused the curiosity of the

human derelict in the ditch. He investigated and, after a short
search, discovered the ring! That is Kellett's story. It's only fair to
say that Lowen denies it utterly, and of course the word of a man like
Kellett can't be relied upon in the slightest. It's within the bounds
of possibility that he met Davenheim in the lane and robbed and
murdered him."

Poirot shook his head.

"Very improbable, *mon ami*. He had no means of disposing of the
body. It would have been found by now. Secondly, the open way in
which he pawned the ring makes it unlikely that he did murder to
get it. Thirdly, your sneak thief is rarely a murderer. Fourthly, as he
has been in prison since Saturday, it would be too much of a
coincidence that he is able to give an accurate description of Lowen."

Japp nodded. "I don't say you're not right. But all the same, you
won't get a jury to take much note of a jailbird's evidence. What
seems odd to me is that Lowen couldn't find a cleverer way of disposing of the ring."

Poirot shrugged his shoulders. "Well, after all, if it were found
in the neighborhood, it might be argued that Davenheim himself
had dropped it."

"But why remove it from the body at all?" I cried.

"There might be a reason for that," said Japp. "Do you know
that just beyond the lake, a little gate leads out on to the hill, and
not three minutes' walk brings you to—what do you think?—*a lime
kiln.*"

"Good heavens!" I cried. "You mean that the lime which de-
stroyed the body would be powerless to affect the metal of the ring?"

"Exactly."

"It seems to me," I said, "that that explains everything. What a
horrible crime!"

By common consent we both turned and looked at Poirot. He
seemed lost in reflection, his brow knitted, as though with some
supreme mental effort. I felt that at last his keen intellect was assert-
ing itself. What would his first words be? We were not long left in
doubt. With a sigh, the tension of his attitude relaxed, and turning
to Japp, he asked:

"Have you any idea, my friend, whether Mr. and Mrs. Davenheim
occupied the same bedroom?"

The question seemed so ludicrously inappropriate that for a moment we both stared in silence. Then Japp burst into a laugh. "Good
Lord, Monsieur Poirot, I thought you were coming out with something startling. As to your question, I'm sure I don't know."

"You could find out?" asked Poirot with curious persistence.

"Oh, certainly—if you *really* want to know."

"*Merci, mon ami.* I should be obliged if you would make a point of it."

Japp stared at him a few minutes longer, but Poirot seemed to have forgotten us both. The detective shook his head sadly at me, and murmuring, "Poor old fellow! War's been too much for him!" gently withdrew from the room.

As Poirot still seemed sunk in a daydream, I took a sheet of paper, and amused myself by scribbling notes upon it. My friend's voice aroused me. He had come out of his reverie, and was looking brisk and alert.

"*Que faites vous là, mon ami?*"

"I was jotting down what occurred to me as the main points of interest in this affair."

"You become methodical—at last!" said Poirot approvingly. I concealed my pleasure. "Shall I read them to you?"

"By all means."

I cleared my throat.

" 'One: All the evidence points to Lowen being the man who forced the safe.

" 'Two: He had a grudge against Davenheim.

" 'Three: He lied in his first statement that he had never left the study.

" 'Four: If you accept Billy Kellett's story as true, Lowen is unmistakably implicated.' "

I paused. "Well?" I asked, for I felt that I had put my finger on all the vital facts.

Poirot looked at me pityingly, shaking his head very gently. "*Mon pauvre ami!* But it is that you have not the gift! The important detail, you appreciate him never! Also, your reasoning is false."

"How?"

"Let me take your four points.

"One: Mr. Lowen could not possibly know that he would have the chance to open the safe. He came for a business interview. He could not know beforehand that Mr. Davenheim would be absent posting a letter, and that he would consequently be alone in the study!"

"He might have seized his opportunity," I suggested.

"And the tools? City gentlemen do not carry round housebreaker's tools on the off chance! And one could not cut into that safe with a penknife, *bien entendu!*"

"Well, what about Number Two?"

"You say Lowen had a grudge against Mr. Davenheim. What you mean is that he had once or twice got the better of him. And presumably those transactions were entered into with the view of benefiting himself. In any case you do not as a rule bear a grudge against a man you have got the better of—it is more likely to be the other way about. Whatever grudge there might have been would have been on Mr. Davenheim's side."

"Well, you can't deny that he lied about never having left the study?"

"No. But he may have been frightened. Remember, the missing man's clothes had just been discovered in the lake. Of course, as usual, he would have done better to speak the truth."

"And the fourth point?"

"I grant you that. If Kellett's story is true, Lowen is undeniably implicated. That is what makes the affair so very interesting."

"Then I did appreciate *one* vital fact?"

"Perhaps—but you have entirely overlooked the two most important points, the ones which undoubtedly hold the clue to the whole matter."

"And pray, what are they?"

"One, the passion which has grown upon Mr. Davenheim in the last few years for buying jewelry. Two, his trip to Buenos Aires last autumn."

"Poirot, you are joking!"

"I am most serious. Ah, sacred thunder, but I hope Japp will not forget my little commission."

But the detective, entering into the spirit of the joke, had remembered it so well that a telegram was handed to Poirot about eleven o'clock the next day. At his request I opened it and read it out:

HUSBAND AND WIFE HAVE OCCUPIED SEPARATE ROOMS
SINCE LAST WINTER

"Aha!" cried Poirot. "And now we are in mid-June! All is solved!"
I stared at him.

"You have no moneys in the bank of Davenheim and Salmon, *mon ami?*"

"No," I said, wondering. "Why?"

"Because I should advise you to withdraw it—before it is too late."

"Why, what do you expect?"

"I expect a big smash in a few days—perhaps sooner. Which

reminds me, we will return the compliment of a *dépêche* to Japp. A
pencil, I pray you, and a form. *Voilà!* 'Advise you to withdraw any
money deposited with firm in question.' That will intrigue him, the
good Japp! His eyes will open wide—wide! He will not comprehend
in the slightest—until tomorrow, or the next day!"

I remained skeptical, but the morrow forced me to render tribute
to my friend's remarkable powers. In every paper was a hugh headline telling of the sensational failure of the Davenheim bank. The
disappearance of the famous financier took on a totally different
aspect in the light of the revelation of the financial affairs of the
bank.

Before we were halfway through breakfast, the door flew open and
Japp rushed in. In his left hand was a paper; in his right was Poirot's
telegram, which he banged down on the table in front of my friend.

"How did you know, Monsieur Poirot? How the blazes could you
know?"

Poirot smiled placidly at him. "Ah, *mon ami,* after your wire, it
was a certainty! From the commencement, see you, it struck me
that the safe burglary was somewhat remarkable. Jewels, ready
money, bearer bonds—all so conveniently arranged for—whom?
Well, the good Monsieur Davenheim was of those who 'look after
Number One' as your saying goes! It seemed almost certain that it
was arranged for—himself! Then his passion of late years for buying
jewelry! How simple! The funds he embezzled he converted into
jewels, very likely replacing them in turn with paste duplicates, and
so he put away in a safe place, under another name, a considerable
fortune to be enjoyed all in good time when everyone has been
thrown off the track. His arrangements completed, he makes an
appointment with Mr. Lowen (who has been imprudent enough in
the past to cross the great man once or twice), drills a hole in the
safe, leaves orders that the guest is to be shown into the study, and
walks out of the house—where?" Poirot stopped, and stretched out
his hand for another boiled egg. He frowned. "It is really insupport-
able," he murmured, "that every hen lays an egg of a different size!
What symmetry can there be on the breakfast table? At least they
should sort them in dozens at the shop!"

"Never mind the eggs," said Japp impatiently. "Let 'em lay 'em
square if they like. Tell us where our customer went to when he left
The Cedars—that is, if you know!"

"*Eh bien,* he went to his hiding place. Ah, this Monsieur Davenheim, there may be some malformation in his gray cells, but they
are of the first quality!"

"Do you know where he is hiding?"

"Certainly! It is most ingenious."

"For the Lord's sake, tell us, then!"

Poirot gently collected every fragment of shell from his plate, placed them in the egg cup, and reversed the empty egg shell on top of them. This little operation concluded, he smiled at the neat effect, and then beamed affectionately on us both.

"Come, my friends, you are men of intelligence. Ask yourselves the question which I asked myself. 'If I were this man, where should *I* hide?' Hastings, what do you say?"

"Well," I said, "I'm rather inclined to think I'd not do a bolt at all. I'd stay in London—in the heart of things, travel by tubes and buses; ten to one I'd never be recognized. There's safety in a crowd."

Poirot turned inquiringly to Japp.

"I don't agree. Get clear away at once—that's the only chance. I would have had plenty of time to prepare things beforehand. I'd have a yacht waiting, with steam up, and I'd be off to one of the most out-of-the-way corners of the world before the hue and cry began!"

We both looked at Poirot. "What do *you* say, monsieur?"

For a moment he remained silent. Then a very curious smile flitted across his face.

"My friends, if *I* were hiding from the police, do you know *where* I should hide? *In a prison!*"

"*What?*"

"You are seeking Monsieur Davenheim in order to put him in prison, so you never dream of looking to see if he may not be already there!"

"What do you mean?"

"You tell me Madame Davenheim is not a very intelligent woman. Nevertheless I think that if you took her to Bow Street and confronted her with the man Billy Kellett, she would recognize him! In spite of the fact that he has shaved his beard and mustache and those bushy eyebrows, and has cropped his hair close. A woman nearly always knows her husband, though the rest of the world may be deceived!"

"Billy Kellett? But he's known to the police!"

"Did I not tell you Davenheim was a clever man? He prepared his alibi long beforehand. He was not in Buenos Aires last autumn—he was creating the character of Billy Kellett, 'doing three months,' so that the police should have no suspicions when the time came. He was playing, remember, for a large fortune, as well as liberty. It was worth while doing the thing thoroughly. Only——"

"Yes?"

"*Eh bien,* afterwards he had to wear a false beard and wig, had to *make up as himself* again, and to sleep with a false beard is not easy—it invites detection! He cannot risk continuing to share the chamber of madame his wife. You found out for me that for the last six months, or ever since his supposed return from Buenos Aires, he and Mrs. Davenheim occupied separate rooms. Then I was sure! Everything fitted in. The gardener who fancied he saw his master going around to the side of the house was quite right. He went to the boathouse, donned his 'tramp' clothes, which you may be sure had been safely hidden from the eyes of his valet, dropped the others in the lake, and proceeded to carry out his plan by pawning the ring in an obvious manner, and then assaulting a policeman, getting himself safely into the haven of Bow Street, where nobody would ever dream of looking for him!"

"It's impossible," murmured Japp.

"Ask Madame," said my friend, smiling.

The next day a registered letter lay beside Poirot's plate. He opened it, and a five-pound note fluttered out. My friend's brow puckered.

"*Ah, sacré!* But what shall I do with it? I have much remorse! *Ce pauvre Japp!* Ah, an idea! We will have a little dinner, we three! That consoles me. It was really too easy. I am ashamed. I, who would not rob a child—*mille tonnerres! Mon ami,* what have you, that you laugh so heartily?"

Green Ice

Few and far between were the passers-by on Manhattan's Fifty-seventh Street that rainy Saturday afternoon, but still not few enough for the purpose of the man in the tan raincoat. He loitered until the glint of brass buttons had disappeared inside the cigar store on the corner, and then pulled his hat over his eyes and strolled casually toward the glittering windows of VANDERBOCK ET CIE., JEWELERS, FOUNDED PARIS 1890.

He paused there briefly, and then passed hurriedly on, leaving behind him one neatly-wrapped brick, one smashed plate-glass window, and no diamonds.

As the burglar alarms let go with a nerve-paralyzing clatter, the man in the raincoat ran out into the street and leaped lightly to the side of a small shiny roadster which happened to be rolling conveniently along there, driven by what was later described as "a blonde dame with sun-glasses." The roadster picked up speed, but then from the cigar store on the corner rushed a uniformed officer, shouting "Halt!" and fumbling with the catch of his holster. There was the sharp dry slap of a pistol shot. Brass buttons collapsed on the wet pavement, and with a screech of tortured rubber the car rounded the corner and disappeared north toward the park.

The burglar alarms continued, and then the wail of sirens swelled the ear-splitting din. A radio car slammed on its brakes beside the crumpled figure in the gutter, but the doctor who jumped down out of the following ambulance shook his head and said "Dead on arrival."

Humanity appeared in considerable numbers, blocking the street and trampling in the broken glass outside the jewelers' window. Precinct detectives were very busy, and then stood back as a sharp-nosed lieutenant from Uptown Robbery Detail took charge. And finally nothing less than a big black limousine from Headquarters appeared, from which climbed a wiry, gray little Irishman with a gold badge cupped in his right hand. The murder of a police officer in the line of duty is taken very seriously by the force.

The lieutenant, who had been staring gloomily into the looted window, now turned and saluted. "Grosskopf, lieutenant—Robbery Detail," he introduced himself.

"Inspector Piper. And Sergeant Mains," said the man from downtown, waving at the curly-headed but extremely serious youngster who had driven the car. "We're only kibitzing, Lieutenant. Go right ahead."

"It's simple smash-and-grab," the lieutenant said. "Like the other cases we've been having. Only this time old Sam Bodley had to get blasted as they were making their getaway."

"Someday these jewelers will learn to use safety glass," Piper observed. "Any witnesses?"

Lieutenant Grosskopf shrugged, and pointed inside the store. "There's the doorman at Carnegie, and a dame," he said, making it clear that he was unimpressed with the showing. The inspector moved toward the door, and then winced as a clear and familiar feminine voice sounded above the noise of the crowd.

"Yoo hoo! Oscar!"

The inspector turned, as if to seek shelter, but it was too late. Pushing through the ranks of the curious, ducking beneath the rope barrier to the detriment of her somewhat amazing hat, came a lean, angular lady brandishing a black-cotton umbrella. "Oscar, I simply *must* tell you—"

"Oh, it's you!" muttered the inspector, without enthusiasm, as he turned to face Miss Hildegarde Withers. "You know, someday I'm going to smash that radio of yours, so help me."

"I wasn't listening in on your old police calls," snapped the maiden schoolteacher indignantly. "I was right here in the neighborhood, shopping for an apartment, and I heard the sirens—"

"All right, all right," he told her. "Run along." Lieutenant Gross-kopf now interrupted, bearing a brick partially wrapped in white tissue paper, with festive red string and gilt stickers. "That's what the guy used, eh?" Piper took the brick, hefted it, and then handed it into the custody of the handsome young sergeant, in spite of Miss Withers's obvious interest. "Stop trying to act like a detective, Hildegarde," Piper went on. "There's no tracing a used brick."

He passed on inside the jewelry store, intent upon finding the witnesses to the crime. The sergeant followed, with notebook in readiness, and Miss Withers, trying to look as much like the Invisible Man as possible, tagged along.

There wasn't too much to be got from the witnesses. John Asch, doorman at Carnegie Hall, had heard the alarms and the shot, and had looked down the street in time to glimpse the departing roadster, which he thought was a 1938 Ford coupé. "It all happened so quick!" he complained. "A blonde dame with goggles was driving."

Miss Marcia Lee Smith, who admitted that she was late of Savannah, Georgia, and now in New York to take up the study of the violin, was making the most of her adventure. "I was jus' walking along the street, to save taxi fare, you know, and I heard a great tremendous crash and the alarms and everything. I looked up and there was a man—a great, tall, dark man, sort of foreign-looking—and he ran out into the street and jumped in the car and away they went. Ooh, was I scared!"

Marcia Lee's round young shoulders shivered deliciously to indicate how scared she had been. She was doubtful about the make of the car, but very positive about her description of the bandit. "He was awful tall—taller even than this gentleman heah," she insisted, looking up at Sergeant Mains and letting her lashes fall across her dimpled cheek.

"Okay, folks. Leave your names and addresses with the sarge, and then you can go." Inspector Piper turned away, then suddenly confronted Miss Hildegarde Withers. "Now what are you sleuthing at?" he demanded. "I thought I told you—"

"Nothing, Oscar. Nothing at all," she insisted. Which was mostly true. It had occurred to her that the sergeant ought to be taking Marcia Lee Smith's address and telephone number down in his official notebook instead of in the little red address book which he had produced from an inner pocket, but that was nobody's business but his own.

The last witness to be interviewed was the Vanderbock in charge of the store, a dapper, narrow-shouldered young man in spats, who

had been the only one in the place to have even a fleeting glimpse of
the bandit, and who seemed very vague about that.

"I was in the rear of the store with the staff, making plans for the
anniversary sale tomorrow," he admitted. "I heard the tinkle of glass,
and looked up to see a man—a man with a hat—grabbing things
out of the display window. Then he was gone." Vanderbock shrugged. "Anyway, the most valuable piece in the window, a flawless
twenty-five-carat emerald ring, was overlooked by the thief. And
the diamonds he took were fully insured."

"Funny he left that twenty-five-carat hunk of green ice," said
Piper worriedly. "Okay. Make out a complete list and description
of the missing stones." He turned. "Hey, Sarge!"

"I'll be glad to take down the list," Miss Withers hastily offered.
"The sergeant is busy."

The inspector's temper was short today. "Relax, Hildegarde!" he
ordered, gesturing toward the door with his thumb. "Sergeant!"

"But Oscar, I've something—" the maiden schoolteacher tried to
continue.

"Later, Hildegarde! Run along now." And the inspector turned
his back on her. Miss Withers sniffed, shrugged, and marched toward
the door.

"Sergeant, if you're through with the witnesses, will you take down
this list of stolen property?" the inspector was saying. Then he was
interrupted by a policeman, who brought word that the commissioner was on the phone.

"There it starts!" moaned Oscar Piper. He looked around, thinking fast. "Oh—tell him I've just left." And he started for the door,
pausing only long enough to tell the sergeant that he would be at the
drugstore up the street, and that no, it would not be necessary to
drive Witness Marcia Lee Smith home in the Headquarters limousine.

The inspector caught Miss Withers on the sidewalk, a very ruffled
Miss Withers indeed. "Okay, Hildegarde," he apologized. "I'll buy
you a cup of coffee to make up for throwing you out. Only it makes
us all short-tempered to have anything like this happen. A cop shot
down in his tracks—and we don't know a thing about the guy who
did it."

"No, Oscar?" Only slightly mollified, Miss Withers sank down on
a stool in the drugstore. "How about the witnesses?"

"Worthless," he told her. "You know yourself that nine witnesses
out of ten make up a long story about the tall dark foreign-looking
man . . ." She nodded, and he went on. "So we start from nowhere."

"Knowing nothing about the bandit," Miss Withers said thoughtfully as she looked into her coffee cup, "nothing except that he is a man between thirty and forty years of age, about five feet six inches tall, wears a light-tan raincoat and a dark hat, is an experienced crook known to the police, and is new to the jewel racket. And that he is an egomaniac with a twisted sense of humor. That's all?"

The inspector's cup clattered in its saucer. "*What?*"

"Elementary, my dear Oscar. Who else but an egomaniac would wrap the brick as a gift, with HAPPY BIRTHDAY stickers on it, just because it was the jewelry store's fiftieth anniversary? He was an experienced crook because of the neatness and swiftness of the job. Wanted by the police—or else he wouldn't have been desperate enough to shoot his way clear. A first offender asks for mercy and a light sentence. And the bandit is new to the jewel trade, or he wouldn't have missed the big emerald. See?"

Piper nodded slowly. "Shrewd guessing. But the rest of it—his height and age and so on . . ."

"I know that," Miss Withers confessed, "because I *looked.* I came around the corner just as the killer jumped for his car. Oh, don't look at me that way. I tried to tell you. Anyway, no man over forty is spry enough to jump as he jumped. I didn't see his face, or the driver's, because they were headed the other way. But I saw his height, and he was no giant."

"Not bad, Hildegarde, not bad at all," Oscar Piper was forced to confess. "Now if you could work out a trap to catch him . . ."

"Why not an officer in every jewelry store—or staked out across the street?"

Piper shook his head. "They'd scare him off. I don't just want to stop this series of robberies, I want to get the man who shot Sam Bodley. He'll probably strike again—at some one of the big jewelry stores of upper Fifth or Madison or this street." Suddenly the inspector snapped his fingers. "I've got it! The really important jewelry stores are all within a ten-block area. Tiffany's, Black Starr & Gorham and so forth—all of them. Each store has alarm wires to the protective association. We'll reroute those wires straight to the radio dispatcher at Headquarters. Plant men in radio cars, motorcycle units, and stakeouts so that thirty seconds after the next smash-and-grab alarm we have a police cordon drawn tight around the whole section. Nobody gets out, nobody gets in. We tighten the cordon, search everybody, watch for a known crook or somebody acting suspicious." He grinned. "It's a sort of dragnet."

"Or a grab bag," said the schoolteacher. "There'll be complaints."

"But we'll nab the killer of Sam Bodley." Pleased to think that at last he had something concrete to suggest to the commissioner, Oscar Piper borrowed a nickel from Miss Withers and headed for the nearest phone booth.

He was less pleased next morning when he picked up the paper and read the story beneath the banner head Cop Killer Still at Large. It was not that the newspaper story was in error. They had everything, from the photograph of old Sam Bodley face-down in the street to an artist's re-creation of the killer, from Marcia Lee Smith's description. They poked fun at the bandit for taking the diamonds and missing the more valuable emerald. But the story ended with a complete explanation of the "dragnet" which the police were planning to try.

His cigar suddenly went stale in his mouth. A lot of good the dragnet would do, with the quarry forewarned. Oscar Piper shook his head. It was the first time his old friend and sparring partner had let him down. So Hildegarde had to go and talk in front of the reporters!

He reached savagely across his desk and tore off the top sheet of his calendar pad, on which he had written *Call Hildegarde re: dinner.* The rest of the day Piper devoted to perfecting the dragnet plan, for lack of a better idea. When, toward five, Miss Withers called on the phone, he sent word that he was tied up.

A rare thing it was for the normally sunny inspector to carry a grudge overnight, but this one grew and flourished. Over his desk was pinned the picture of Sam Bodley lying dead in the gutter, and that didn't help. Nor did his temper take a turn for the better when two days later, dressed in unaccustomed black, he sat in the funeral parlors with a delegation from Headquarters and heard the last prayers for Sam Bodley. During a lull in the ceremony a well-meaning captain—old Judd from Missing Persons—leaned over and whispered, "If you're still stymied on this case, why don't you call in that school-ma'am pal of yours? She was a ball of fire on that last job." Piper nearly bit him.

On Monday, four days after the shattering of the jewelers' window, Miss Withers marched down Fifty-seventh Street again. She noted in passing that Vanderbock's window was repaired, and that again its glittering treasures tempted the public, even to the big green emerald ring in the center of the display.

But she had other things on her mind besides trying to help a stubborn, pigheaded Irishman out of his muddle. If he wanted to play that way, so be it. She was determined on the business in hand, which was to find an unfurnished apartment within her means and near the Sixth Avenue subway.

There was a remodeled brownstone just around the corner from Fifty-seventh which had caught her eye just before the shriek of the sirens had led her astray the other day. Now she retraced her steps, came up past the neatly lettered sign UNFURNISHED APARTMENTS— NEWLY DECORATED—AGENT ON PREMISES. The door was open, and the lower hall disclosed a jumble of painters' ladders, wallpaper rolls, kegs and tubs and buckets of paint, and all the canvas, plaster, plumbing equipment which could be imagined.

In the midst of all this stood a young girl. She and Miss Withers spoke together, in one voice: "I'm looking for an apartment—are you the agent?" They stopped, blinked, and smiled. Then the girl cocked her head. "Why—I remember *you!*"

It was Marcia Lee Smith, the star witness who had actually seen the jewel bandit in the act of departing. They discussed the coincidence of meeting like this. "After all," Marcia Lee said, "it's the only attractive building around here with any vacancies. I was out looking the other day, when it all happened."

She had been waiting here some time, hoping for the rental agent to show up. There was a sign on the door, *Gone to lunch, back in half an hour,* but it didn't say half an hour from any set time. "Anyway," said Miss Withers, "I don't need a rental agent to tell me whether or not I like an apartment. I'm going upstairs."

Marcia Lee tagged along. She was living now at the Martha Washington, but she hoped to find an apartment where she could entertain. "Entertain good-looking young detective sergeants?" Miss Withers pressed, and struck home, because the girl came as near to blushing as girls ever come nowadays. They poked through the second-floor apartment, praised the new Venetian blinds, the wide fireplace, the big shining refrigerator which, Marcia Lee pointed out, would make sixty-four ice cubes at once.

The schoolteacher liked everything except the walls, which were a somewhat glaring shade of ivory. "It should be a rather quiet apartment, too," she pointed out. "Set well back. . . ."

It was not a quiet apartment at the moment, because the sirens were howling again. A radio car went up the street screaming bloody murder. From farther off other sirens took up the sound, like hounds on a scent. . . .

Miss Withers, who had started to leap toward the stairs like a fire-horse at the first alarm, now held herself in check. "Let them shriek," she said. "I'm not going to mess into it."

"But—" Marcia Lee said. "It's—it's—"

Evidently the girl was more impressed and thrilled with the activities of the force than was Miss Withers. "I used to feel that way, too," she confessed. "But I've decided that the police are a lot of nincompoops."

"Not all of them!" Marcia Lee said definitely. She edged toward the stairs, started running down so fast that she tripped and slid the last few steps, spilling her handbag and vanity on the floor. The schoolteacher helped her up.

"And the sergeant may not even be on this case!" pointed out Miss Withers. But Marcia Lee was gone. Miss Withers waited, using all her self-control to keep from rushing after the sirens. Finally the rental agent, a baldish, gum-chewing young man, put in an appearance.

"My name is Leach, Al Leach," he said. "Sorry I'm late, but on my way back from lunch I stopped to see the excitement up on Fifty-seventh." Miss Withers waited. "Oh, it wasn't much," he continued. "Some fellow just smashed a window at Vanderbock's and grabbed an emerald ring."

"Imagine!" said Miss Withers. "Did they catch him?"

Leach shook his head. "He ducked around the corner, so a man told me. But everybody says that the police have drawn a sort of dragnet around the whole section. When you leave you'll have to be searched."

"Will I?" gasped the schoolteacher.

"Now about the apartments," he continued. "The painters and decorators will be finished in a day or so. I phoned the agencies to send every man they could dig up. The rent's eighty-five on a year's lease—and if you want any special shade on the paint now's the time to say so." Miss Withers hesitated, and he cocked his head. "I could let you have the top floor a bit cheaper—say seventy-five? It's had a first coat in a slightly darker tone, and the floor's been polished . . ."

Miss Withers hadn't thought about going that high. But it was worth looking into. "You go right ahead," he said. "I got to stay here a minute and give those painters hell for taking so long for lunch." He headed for the front door where outside a truck was backing up.

Up the stairs, all three flights of them, went Miss Hildegarde Withers. She opened the door of the top-floor apartment, and entered. Instantly the pleasant smile with which she had been intending to greet her future home was erased by a quick gasp. She walked slowly forward into the big living room, stepping gingerly like a cat on a damp floor.

It was the walls. On the creamy white of the smooth surface some-one had painted a great blue eye, which wept red tears on the base-board. Beside it was a pink tree with a mermaid's tail instead of roots, and across one branch, limply twisted like a piece of warm butter-scotch, was a curious object which was—which must be!—a pocket watch with hands pointing to five o'clock.

Miss Withers drew back and sniffed. This was not even good sur-realist art. Then she realized that she was not alone. There was a man standing beside her, breathing rather warmly on the back of her neck. He wore streaked white coveralls and carried a pail of paint. His face, too, was well smeared.

"Now tell me honestly what you think!" he begged, waving at the wall. "Have I got something there, or not?"

"Why—" Miss Withers backed away a little, not sure whether a laugh or a scream was indicated. The man wasn't drunk, because the rank smell about him was linseed oil, not alcohol.

"You mustn't go," he said thickly. There was pleading in his voice. "I have to explain about the white, white walls. Nobody can go on forever painting white, white, white. . . ." He stopped suddenly. "I'd like to paint you. I'd like to do you all pale blue, with your hair a rich yellowish-green." His smile faded, and the dreamy, puffy eyes widened. "It won't hurt!"

There was no getting past him to the door. Miss Withers had her umbrella, and now she raised it like a lance. "Stand back!"

"Don't scream, lady!" But she did scream, a goodly yip. Her voice echoed hollowly in the empty room. "Don't do that, lady!" he shouted, raising the pail of paint as if to hurl it.

"Mister Leach!" shrieked Miss Withers. There was the pounding of footsteps on the stairs. The painter, ignoring the paralyzed school-ma'am, turned toward the door, waiting. An expression of innocent enjoyment marked his face. He lifted the pail.

"Look out!" Miss Withers cried. "Don't!" But poor Leach came rushing into the room. His eyes took in the scene, his brain reacted, but his legs of their own volition took him three steps closer before they stopped. And by that time the pail of paint was over him. He lurched back, reeling and pawing at his eyes. Then he turned, stum-bled, and half fell down the stairs.

The painter turned back toward Miss Withers, but that lady had seized her opportunity and was now disappearing into the bathroom. The lock clicked behind her.

"Come on out, lady!" howled the painter. "The paint won't hurt you. If you don't like it you can wash it off!" He pounded on the door, kept on pounding until Leach came back up the stairs with two other painters and the nearest patrolman. Miss Withers even then did not unlock the door, not until the painter had been overpowered and pinned to the paint-covered floor. An ambulance arrived, and the doctor took one look and whipped out a hypodermic needle.

"Two minims of hyoscine m.c.," he observed cheerily, "and sleepy-by is what he needs."

"Do they ever get over it?" Miss Withers wanted to know.

"Lead poisoning? Why, sure. Give him a nice stomach wash of magnesium sulphate and he'll be good as new in a week, maybe sooner. Lots of painters get it—the lead in paint, you know. Delusions and so forth. It often takes the form of mild mania."

"Mild!" said Miss Withers bitterly. She gathered herself together as best she could, waded through the pools of spilled paint, and then stopped short in the doorway as Inspector Oscar Piper thundered up the stairs, followed by the young sergeant and a policeman. Piper was curious.

"What's that ambulance doing outside, and what's going on here, and—"

"How nice of you to drop over," said the schoolteacher sweetly. "You're only about ten minutes late."

The inspector listened to what had happened, and shook his head. "You know, Hildegarde, wherever you are, there's trouble. You breed it, like stagnant water breeds mosquitoes."

"Hmmp!" Miss Withers started down the stairs, stood aside to let the stretcher go past her. The inspector followed her, almost amused now.

"It must have been funny, though," he observed. "Your walking in on that screwball painter. It could happen to nobody but you, nobody in the world."

They came into the lower hall. "At least," she said tartly, "you can't blame me for what happened up on Fifty-seventh Street today. So lightning struck twice in the same place, eh? And is your dragnet working?"

He shrugged. "We can't tell yet. I think we'll get the guy—in spite of your tipping off the whole thing to the papers."

"I hope you do," she said sweetly. Then her head jerked back, like that of a startled horse. "What?"

Doggedly, he repeated it. And she stood there, rigid with indignation, while the inspector turned to confer with his aides and with the doctor. There was some question, it seemed, about the identity of the ambulance patient. "Book him at the hospital as John Doe for the time being," he ordered. "Mains, you can check with the employment office and the painters' union and find out who he is." He turned back to Miss Withers. "Hey, where are you going?"

"Home!" said that lady, very definitely.

"Well, you better let me send Sergeant Mains to pass you through the cordon, or—"

"I want no favors from you!" she snapped. "The idea of your thinking *I* blabbed to the papers!"

"Well?" shrugged Piper. "Nobody knew about the dragnet, outside of the department, except you and the commissioner."

"I knew—and the *commissioner!*" she exploded. "Of course, *I* must be the one. *I* have so many reporters in *my* outer office, and *I'm* in politics and need the good will of the papers, and . . ." The inspector was trying to talk, but she was not in the mood to listen. "And all right for you, Oscar Piper. You stood me up for dinner the other night. Well, now you can stew in your own juice. Go back to your precious dragnet, and see what it brings you. And when it fails, don't come to *me!*"

"That, my boy," said the inspector slowly, "is what they call giving somebody a piece of one's mind." Sergeant Mains stood beside him, looking dubiously after the departing schoolma'am. "The sad part about it is that she's right," Piper finished.

Consciousness of rectitude gave Miss Hildegarde Withers no inner feeling of satisfaction whatever on her homeward march, which was interrupted for nearly twenty minutes while she stood in line to have her handbag searched. The cordon was tight, no doubt about that.

She flounced back into her own apartment in the West Seventies, the apartment which she had decided to vacate in a month. In spite of herself she spent the rest of the afternoon listening in on the police wave-length. At six o'clock she turned back to the regular news broadcast and heard an announcer declaim that today New York had seen its most spectacular manhunt since the capture of Two-gun Crowley—a manhunt which was by this time admittedly a failure.

"I told him so," Miss Withers snapped at her mirror, without pleasure. By the time she had picked at her dinner and done up the dishes, she was definitely uneasy. Somewhere, deep down in the bottom of her mind, the schoolteacher sensed that a signal light was burning, as it had burned so many times before, to tell her that she had missed something. It was an angry red signal. . . .

At nine o'clock the boys cried an extra through the streets, with headlines Cop Killer Returns—Gets Rest of Loot. There were remarks about butter-fingered police, and the need for a shakeup at Centre Street.

Much to her surprise, Miss Withers was not surprised at all when her doorbell rang some time later, and she found the inspector outside. He was a very tired and gray and deflated inspector.

"Oh," she said. "Come in."

He hesitated. "I thought of sending you flowers, only all the florists are closed. And I was going to have a Western Union messenger come up and sing you something, only they don't know the songs with the right words." He smiled wanly. "You see, it *was* the commissioner that gave out that story to the press."

"Come on in!" she insisted. "For heaven's sake, come on in." She stared at him. "Oscar Piper, have you eaten anything today?"

He shrugged. "I don't remember." But he came inside, sank into a chair. "I'm not hungry," he insisted. "Would you be hungry if they were going to take away your badge tomorrow morning? I'll be back at a precinct desk, see if I'm not."

"No luck at all with the dragnet?"

"None. We picked up three or four crooks we'd been looking for, but none of them is up to this sort of crime. And no trace anywhere of that emerald—that hunk of green ice!"

She fed him scrambled eggs, made him clean up the plate. She even insisted on his smoking one of his long greenish-brown cigars, a privilege hitherto denied him in her domain. Oscar Piper stared unhappily at the smoke as it rose.

"It's the same crook," he observed. "With the same twisted sense of humor. He made a laughing stock of me and the entire force."

"An egomaniac," agreed the schoolteacher. Now the red bulb in the back of her mind was flashing and glowing like a neon sign. "A maniac—" She gulped. "Oscar! Suppose that your dragnet didn't fail! Suppose that it didn't catch your crook because he rode through in an ambulance!"

Piper tensed, then relaxed again. "I checked all that, Hildegarde," he told her. "The painter, you mean. No, he was a real painter, registered and everything. And I called Bellevue and he was really brought in there to the emergency ward, booked for lead poisoning."

"When?"

The inspector thought it was about an hour ago.

She rose suddenly and headed for the bedroom, where her telephone was installed. Oscar Piper puffed unhappily, and she was back before the long gray ash had fallen from his cigar. "Oscar!" she announced. "Bellevue released that man twenty minutes ago, to a nurse from the Painters' Union Clinic!"

"Well? What's wrong with that?"

"Nothing at all. Except that I called Information, and there *is no* Painters' Union Clinic."

The inspector rocked back on his heels as if he had run into a haymaker. "That does it! Now I know I ought to quit the force and get a job as understudy to an idiot!" He started pacing the floor. "We had him! We had him, and just because he put on an act with a bucket of paint we sent him off in an ambulance with our blessing! Good gravy!"

"What about the emerald?" Miss Withers suggested.

"He swallowed it, probably. Anyway, it's gone and so is he . . ."

She shook her head. "A man as smart as that wouldn't risk swallowing the jewel, not when he faced the prospect of stomach pumps at the hospital. No, Oscar."

"Well, then?"

The red light flared again in the back of her mind, flared into an electric sign as clear as the messages which went twinkling around the *Times* Building.

"Oscar! The deadline or dragnet or whatever it is—it's all over?"

He nodded. "We had to order the men back to their regular duty, after they'd all met in the middle of the area and reported a blank." Miss Withers was grabbing her hat. "Hey—"

"Come on!" she cried. "Get a taxi."

The taxicab was not necessary, as it developed that young Sergeant Mains and a Headquarters car waited below. They piled in and Miss Withers gave an address. "And please, no siren!" she begged. "I know you all love the things, the way small boys love a whistle, but just this once . . ."

They cut south along Central Park West, red lights blazing, and then left at the Circle. . . . And then they were outside the remodeled brownstone, with its UNFURNISHED APARTMENTS sign. "Wait here," ordered Piper, looking at the sergeant. Miss Withers was already rushing up the steps, and he hurried after her. The front door was half open, and in the lower hall with its muddle of equipment one pale light bulb gleamed. Most particularly did it gleam down upon Miss Marcia Lee Smith, who seemed a bit startled.

"Still looking for the rental agent?" quizzed the schoolma'am. Marcia Lee gasped, blinked, and answered. "Oh, it's you! I—why— I—" She was peering toward the door. "You 'member when we were here this afternoon? And I spilled my bag? Well, I lost eighty-five dollars somehow. I must have, because it's gone. You didn't see it, did you?"

Miss Withers said that it had been years since she had seen that much money all at one time. The inspector pushed into the scene. "What makes, anyway?"

"You remember Miss Smith," said the schoolteacher. "She and I were looking for apartments the other day, and we met again today. Our paths are always crossing."

"You haven't seen anybody hanging around upstairs?" Piper demanded of the girl.

"I haven't been upstairs," the girl admitted. "It was so dark and lonesome—I had just about decided I'd run along home and come back and look for my money in the morning."

"A very good idea," agreed Miss Withers. "It's a bit late for you to be out. But, by the way—" she lowered her voice—"there's a friend of yours outside in the car."

The inspector was already on his way up the stairs, and Miss Withers hurried along after him. They approached the top-floor apartment on tiptoe, entered softly in the wake of the round beam cast by Piper's flashlight. The big living room was empty, except for the half-dried puddles of paint not yet cleared away. The kitchen, the bath, the bedroom, the closets—all empty.

"Maybe we're too late," Piper said. "Maybe he's been and gone, with the emerald." But Miss Withers thought not. They began to search. An empty apartment offers few hiding places. Piper looked under the drain in each bit of plumbing. He looked up the flue of the fireplace, and behind the Venetian blinds. He even raised each window, making sure that the emerald had not been hung outside on a thread.

Finally they both admitted failure. "I wonder," Miss Withers began, "if we might not get some information from that girl. Of course she's outside talking to your handsome sergeant."

Of course she was—they could look down from the window. But even as Piper started to lead the way out of the place, Miss Withers froze. "My ankles!" she whispered. "They feel a draft."

Oscar Piper halted, looking dubious. "Oscar, the back door! Somebody just opened it . . ." she insisted.

He nodded. Then, motioning her to stay behind him, Oscar Piper went softly back into the apartment. He crossed the living room, came into the kitchen. The rear door was closed and locked, but that didn't prove anything. He started to turn. . . .

"Up!" came a voice behind him. "Up high—higher than that!"

The bathroom door opened, and a man came out, a smallish man, no more than five feet six. He was in his middle thirties, and his mouth was twisted in a curious smile. He held an automatic pistol in his right hand.

"Back up!" was the order. "Now go on—both of you!" It was the mad painter, only he wasn't really mad. It was the jewel thief, the murderer of Sam Bodley, the man in the tan raincoat who had jumped so lightly to the waiting car. . . .

"Don't make any moves, copper!" he said.

"What do you think this will get you?" asked Inspector Piper slowly, as he backed into the living room. "Why don't you drop that gun and give yourself up? I know you. You're Joe Swinton . . . Swinnerton? . . . Swinston, that's it!"

There was a difficult pause. "That's too bad," said the man with the gun. "Sorry you recognized me, copper. Because now I've got to knock you over, and I wasn't going to do that . . ."

Oscar Piper may have been worried, but he did not show it. "You haven't nerve enough to shoot."

"I've got more nerve than you," Swinston told him, and looked it. Miss Withers, who had been edging imperceptibly toward the front window, realized that of all the tough spots they had ever been in, this was about the toughest.

The inspector's body was as tense as a coiled spring, but he kept his voice easy. "Come on, Joe, where did you stash the emerald?"

Swinston didn't take the bait. "What good would it do you to know, copper? *You* aren't going looking for that hunk of green ice. . . ." His mouth was smiling, but his eyes squinted narrowly, and he tightened in preparation for the recoil of the gun. It's now or never, said Hildegarde Withers to herself, and grasped the cord of the Venetian blind. It fell with a most terrific clatter. Swinston, caught off guard, turned and fired blindly. At almost the same instant he was kicked most deftly in the stomach by Oscar Piper, who had his own ideas about the amount of courtesy which should be extended to cop killers.

"Not exactly sporting, Oscar, but well-timed," observed the schoolteacher, as the inspector slipped bracelets on the writhing bandit.

He looked up at her. "You all right?"

"It's about time you wondered," she told him, eyeing the neat round hole in the wall beside her left ear. But what interested her most was the sequence of events down on the sidewalk. The inspector came up beside her at the window, and they both stared down, wide-eyed.

Far below them, beside the Headquarters car, Sergeant Mains was embracing Marcia Lee Smith. And a curious embrace it was, for he had her arm pinned behind her back and was, at the moment, twisting it.

"When the shot went off she tried to swing a sap on me!" complained the bewildered young sergeant later, as they waited at the curb for the Black Maria, prisoners handcuffed together.

Piper grinned. "You've been monkeying with a buzz saw, Romeo. This dame is the one who drove the getaway car, in blonde wig and glasses. Then she hopped out and came back to give us a wrong steer on the description of her boy friend. Didn't you, honey chile?"

Marcia Lee swore at him in a South Brooklyn accent. "Don't talk," Joe Swinston told her.

"You'll talk," the Inspector said, "when we find that emerald." He suddenly jumped as something cold and wet was dropped into his hand by Miss Hildegarde Withers, who had lingered in the apartment for a moment while he was shoving his captive down the stairs. "What the blazes—"

"Of course," Miss Withers said. "Mr. Swinston here has just the type of mind that would see humor in hiding the emerald—the green ice—where he did. I should have figured it out sooner." She pointed to what Piper held gingerly in his hand.

They all looked down and saw, by the pale light of the street lamp, a melting ice cube in which glittered a big square drop of green fire.

MacKINLAY KANTOR

The Grave Grass Quivers

We were alone, out there in the soft spring sunshine. There was no one to disturb us. We dug silently, carefully.

The clinging, black earth came up at every shovelful—moist and alive with the richness of the prairies. We had been digging for ten minutes, when my shovel struck against something, and something cracked.

After that, it wasn't long before we began to uncover things. "Murdered," Doc said, once, and then he didn't talk any more.

It began in Doc Martindale's office, which, as soon as he retired, was to be my office, on a cool spring afternoon in 1921.

"How's it going?" asked Doc.

"I guess it'll be pretty slow here, to live," I said, childishly.

"Not much excitement," agreed Doc. He went to the door and picked up a copy of the *Cottonwood Herald* which a boy had just tossed over the banisters. . . . "Yes, local news is slow, pretty slow. There's a sample of a Cottonwood thriller."

It told of the plans for Arbor Day. The children of the public schools were going to set out some trees as a memorial to the local boys who had died in the World War.

. . . and selected as their choice, American elms. The trees will be planted on the Louis Wilson farm, above the Coon River. Mr. Wilson has agreed to donate a small plot of ground for this purpose. It is thought that these trees, standing on a high hill above the river and overlooking a majestic view of our city, will be a fitting memorial.

Ceremonies are to begin at 2 p.m., and it is urged that all local people attend. Rev. J. Medley Williams of the Baptist Church will deliver a—

Doc pulled his gray beard and laughed. "A few meetings, a church social, once in a while a fire or an auto accident! Once in a blue moon we have a divorce. Life comes—and goes—without much hullabaloo."

Then I had to laugh also, and a bit sheepishly. "I guess I'm rather silly. Of course those are the important things in most people's lives. But I would like to get called in on a nice, exciting murder once in a while!"

Doc was silent for a moment. He appeared to be thinking heavily, as if he had taken me seriously. "Murders," he said, after a moment. "Once before the war, a Mexican section worker stabbed his wife. Then back in '96, an insane farmer shot his neighbor. But, come to think about it, those are the only murders we've ever had here in all my years of practice." He seemed much impressed. "Think of that, think of that! Only two murders since 1861."

"And who," I inquired idly, "was murdered in 1861?"

He tugged at his beard again, and cleared his throat. "Well," he said, slowly, "it was my father and my brother."

"Oh." And I scarcely knew what to say. "I'm sorry, Doctor, I—"

"No matter." He shrugged. "It's a long time. I was just a boy then."

My curiosity was aroused. "What are the details, Doctor? That is, if you don't—"

"Oh, I don't mind. . . . Sit down and take it easy." He fumbled around for his matches, and his fat, brown cigar had been fogging the room for several minutes before he began.

"My brother Titus—he was a lot older—had run away from home when he was small, and gone West with some folks. He didn't come back until the spring of '61. And when he came, what a time!"

He laughed his short, dry laugh.

"Titus had struck it rich. He had about seven thousand dollars in gold with him.

"Pa and Titus decided to take the gold to Hamilton. There was a sort of bank opened up there, and the folks were afraid to risk keeping so much money around home.

"They were pretty careful, too, and didn't tell around town much about what they planned. They started out at night, figuring to get clear away from Cottonwood, and the settlers who knew them, before daylight. Pa and Titus were big strapping men. They looked very strong, setting up on the board laid across the plank wagon box, and Titus carried a navy revolver on his hip and a Sharps rifle across his knees."

Doc Martindale shifted his fat, bumpy body in his old swivel chair. "And that," he said, "was the last we ever saw them.

"On the evening of the second day after my folks left," Dr. Martindale continued, "a farmer from the Salt Creek neighborhood rode up in front of our house, and said that he had seen our team down in a clump of willows by Little Hell Slough, hitched to a wagon, and that the men folks were not with the wagon. The team had been dragging around, and tried to go home, but they got hung up in the willows."

Old Doc was silent for several minutes.

"That was a terrible night," he said, simply. "Before we all got down to Little Hell Slough—most of the neighbors were with us— we found the team in those willows, pretty muddy and hungry, and tangled up in the harness, too.

"None of the stuff in the wagon had been taken except—sure: the gold was gone. The blankets were still there, and Titus's rifle, but his navy revolver wasn't anywhere around. And there was no other sign of Pa and Titus.

"I drove Ma and the girls home, in that wagon. Ma sat there beside me on the board, stiff and solemn. Once she said, 'Georgie, if they're gone and gone for good, you'll get the man who did it. Won't you?' I began to cry, of course. I says, 'Yes, Ma. I'll take care of you always, Ma. . . . But if they're dead, it wasn't a man who killed 'em. It was men. One man wouldn't be a match for Titus alone.' "

Doc was buried in the thickening shadows of the office. I couldn't see his face any more.

"Then I went back with the men. We searched the river, up and down the hills around Cottonwood, too, clear down the East Fork. And never found a thing.

"In that wagon there was just one clue—just one thing which made it certain in our minds that they were dead. That was a little spot of dried blood on the floor of the wagon, right behind the seat. About half as big as your hand. Seemed like, if they'd been shot off the wagon, there'd have been more blood. Then, too, the horses were a fairly young team and they might have cut loose and run away if any shooting had started.

"It was always the general opinion that the murderers had disposed of the bodies in the river. But, personally, I always hung to the idea that Titus and Pa were killed in some mysterious way, and their bodies buried. The fact is that the entire community searched for a week, and then gave it up. No other clue was ever discovered, and no further information of any kind was ever unearthed.

"I didn't quit searching for months. Eli Goble helped me, too; he worked like grim death. But we couldn't find a thing."

I asked, "Who was Eli Goble?"

There was the dull scraping of Doc's shoes on the floor. "Seems to me that you cashed a check this noon, boy. Where did you cash it?"

Somewhat perplexed, I told him. "At the bank across the street."

"Well, that's Eli Goble. And where are you living temporarily—until you can find rooms or an apartment to your liking?"

"At the—Oh, of course, Doctor. The Goble Hotel."

He chuckled. "Everything in this town's Goble, boy. He came here in '59 with a man named Goble, but that wasn't Eli's real name. He had heard that his folks came from Ohio, but didn't know anything about it. You see, his family was killed in the Mint Valley massacre, about 1840, and he had been kidnaped by the Indians. Lived with the Sioux until he was sixteen—could talk the language like a native, too. In fact, lots of folks used to think he was part Indian. But he wasn't. And during the search, he thought all the trailing experience which he had had when among the Indians might be of some account. But even that didn't help. We couldn't find a thing."

I said, slowly, "He's rich, now?"

Doc sighed, and began to hunt around for the light switch. "Suspecting Eli Goble, are you?" He chuckled. "I don't believe anybody ever did, before. He never had a cent to his name for years after that. A few months later he enlisted in the army, served all through the war, and didn't come back here till 1867. In the meantime, through someone he met in the army, he had been trying to get track of his family. And eventually he succeeded. Found the original family, back in Ohio. He got what money was coming to him, brought it out here to Cottonwood, invested it carefully, and made good. He retained the name of Goble for convenience's sake. Now he's almost ninety, but he's one of the richest men in the state, and one of the tightest. He never lets go of a nickel until the Goddess of Liberty yells for mercy."

The big yellow light hissed into being. It glared down on the white-enameled table, the glistening cabinets and instruments, the old desk and rows of books. Doc Martindale stood there in the middle of the office and nodded his head. "That's the story, boy. Real live mystery, just sixty years old this spring. . . ."

We were just putting on our hats, and Doc was struggling into his old brown slicker, when the telephone rang. Martindale took up the receiver. "Doctor Martindale speaking."

"Oh," he said, after a moment. "Well." And then he winked quickly at me above the telephone. "Did you use any of that stimulant I left last time? . . . Yes. I'm leaving the office now, to go home, and I'll stop in. Yes."

He replaced the receiver on its hook. "Speak of the devil," he said. "Eli Goble's just had another heart attack. Nothing to get excited about. He has them frequently, but in between times he's up and down and around. We'll stop in to see him for a minute."

The Goble house was only a few minutes' drive from the main business streets. . . . Lights glowed from most of the windows as we came up the sidewalk. "You can tell that Eli's flat on his back," said Doc. "If he was around, he wouldn't let them burn all that electricity."

The old man watched us from his pillow, with black, red-rimmed eyes deeply sunk beneath the moldy fuzz of his eyebrows. . . . He was breathing heavily.

"Well, Eli. How do you feel? This is Dr. Patterson, Eli."

The old man seemed to glare broodingly at me.

"Don't feel—so—good," Goble manged with difficulty. "Plagued heart seems—like—played out on me."

Martindale began to open his bag. "Oh, nothing to worry about, Eli. We'll fix it all up right." He made a perfunctory examination. "You'll feel better soon, Eli. Sleep tight."

The old man mumbled and coughed; and we went down the shadowy stairway, through the gloomy, over-ornate hall, and out to the front door.

It was four o'clock the next afternoon when Doc Martindale and I arrived at the office, following a round of calls on widely separated cases. Beyond a few hasty reports to the girl whom Doc Martindale kept in his office during the midday hours, we had enjoyed no contact with the town of Cottonwood since 10 a.m.

When we returned in Doc's old touring car, it was to find the *Cottonwood Herald* spread on the table with plenty of black ink decorating the front page.

ELI GOBLE GIVES PARK TO CITY
Local Businessman and Pioneer Settler Decides on Memorial
Plans Changed for Tomorrow's Dedication

At a special meeting of the city council this afternoon, it was unanimously agreed to accept the gift tendered by Eli Goble, revered Civil War veteran and early settler in Cottonwood, who today offered to give the town of Cottonwood some thirty acres of beautiful woodland, to be known as "Goble Memorial Park."

It is understood that Mr. Goble has been ill, and that is the reason for a delay in his plans.

"The grand old man of Crockett County" stipulated in the terms of his gift that the proposed Memorial Grove of trees should be set out somewhere in the new park area. This necessitated a hasty change in plans. Instead of being planted on the north hill, on the Louis Wilson farm above the Coon River, the trees will be set out on the brow of the east hill, which is included in the thirty acres donated by Mr. Goble.

A big parade, forming in the city hall square, and proceeding across the east bridge toward the new park, will officially open the Arbor Day ceremonies at two o'clock tomorrow afternoon. Following an invocation by Rev. J. Medley Williams, the Cottonwood city band will—

We leaned there, side by side with our hands upon the desk, and read that newspaper story.

Doc tapped the paper with his forefinger. "I'll go on record as saying," he declared, "that this is the first thing Eli Goble ever gave away in his life—at least the first thing in which there wasn't some chance of his getting value received out of it. And I don't see what he can get out of this, except glory. . . . Eli doesn't care a rap for glory. Listen to Editor Nollins calling him 'the grand old man of Crockett County.' That's because Eli holds a mortgage on the *Herald* building."

Two patients drifted in for examination. . . . When I left, an hour later, I looked back to see Doctor Martindale sitting there in his swivel chair, a tired hulk, still reading the *Cottonwood Herald*.

At five-thirty in the morning, Old Doc was beating on my door. I arose, startled, and feeling that nothing short of peritonitis or a breech delivery could have made him summon me so insistently.

He came into the hotel room and waited while I threw on my clothes. "What is it?" I asked, between splashes of cold water.

"We're going out and do a little digging," he said.

I nodded. "Appendectomy? Or what?"

"Nothing so unimportant," Doc replied. And his eyes looked as if he had been awake all night—red-rimmed and circled. . . . "Real digging. No one will know where we are. If Mrs. Gustafson takes a notion to sink and die while we're away, she'll just have to sink and die." He said it with seeming brutality. I was still too sleepy to press him for more details, or to wonder what it was all about.

But when we got out to the curbing in front of the hotel, and I glanced into the rear seat of Doc's car, there lay two spades, a scoop-shovel and a pickax.

I turned with an exclamation of astonishment.

"Get in," said Doc. And I did, without any more words. He drove down Main Street, north on Kowa Avenue, and under the Burling-ton viaduct. We seemed to be heading north of town. Two minutes later our car was making the Coon River bridge rattle and bang in every loose joint.

"This is the Louis Wilson farm," said Doc. "Hm. I reckon we can turn here past the Cedar school, and drive down the lane past the timber."

At the furthest corner of the cornfield we climbed out, taking the shovels and ax with us. Doc was breathing hoarsely, but the strange pallor had left his face. . . . His eyes were bright and intent; there was something almost furious in their gleam.

He led me through a fringe of oak timberland, skirting two brushy ravines, and coming out on a sloping knoll where one solitary oak tree stood, stunted and twisted by many winds. The grass beneath our feet was coarse, tangled, flat-bladed. Native prairie sod, without a doubt. . . . Far away, a band of crows was circling over the river, cawing with faint and raucous cries.

"This is the north hill," said Doc. "There's the town."

It was a very high hill, this bald mound on which we stood. Beneath us the Coon River swung in a flat band of glistening brown.

The thin, brittle grass of the barren hill was tufted with hundreds of pale, lilac-pastel flowers. The blossoms grew on short, fuzzy stems; the petals shaded from white to purple, with a heart of yellow in each flower.

"They're beautiful," I said. "I never saw anything like them before. What are they?"

"Wind-flowers. Easter flowers. Or I guess the more modern name is pasque-flower. Pretty things, aren't they? One of the earliest we have around here. . . . Well, I'm going to get busy."

Doc dropped the shovel he was carrying, and I was just as willing to relinquish the heavy load in my own arms. I went over and sat down against the gnarled oak tree, which was the only tree on all that bald, brownish hill. A million facts and statements and conjectures seemed to be boiling in my brain; I could make nothing out of them.

Before my eyes, Doc Martindale was behaving in a very strange manner. He was walking slowly in vague, indefinite circles, his eyes staring at the ground in front of him. Occasionally he would move up beyond the brow of the hill and sweep the surrounding area with his eyes. I had the strange notion that Doctor George Martindale, after unloading the sad story of his youth, had taken two days in going deliberately and completely insane.

He thrust a small piece of stick into the ground, moved away, surveyed the spot carefully, and then came back to set up another stick, several feet from the first. He repeated this process two more times. He now had an uneven rectangle, eight or ten feet long, marked at its corners by the bits of stick. "We'll try it here," he said.

Without another word, he removed his coat, lifted the pickax, and sent its point into the ground.

I cried, "Wait a minute! Won't people down in the town see us up here?"

"They'll think we're cows or pigs," said Doc.

And, as I have said before, we were alone—out there in the thin sunshine of early morning. We dug silently. Neither of us spoke a word. After Doc had penetrated some two feet in depth, at one side of the rectangle, he moved out toward the middle of the space he had marked. I followed, with my shovel.

We had been digging for about ten minutes when we began to find things.

"Murdered," said Doc.

We were finding them, picking out the disordered relics from the rich earth where they had lain so long. Tibiae, ribs . . . phalanges . . . the rusty remains of an ancient revolver.

Doc straightened up, and spoke to me gently. His face was set and strained; it might have been cast in iron. "There's a sheet and a grain sack or two in the car," he said. "Will you go over and bring them?"

I was glad of the opportunity to get away for a few minutes. When I came back, Doc had most of the bones covered with his coat. The knees of his trousers were dark and earthy; he had been kneeling in the loose mold of the grave, picking out the smaller fragments.

"I want a witness," he said, shortly. "Take a look at this." From beneath the coat he withdrew a human skull and turned it slowly for me to see. There was a complete and noticeable fracture, such as

might have been caused by the blow of a sharp ax. "The other is the same way," he added, and replaced the skull tenderly.

Then I spoke for the first time. "Can you identify them?"

"Easily," he said. "There's a Masonic pocket-piece, the revolver, and knives and things. . . . The pocket-piece is the best bet. It's engraved with Pa's name. Not corroded at all. I rubbed it up and could read the engraving."

Wisely, he made no attempt to identify or isolate the separate skeletons. The bones made awkward bundles in the grain sacks. We worked slowly, carrying them and the shovels back to the car. I was too stunned by the grim reality to ask any questions. We went away and left that uneven black hole in the middle of the blooming wind-flowers.

Back in town, we went to Doc Martindale's garage, behind his little house on Omaha Street, and left the bundles there. Then we hurried to the office; fortunately there had been no phone calls at either house or office. It was after seven o'clock, and yet I had no desire for breakfast.

Doc sat at his desk and thumbed through a stack of old letters and notebooks. "Clell Howard's living in Long Beach," he muttered. "Got his address somewhere. . . . And Eph Spokesman is with his niece out in Portland. I've got to send telegrams right away." Then, strangely enough, he seemed to discover me standing there. "You go around and look at Mrs. Gustafson and that greenstick fracture and the little Walker boy; tell them I'm busy on an emergency case. Don't say a word to anybody."

"I won't," I promised.

He said, "And be sure you don't forget the parade. It forms at 2 p.m., at the city hall square. You'll want to see that." And then he turned back to his rummaging.

I had all of the bedfast patients bandaged and dosed and sprayed and examined before 1:30 p.m. At two o'clock I was standing with a group of pleasant and gossipy citizens on the steps of the Cottonwood city hall. The triangular "square" was blooming with the gay sweaters and dresses of hundreds of school-children who darted wildly underfoot, seething and yelling in a mad half-holiday.

At twenty minutes after two, the crowd was somewhat impatient. There had been a large turnout; the Boy Scouts were there, and the members of the American Legion, chafing and shifting in line. There was even a huge truck, splashed with vivid bunting, on which were the grove of memorial elms all ready to be set out, their dirt-encrusted roots sticking from beneath the scarlet shimmer of flags like so many witches' claws.

This crowd was waiting for Eli Goble, albeit waiting impatiently. If a man was so kind as to give away thirty acres of land, one could at least expect him to show up for the dedication.

It was almost two-thirty before a big Cadillac touring car slid around the corner of the Phillips's oil station, and the crowds in that vicinity began a desultory hand-clapping. Yes, it was Eli Goble. I could see that bearded, skeleton shape sitting hunched in the rear seat, a Navajo blanket across his knees. His narrow-eyed son, vice-president of the bank, was driving.

Some fortunate fate had directed me to take up my station on those steps, above the mass of children. For I had a clear and un-obstructed view of Doc Martindale, accompanied by a fat, pink-faced man who seemed very nervous, emerging from a dark stairway across the street.

I vaulted over the concrete railing beside me, and shouldered through the knotted humanity. Once or twice I had a quick glance at Doc and the pink-faced man, over the heads of the crowd. They were walking rapidly toward the corner where the Goble car was parked; the pink-faced man was drawing a folded paper from his pocket, and he seemed more nervous than ever.

We reached the corner simultaneously. A benign citizen who wore a white silk badge, "Chairman," fluttering from his coat, was lean-ing at the side of the car, conversing with Eli Goble and his son.

"Daniel," said Doc Martindale.

The chairman turned.

"Get up on the city hall steps," Doc directed him, "and announce to the crowd that Mr. Goble's physician refuses to allow him to par-ticipate in the exercises. Then get them started with their parade."

Daniel began to stammer and sputter.

"Go 'long with you," ordered Doc, firmly. He opened the door of the back seat, and he and the pink-faced man slid in beside Eli Goble. And then Doc saw me standing there. "Get in the front seat, Dr. Patterson," he called, and before I knew it I was sitting beside Vincent Goble, who was too excited even to bow.

"I don't understand this," he said importantly. "You're carrying things off with a very high hand, Doctor Martindale. It is my father's wish that—"

Doc's lips were thin and firm beneath his scraggly beard. "You keep your mouth shut, Vincent," he said. Vincent Goble gasped.

"Drive around the corner on Queen Street, out of this crowd, and pull up at the curb."

The younger man's face was flaming with rage, but he obeyed the command. The Cadillac purred ahead, past the corner, past the alley, past the crowd. A block away it drew up beside the curb.

Vincent Goble and I swung around to face the trio in back. Eli Goble sat in the middle, clutching and contracting his hands against the red triangles of the Navajo blanket.

"Go ahead, Ed," said Doctor Martindale.

The little pink-faced man gasped apologetically, and fluttered the folds of the paper in his hand. He began a whispered jumble of phrases: "As sheriff of Crockett County, it is my duty to place you, Eli Goble, under arrest. You are charged with the murder of Titus Martindale, and William Martindale, on or about the twenty-fourth of April, in the year 1861—"

Vincent Goble snarled. The old man still sat there, motionless except for the parchment hands which twisted in his lap. "Ain't true," he managed to whisper. "It—ain't true."

"You cowards!" cried his son. The banker's face was livid. "You'd devil the very life out of an old man with some crazy superstition like that! You'd—"

Doc Martindale said, "Drive up to the sheriff's office, Vincent. We want to talk things over."

"Like hell I will! Like—"

Ed Maxon, the sheriff, gulped fearfully. "Yes, Mr. Goble. That's right. Have to ask you to bring your father up to my office."

And so, we went. Vincent, cursing beneath his breath, Doc Martindale silent as the tomb, Ed Maxon twisting and rubbing a damp hand around his collar. And Eli Goble sitting there under the blanket, his eyes like black caverns, and saying: "I—never done it. You'll see. I never done—that."

"You saw the gold at the house. And made up your mind—"

"No."

"You followed them out there on the east prairie. Or maybe you were lying there, waiting for them."

"I never—done it."

"Say, Doctor Martindale! If my father should have another heart attack and die while you're questioning him—"

"Now, Mr. Goble, you—"

"I'm a physician, Vincent. And Eli's my patient. I'll look out for him if he starts to faint. . . . Eli, you killed them from ambush."

"I never. Never did."

"Then you left the bodies in the wagon, took the team, and drove out to the north hill. It was a long drive—must have taken hours to get out there. But you figured that nobody ever went up there, and it was away from the beaten track, and would be a good place to hide the bodies."

"I—I—George, I'm an old man. I—"

"Damn you, Martindale! You—"

"Sit down, Vincent, and shut up. I'm not going to fool with anybody today. . . . Let's take your pulse, Eli. . . . Hm. Guess you can stand it. All right. You buried them out on the north hill. Maybe you drove the wagon back and forth over the grave—an Indian trick. Trick you learned from the Sioux. And probably you scattered lots of grass and brush around."

"No. *No.*"

"Titus had his gun strapped on; you left them in the ground, just as they were. You didn't take anything out of the wagon except those buckskin bags. Then you drove clear around town again, forded the river opposite Salt Creek, and drove over by Little Hell Slough. You left the team there, and skinned out. Took the gold somewhere and hid it, probably."

"Ain't so. Lie. . . ."

"Then you laid low, and waited to join in the search. You were clever, Eli. Clever as an Indian. . . . You helped me search, too. Oh, how we searched! We even went right across that north hill. But we never saw anything that looked like a grave. . . . You kept it covered up, Eli. You were smart."

"Don't. . . . Don't talk so—I can't—"

"By God, you let my father alone!—"

"Now, Mr. Goble. Please. Control yourself. Please—"

"You concluded that seven thousand dollars was a big fortune. Well, it was. Worth waiting for. So you enlisted in the army, took your chances—I'll give you credit for nerve there, Eli—and turned up after the war with that story about finding your relatives and your family property back in Ohio. Yes, you were smart."

"I never—never done it."

"Why did you give this park to the city?"

"Mmmmm. I—"

"The *Herald* carried that Arbor Day announcement night before last. And right away you had a heart attack. And the next morning you came out with that gift to the city. *Provided—*"

"Vincent. Vincent. Make 'em let me—"

"I'll—"

"Here, hold him!"

"I've got him. Now, Mr. Goble, you'll have to sit down."

"Don't be a fool, Vincent. This is true—all true. It's taken me sixty years to find out, but I've found out. . . . You gave that park to the city of Cottonwood, Eli Goble, *provided* that they set out the memorial grove over there, on the east hill, instead of on the north hill. You didn't want anybody digging on the north hill, did you? It had never occurred to you to buy Louis Wilson's farm, so there wouldn't be a chance of people digging that ground up."

"No. . . . Don't talk so, George!. . . Old. I'm an old an'—"

"Well, it was the first thing you ever gave away in your life. And it set me to thinking. I thought, 'Why didn't Eli want that memorial grove planted up there?' And then I began to understand things. I went up there this morning. Doctor Patterson was with me—I have a witness to what I am now about to relate. He saw me dig; he saw me find things. I found *them*, Eli."

Vincent Goble was slumped forward, his head buried in his hands. Eli sat there in the sheriff's big chair, staring across the table. He seemed to be looking squarely through the opposite wall.

"They were murdered, Eli. Their skulls had been broken. A heavy, sharp blow at the back of each skull. I found them."

The old man's lips were gray and rubbery. He whispered. "No, I never done it. Can't prove it was me."

"A hatchet, Eli. Someone had thrown a hatchet—or maybe two hatchets, in quick succession. They were sitting on that wagon board, in the bright moonlight. It would have been easy for anyone who could throw a tomahawk."

Doc fumbled in the breast pocket of his coat, and brought out three folded squares of yellow paper. "I'll read to you all," he said calmly. "Three telegrams. The first one I sent myself, early this morning, to Clell Howard, in Long Beach, California, and to Ephriam Spokesman in Portland, Oregon. . . . Remember those names, Eli? . . . Clell was mayor here once. And Eph Spokesman— everybody knew him. Here's my telegram: 'Please reply by wire completely and at my expense. During the old days at Cottonwood, what man was skillful at throwing a knife or hatchet. Search your recollection and reply at once.'

"Here's the first reply I got. It came from Ephraim Spokesman's niece. Came about eleven o'clock. You can read it yourself, gentlemen. It says, 'Uncle Eph very sick but says man named Goble thought to be a half-breed was only one who could throw hatchet.

Wants to hear full details why you ask.'

"Along about eleven-forty-five, I got a telegram from Clell Howard. Here it is: 'Hello old neighbor regards to you. Am almost ninety but recall perfectly how I lost five dollars betting Eli Goble couldn't stick hatchet ten times in succession in big tree by Halsey blacksmith shop.' "

The room was perfectly still except for the hoarse sputtering in Eli Goble's throat. "No," he whispered tremulously. "No."

Doc Martindale pointed to the further corner of the dusty old room. There was a table, which none of us had noticed before, and on that table was a white sheet, rumpled and bulky. . . . "Eli," said Doc, quietly. "They're over there. In the corner."

The aged man stiffened in his chair. His back arched up, the shoulders quaking; his claw hands seemed to be wrenching a chunk of wood from the table in front of him.

"Father!" his son cried.

Eli Goble shook his head, and dropped back in his chair, his deep-set eyes dull with a flat, blue light. "The dead," he whispered. "They found me. . . . They're here in this room. I done it. I killed them. Titus and Bill. Yes. Yes."

Vincent Goble dropped down, his head buried in his arms, and began to sob—big, gulping sobs. The sheriff twisted nervously in his seat.

"George. You—you gonna send me to—prison? You gonna have them—hang me? I'm old . . . I done it. Yes."

Doc Martindale cleared his throat. "Yes, you are old, Eli. Lot older than I am. It's too late, now, to do anything about it. I told my mother I'd get the man, and—But I can't see what good it would do, now, to send you to jail or even try you for murder."

Sheriff Maxon wiped his forehead. "The law," he said shrilly, "the law must take its course! Eli Goble, you must—"

"No," said Old Doc, decisively. "I'm running this show, Ed. Without me, without my testimony and the case I've built up, there isn't any show against Eli. I won't prosecute him, or furnish evidence."

"But he confessed to this murder!" shrilled Maxon. "He—"

Doc nodded. "Orally. Yes, but what if Vincent and Dr. Patterson and myself all swear that he never confessed? What if I destroy—the evidence!"

Maxon shook his head and bit his lips.

"How much is your father worth?" asked Doc of Vincent Goble.

The banker lifted his face, on which the weary, baffled tears were still wet. "Couple of million, I guess."

"All yours," whispered Eli.

"Maybe," Doc nodded. "Seven thousand dollars. Quite a nest egg, in those days. Like fifty thousand, now. Or even more. . . . No, gentlemen. Money won't do me any good. It can't bring back Titus and my father. But it can still do good. Yes."

Eli Goble's eyes had closed, like dark windows on which ragged curtains had been drawn. "I've seen 'em—I've seen 'em. Always. Since I got old—they come back. . . . I had to give in. Yes."

"You'll go home," said Doc. "I'll give you something to put you to sleep. Then, after you have a little rest and get your strength back, you'll have a lawyer up at your house. . . . You will give, to this county in which you live, one million dollars for the purpose of founding and endowing a modern hospital, where every inhabitant can secure the best medical and surgical attention, free of charge. How does that sound?"

Head still buried in his arms, Vincent Goble nodded drunkenly. His father had opened his eyes and was shivering, still staring through the blank wall ahead of him. "Yes. Anything. . . . I give—anything. But take me away. I want to go—home. . . . I'm old. I don't want to stay in—this room. I don't want to stay with—*them.*"

After Eli Goble was in bed, and asleep, Doc and I came out into the damp warmth of the spring afternoon. Martindale looked ten years older than he had the day before. "After this," he said, "after everything is taken care of, I'll let things go. . . . You look after the practice beginning next Monday."

Our feet sounded flat and talkative, echoing on the long sidewalk. "One thing," I said. "I can't understand how you found the place. I can see how you reasoned out the rest—about that grove and about Eli Goble's not wanting the trees planted up there. But how did you know where to dig? We could have been up there for days, turning the soil."

Doc felt in his pocket for a cigar which wasn't there. "Wind-flowers," he said quietly. "They were scattered all over that hill. Beautiful, like you said. · . . . But I knew enough to dig where there were no wind-flowers. The grass on that hill looked pretty much alike, all over, but there weren't any flowers growing in that place I marked off. Those little purple flowers are funny. They only grow on native soil. You can't get them to grow where the sod has ever been turned."

ERLE STANLEY GARDNER

The Case
of the Irate Witness

The early-morning shadows cast by the mountains still lay heavily on the town's main street as the big siren on the roof of the Jebson Commercial Company began to scream shrilly.

The danger of fire was always present, and at the sound, men at breakfast rose and pushed their chairs back from the table. Men who were shaving barely paused to wipe lather from their faces; men who had been sleeping grabbed the first available garments. All of them ran to places where they could look for the first telltale wisps of smoke.

There was no smoke.

The big siren was still screaming urgently as the men formed into streaming lines, like ants whose hill has been attacked. The lines all moved toward the Jebson Commercial Company.

There the men were told that the doors of the big vault had been found wide open. A jagged hole had been cut into one with an acetylene torch.

The men looked at one another silently. This was the fifteenth of the month. The big, twice-a-month payroll, which had been brought up from the Ivanhoe National Bank the day before, had been the prize.

Frank Bernal, manager of the company's mine, the man who ruled Jebson City with an iron hand, arrived and took charge. The responsibility was his, and what he found was alarming.

Tom Munson, the night watchman, was lying on the floor in a back room, snoring in drunken slumber. The burglar alarm, which had been installed within the last six months, had been by-passed by means of an electrical device. This device was so ingenious that it was apparent that, if the work was that of a gang, at least one of the burglars was an expert electrician.

Ralph Nesbitt, the company accountant, was significantly silent. When Frank Bernal had been appointed manager a year earlier, Nesbitt had pointed out that the big vault was obsolete.

Bernal, determined to prove himself in his new job, had avoided the expense of tearing out the old vault and installing a new one by investing in an up-to-date burglar alarm and putting a special night watchman on duty.

Now the safe had been looted of a hundred thousand dollars, and Frank Bernal had to make a report to the main office in Chicago, with the disquieting knowledge that Ralph Nesbitt's memo stating that the antiquated vault was a pushover was at this moment reposing in the company files. . . .

Some distance out of Jebson City, Perry Mason, the famous trial lawyer, was driving fast along a mountain road. He had planned a week-end fishing trip for a long time, but a jury which had waited until midnight before reaching its verdict had delayed Mason's departure and it was now eight thirty in the morning.

His fishing clothes, rod, wading boots and creel were all in the trunk. He was wearing the suit in which he had stepped from the courtroom, and having driven all night he was eager for the cool, piny mountains.

A blazing red light, shining directly at him as he rounded a turn in the canyon road, dazzled his road-weary eyes. A sign, *STOP— POLICE,* had been placed in the middle of the road. Two men, a grim-faced man with a .30–30 rifle in his hands and a silver badge on his shirt and a uniformed motorcycle officer, stood beside the sign.

Mason stopped his car.

The man with the badge, deputy sheriff, said, "We'd better take a look at your driving license. There's been a big robbery at Jebson City."

"That so?" Mason said. "I went through Jebson City an hour ago and everything seemed quiet."

"Where you been since then?"

"I stopped at a little service station and restaurant for breakfast."

"Let's take a look at your driving license."

Mason handed it to him.

The man started to return it, then looked at it again. "Say," he said, "you're Perry Mason, the big criminal lawyer!"

"Not a criminal lawyer," Mason said patiently, "a trial lawyer. I sometimes defend men who are accused of crime."

"What are you doing up in this country?"

"Going fishing."

The deputy looked at him suspiciously. "Why aren't you wearing your fishing clothes?"

"Because," Mason said, and smiled, "I'm not fishing."

"You said you were going fishing."

"I also intend," Mason said, "to go to bed tonight. According to you, I should be wearing my pajamas."

The deputy frowned. The traffic officer laughed and waved Mason on.

The deputy nodded at the departing car. "Looks like a live clue to me," he said, "but I can't find it in that conversation."

"There isn't any," the traffic officer said.

The deputy remained dubious, and later on, when a news-hungry reporter from the local paper asked the deputy if he knew of anything that would make a good story, the deputy said that he did.

And that was why Della Street, Perry Mason's confidential secretary, was surprised to read stories in the metropolitan papers stating that Perry Mason, the noted trial lawyer, was rumored to have been retained to represent the person or persons who had looted the vault of the Jebson Commercial Company. All this had been arranged, it would seem, before Mason's "client" had even been apprehended.

When Perry Mason called his office by long-distance the next afternoon, Della said, "I thought you were going to the mountains for a vacation."

"That's right. Why?"

"The papers claim you're representing whoever robbed the Jebson Commercial Company."

"First I've heard of it," Mason said. "I went through Jebson City before they discovered the robbery, stopped for breakfast a little farther on, and then got caught in a roadblock. In the eyes of some officious deputy, that seems to have made me an accessory after the fact."

"Well," Della Street said, "they've caught a man by the name of Harvey L. Corbin, and apparently have quite a case against him. They're hinting at mysterious evidence which won't be disclosed until the time of trial."

"Was he the one who committed the crime?" Mason asked.

"The police think so. He has a criminal record. When his employers at Jebson City found out about it, they told him to leave town. That was the evening before the robbery."

"Just like that, eh?" Mason asked.

"Well, you see Jebson City is a one-industry town, and the company owns all the houses. They're leased to the employees. I understand Corbin's wife and daughter were told they could stay on until Corbin got located in a new place, but Corbin was told to leave town at once. You aren't interested, are you?"

"Not in the least," Mason said, "except that when I drive back I'll be going through Jebson City, and I'll probably stop to pick up the local gossip."

"Don't do it," she warned. "This man Corbin has all the earmarks of being an underdog, and you know how you feel about underdogs."

A quality in her voice made Perry suspicious. "You haven't been approached, have you, Della?"

"Well," she said, "in a way. Mrs. Corbin read in the papers that you were going to represent her husband, and she was overjoyed. It seems that she thinks her husband's implication in this is a raw deal. She hadn't known anything about his criminal record, but she loves him and is going to stand by him."

"You've talked with her?" Mason asked.

"Several times. I tried to break it to her gently. I told her it was probably nothing but a newspaper story. You see, Chief, they have Corbin dead to rights. They took some money from his wife as evidence. It was part of the loot."

"And she has nothing?"

"Nothing. Corbin left her forty dollars, and they took it all as evidence."

"I'll drive all night," he said. "Tell her I'll be back tomorrow."

"I was afraid of that," Della Street said. "Why did you have to call up? Why couldn't you have stayed up there fishing? Why did you have to stop and get your name in the papers?"

Mason laughed and hung up.

*   *   *

Paul Drake, of the Drake Detective Agency, came in and sat in the big chair in Mason's office and said, "You have a bear by the tail, Perry."

"What's the matter, Paul? Didn't your detective work in Jebson City pan out?"

"It panned out all right, but the stuff in the pan isn't what you want, Perry," Drake explained.

"How come?"

"Your client's guilty."

"Go on," Mason said.

"The money he gave his wife was some of what was stolen from the vault."

"How do they know it was the stolen money?" Mason asked.

Drake pulled a notebook from his pocket. "Here's the whole picture. The plant manager runs Jebson City. There isn't any private property. The Jebson company controls everything."

"Not a single small business?"

Drake shook his head. "Not unless you want to consider garbage collecting as small business. An old coot by the name of George Addey lives five miles down the canyon; he has a hog ranch and collects the garbage. He's supposed to have the first nickel he ever earned. Buries his money in cans. There's no bank nearer than Ivanhoe City."

"What about the burglary? The men who did it must have moved in acetylene tanks and—"

"They took them right out of the company store," Drake said. And then he went on: "Munson, the watchman, likes to take a pull out of a flask of whisky along about midnight. He says it keeps him awake. Of course, he's not supposed to do it, and no one was supposed to know about the whisky, but someone did know about it. They doped the whisky with a barbiturate. The watchman took his usual swig, went to sleep, and stayed asleep."

"What's the evidence against Corbin?" Mason asked.

"Corbin had a previous burglary record. It's a policy of the company not to hire anyone with a criminal record. Corbin lied about his past and got a job. Frank Bernal, the manager, found out about it, sent for Corbin about eight o'clock the night the burglary took place, and ordered him out of town. Bernal agreed to let Corbin's wife and child stay on in the house until Corbin could get located in another city.

"Corbin pulled out in the morning, and gave his wife this money. It was part of the money from the burglary."

"How do they know?" Mason asked.

"Now there's something I don't know," Drake said. "This fellow Bernal is pretty smart, and the story is that he can prove Corbin's money was from the vault.

"The nearest bank is at Ivanhoe City, and the mine pays off in cash twice a month. Ralph Nesbitt, the cashier, wanted to install a new vault. Bernal refused to okay the expense. So the company has ordered both Bernal and Nesbitt back to its main office at Chicago to report. The rumor is that they may fire Bernal as manager and give Nesbitt the job. A couple of the directors don't like Bernal, and this thing has given them their chance. They dug out a report Nesbitt had made showing the vault was a pushover. Bernal didn't act on that report." He sighed and then asked, "When's the trial, Perry?"

"The preliminary hearing is set for Friday morning. I'll see then what they've got against Corbin."

"They're laying for you up there," Paul Drake warned. "Better watch out, Perry. That district attorney has something up his sleeve, some sort of surprise that's going to knock you for a loop."

In spite of his long experience as a prosecutor, Vernon Flasher, the district attorney of Ivanhoe County, showed a certain nervousness at being called upon to oppose Perry Mason. There was, however, a secretive assurance underneath that nervousness.

Judge Haswell, realizing that the eyes of the community were upon him, adhered to legal technicalities to the point of being pompous both in rulings and mannerisms.

But what irritated Perry Mason was the attitude of the spectators. He sensed that they did not regard him as an attorney trying to safeguard the interests of a client, but as a legal magician with a cloven hoof. The looting of the vault had shocked the community, and there was a tight-lipped determination that no legal tricks were going to do Mason any good *this* time.

Vernon Flasher didn't try to save his surprise evidence for a whirlwind finish. He used it right at the start of the case.

Frank Bernal, called as a witness, described the location of the vault, identified photographs, and then leaned back as the district attorney said abruptly, "You had reason to believe this vault was obsolete?"

"Yes, sir."

"It had been pointed out to you by one of your fellow employees, Mr. Ralph Nesbitt?"

"Yes, sir."

"And what did you do about it?"

"Are you," Mason asked in some surprise, "trying to cross-examine your own witness?"

"Just let him answer the question, and you'll see," Flasher replied.

"Go right ahead and answer," Mason said to the witness.

Bernal assumed a more comfortable position. "I did three things," he said, "to safeguard the payrolls and to avoid the expense of tearing out the old vault and installing a new vault in its place."

"What were those three things?"

"I employed a special night watchman; I installed the best burglar alarm money could buy; and I made arrangements with the Ivanhoe National Bank, where we have our payrolls made up, to list the number of each twenty-dollar bill which was a part of each payroll."

Mason suddenly sat up straight.

Flasher gave him a glance of gloating triumph. "Do you wish the court to understand, Mr. Bernal," he said smugly, "that you have the numbers of the bills in the payroll which was made up for delivery on the fifteenth?"

"Yes, sir. Not *all* of the bills, you understand. That would have taken too much time, but I have the numbers of all the twenty-dollar bills."

"And who recorded those numbers?" the prosecutor asked.

"The bank."

"And do you have that list of numbers with you?"

"I do. Yes, sir." Bernal produced a list. "I felt," he said, glancing coldly at Nesbitt, "that these precautions would be cheaper than a new vault."

"I move the list be introduced in evidence," Flasher said.

"Just a moment," Mason objected. "I have a couple of questions. You say this list is not in your handwriting, Mr. Bernal?"

"Yes, sir."

"Whose handwriting is it, do you know?" Mason asked.

"The assistant cashier of the Ivanhoe National Bank."

"Oh, all right," Flasher said. "We'll do it the hard way, if we have to. Stand down, Mr. Bernal, and I'll call the assistant cashier."

Harry Reedy, assistant cashier of the Ivanhoe Bank, had the mechanical assurance of an adding machine. He identified the list of numbers as being in his handwriting. He stated that he had listed the numbers of the twenty-dollar bills and put that list in an envelope which had been sealed and sent up with the money for the payroll.

"Cross-examine," Flasher said.

Mason studied the list. "These numbers are all in your handwriting?" he asked Reedy.

"Yes, sir."

"Did you yourself compare the numbers you wrote down with the numbers on the twenty-dollar bills?"

"No, sir. I didn't personally do that. Two assistants did that. One checked the numbers as they were read off, one as I wrote them down."

"The payrolls are for approximately a hundred thousand dollars, twice each month?"

"That's right. And ever since Mr. Bernal took charge, we have taken this means to identify payrolls. No attempt is made to list the bills in numerical order. The serial numbers are simply read off and written down. Unless a robbery occurs, there is no need to do anything further. In the event of a robbery, we can reclassify the numbers and list the bills in numerical order."

"These numbers are in your handwriting—every number?"

"Yes, sir. More than that, you will notice that at the bottom of each page I have signed my initials."

"That's all," Mason said.

"I now offer once more to introduce this list in evidence," Flasher said.

"So ordered," Judge Haswell ruled.

"My next witness is Charles J. Oswald, the sheriff," the district attorney announced.

The sheriff, a long, lanky man with a quiet manner, took the stand. "You're acquainted with Harvey L. Corbin, the defendant in this case?" the district attorney asked.

"I am."

"Are you acquainted with his wife?"

"Yes, sir."

"Now, on the morning of the fifteenth of this month, the morning of the robbery at the Jebson Commercial Company, did you have any conversation with Mrs. Corbin?"

"I did. Yes, sir."

"Did you ask her about her husband's activities the night before?"

"Just a moment," Mason said. "I object to this on the ground that any conversation the sheriff had with Mrs. Corbin is not admissible against the defendant, Corbin; furthermore, that in this state a wife cannot testify against her husband. Therefore, any statement she might make would be an indirect violation of that rule. Furthermore,

I object on the ground that the question calls for hearsay."

Judge Haswell looked ponderously thoughtful, then said, "It seems to me Mr. Mason is correct."

"I'll put it this way, Mr. Sheriff," the district attorney said. "Did you, on the morning of the fifteenth, take any money from Mrs. Corbin?"

"Objected to as incompetent, irrelevant and immaterial," Mason said.

"Your Honor," Flasher said irritably, "that's the very gist of our case. We propose to show that two of the stolen twenty-dollar bills were in the possession of Mrs. Corbin."

Mason said, "Unless the prosecution can prove the bills were given Mrs. Corbin by her husband, the evidence is inadmissible."

"That's just the point," Flasher said. "Those bills *were* given to her by the defendant."

"How do you know?" Mason asked.

"She told the sheriff so."

"That's hearsay," Mason snapped.

Judge Haswell fidgeted on the bench. "It seems to me we're getting into a peculiar situation here. You can't call the wife as a witness, and I don't think her statement to the sheriff is admissible."

"Well," Flasher said desperately, "in this state, Your Honor, we have a community-property law. Mrs. Corbin had this money. Since she is the wife of the defendant, it was community property. Therefore, it's partially his property."

"Well now, there," Judge Haswell said, "I think I can agree with you. You introduce the twenty-dollar bills. I'll overrule the objection made by the defense."

"Produce the twenty-dollar bills, Sheriff," Flasher said triumphantly.

The bills were produced and received in evidence.

"Cross-examine," Flasher said curtly.

"No questions of this witness," Mason said, "but I have a few questions to ask Mr. Bernal on cross-examination. You took him off the stand to lay the foundation for introducing the bank list, and I didn't have an opportunity to cross-examine him."

"I beg your pardon," Flasher said. "Resume the stand, Mr. Bernal."

His tone, now that he had the twenty-dollar bills safely introduced in evidence, had a gloating note to it.

Mason said, "This list which has been introduced in evidence is on the stationery of the Ivanhoe National Bank?"

"That's right. Yes, sir."

"It consists of several pages, and at the end there is the signature of the assistant cashier?"

"Yes, sir."

"And each page is initialed by the assistant cashier?"

"Yes, sir."

"This was the scheme which you thought of in order to safeguard the company against a payroll robbery?"

"Not to safeguard the company against a payroll robbery, Mr. Mason, but to assist us in recovering the money in the event there was a holdup."

"This was your plan to answer Mr. Nesbitt's objections that the vault was an outmoded model?"

"A part of my plan, yes. I may say that Mr. Nesbitt's objections had never been voiced until I took office. I felt he was trying to embarrass me by making my administration show less net returns than expected." Bernal tightened his lips and added, "Mr. Nesbitt had, I believe, been expecting to be appointed manager. He was disappointed. I believe he still expects to be manager."

In the spectators' section of the courtroom, Ralph Nesbitt glared at Bernal.

"You had a conversation with the defendant on the night of the fourteenth?" Mason asked Bernal.

"I did. Yes, sir."

"You told him that for reasons which you deemed sufficient you were discharging him immediately and wanted him to leave the premises at once?"

"Yes, sir. I did."

"And you paid him his wages in cash?"

"Mr. Nesbitt paid him in my presence, with money he took from the petty-cash drawer of the vault."

"Now, as part of the wages due him, wasn't Corbin given these two twenty-dollar bills which have been introduced in evidence?"

Bernal shook his head. "I had thought of that," he said, "but it would have been impossible. Those bills weren't available to us at that time. The payroll is received from the bank in a sealed package. Those two twenty-dollar bills were in that package."

"And the list of the numbers of the twenty-dollar bills?"

"That's in a sealed envelope. The money is placed in the vault. I lock the list of numbers in my desk."

"Are you prepared to swear that neither you nor Mr. Nesbitt had access to these two twenty-dollar bills on the night of the fourteenth?"

"That is correct."

"That's all," Mason said. "No further cross-examination."

"I now call Ralph Nesbitt to the stand," District Attorney Flasher said. "I want to fix the time of these events definitely, Your Honor."

"Very well," Judge Haswell said. "Mr. Nesbitt, come forward."

Ralph Nesbitt, after answering the usual preliminary questions, sat down in the witness chair.

"Were you present at a conversation which took place between the defendant, Harvey L. Corbin, and Frank Bernal on the fourteenth of this month?" the district attorney asked.

"I was. Yes, sir."

"What time did that conversation take place?"

"About eight o'clock in the evening."

"And, without going into the details of that conversation, I will ask you if the general effect of it was that the defendant was discharged and ordered to leave the company's property?"

"Yes, sir."

"And he was paid the money that was due him?"

"In cash. Yes, sir. I took the cash from the safe myself."

"Where was the payroll then?"

"In the sealed package in a compartment in the safe. As cashier, I had the only key to that compartment. Earlier in the afternoon I had gone to Ivanhoe City and received the sealed package of money and the envelope containing the list of numbers. I personally locked the package of money in the vault."

"And the list of numbers?"

"Mr. Bernal locked that in his desk."

"Cross-examine," Flasher said.

"No questions," Mason said.

"That's our case, Your Honor," Flasher observed.

"May we have a few minutes' indulgence?" Mason asked Judge Haswell.

"Very well. Make it brief," the judge agreed.

Mason turned to Paul Drake and Della Street. "Well, there you are," Drake said. "You're confronted with the proof, Perry."

"Are you going to put the defendant on the stand?" Della Street asked.

Mason shook his head. "It would be suicidal. He has a record of a prior criminal conviction. Also, it's a rule of law that if one asks about any part of a conversation on direct examination, the other side can bring out all the conversation. That conversation, when Corbin was discharged, was to the effect that he had lied about his past record. And I guess there's no question that he did."

"And he's lying now," Drake said. "This is one case where you're licked. I think you'd better cop a plea, and see what kind of a deal you can make with Flasher."

"Probably not any," Mason said. "Flasher wants to have the reputation of having given me a licking—wait a minute, Paul. I have an idea."

Mason turned abruptly, walked away to where he could stand by himself, his back to the crowded courtroom.

"Are you ready?" the judge asked.

Mason turned. "I am quite ready, Your Honor. I have one witness whom I wish to put on the stand. I wish a subpoena *duces tecum* issued for that witness. I want him to bring certain documents which are in his possession."

"Who is the witness, and what are the documents?" the judge asked.

Mason walked quickly over to Paul Drake. "What's the name of that character who has the garbage-collecting business," he said softly, "the one who has the first nickel he'd ever made?"

"George Addey."

The lawyer turned to the judge. "The witness that I want is George Addey, and the documents that I want him to bring to court with him are all of the twenty-dollar bills that he has received during the past sixty days."

"Your Honor," Flasher protested, "this is an outrage. This is making a travesty out of justice. It is exposing the court to ridicule."

Mason said, "I give Your Honor my assurance that I think this witness is material, and that the documents are material. I will make an affidavit to that effect if necessary. As attorney for the defendant, may I point out that if the court refuses to grant this subpoena it will be denying the defendant due process of law."

"I'm going to issue the subpoena," Judge Haswell said, testily, "and for your own good, Mr. Mason, the testimony had better be relevant."

George Addey, unshaven and bristling with indignation, held up his right hand to be swown. He glared at Perry Mason.

"Mr. Addey," Mason said, "you have the contract to collect garbage from Jebson City?"

"I do."

"How long have you been collecting garbage there?"

"For over five years, and I want to tell you—"

Judge Haswell banged his gavel. "The witness will answer questions and not interpolate any comments."

"I'll interpolate anything I dang please," Addey said.

"That'll do," the judge said. "Do you wish to be jailed for contempt of court, Mr. Addey?"

"I don't want to go to jail, but I—"

"Then you'll remember the respect that is due the court," the judge said. "Now you sit there and answer questions. This is a court of law. You're in this court as a citizen, and I'm here as a judge, and I propose to see that the respect due to the court is enforced." There was a moment's silence while the judge glared angrily at the witness. "All right, go ahead, Mr. Mason," Judge Haswell said.

Mason said, "During the thirty days prior to the fifteenth of this month, did you deposit any money in any banking institution?"

"I did not."

"Do you have with you all the twenty-dollar bills that you received during the last sixty days?"

"I have, and I think making me bring them here is just like inviting some crook to come and rob me and—"

Judge Haswell banged with his gavel. "Any more comments of that sort from the witness and there will be a sentence imposed for contempt of court. Now you get out those twenty-dollar bills, Mr. Addey, and put them right up here on the clerk's desk."

Addey, mumbling under his breath, slammed a roll of twenty-dollars bills down on the desk in front of the clerk.

"Now," Mason said, "I'm going to need a little clerical assistance. I would like to have my secretary, Miss Street, and the clerk help me check through the numbers on these bills. I will select a few at random."

Mason picked up three of the twenty-dollar bills and said, "I am going to ask my assistants to check the list of numbers introduced in evidence. In my hand is a twenty-dollar bill that has the number L 07083274 A. Is that bill on the list? The next bill that I pick up is number L 02327010 A. Here's another one, number L 07579190 A. Are any of those bills on the list?"

The courtroom was silent. Suddenly, Della Street said, "Yes, here's one that's on the list—bill number L 07579190 A. It's on the list, on page eight."

"What?" the prosecutor shouted.

"Exactly," Mason said, smiling. "So, if a case is to be made against a person merely because he has possession of the money that was stolen on the fifteenth of this month, then your office should prefer

charges against this witness, George Addey, Mr. District Attorney."

Addey jumped from the witness stand and shook his fist in Mason's face. "You're a cockeyed liar!" he screamed. "There ain't a one of those bills but what I didn't have it before the fifteenth. The company cashier changes my money into twenties, because I like big bills. I bury 'em in cans, and I put the date on the side of the can."

"Here's the list," Mason said. "Check it for yourself."

A tense silence gripped the courtroom as the judge and the spectators waited.

"I'm afraid I don't understand this, Mr. Mason," Judge Haswell said, after a moment.

"I think it's quite simple," Mason said. "And I now suggest the court take a recess for an hour and check those other bills against this list. I think the district attorney may be surprised."

And Mason sat down and proceeded to put papers in his brief case. . .

Della Street, Paul Drake and Perry Mason were sitting in the lobby of the Ivanhoe Hotel.

"When are you going to tell us?" Della Street asked fiercely. "Or do we tear you limb from limb? How could the garbage man have—?"

"Wait a minute," Mason said. "I think we're about to get results. Here comes the esteemed district attorney, Vernon Flasher, and he's accompanied by Judge Haswell."

The two strode over to Mason's group and bowed with cold formality.

Mason got up.

Judge Haswell began in his best courtroom voice. "A most deplorable situation has occurred. It seems that Mr. Frank Bernal has—well—"

"Been detained somewhere," Vernon Flasher said.

"Disappeared," Judge Haswell said. "He's gone."

"I expected as much," Mason said.

"Now will you kindly tell me just what sort of pressure you brought to bear on Mr. Bernal to—?"

"Just a moment, Judge," Mason said. "The only pressure I brought to bear on him was to cross-examine him."

"Did you know that there had been a mistake in the dates on those lists?"

"There was no mistake. When you find Bernal, I'm sure you will discover there was a deliberate falsification. He was short in his accounts, and he knew he was about to be demoted. He had a desperate need for a hundred thousand dollars in ready cash. He had evidently been planning this burglary, or rather, this embezzlement, for some time. He learned that Corbin had a criminal record. He arranged to have these lists furnished by the bank. He installed a burglar alarm, and, naturally, knew how to circumvent it. He employed a watchman he knew was addicted to drink. He only needed to stage his coup at the right time. He fired Corbin and paid him off with bills that had been recorded by the bank on page eight of the list of bills *in the payroll on the first of the month.*

"Then he removed page eight from the list of bills contained in the payroll *of the fifteenth,* before he showed it to the police, and substituted page eight of the list for the *first of the month* payroll. It was that simple.

"Then he drugged the watchman's whisky, took an acetylene torch, burned through the vault doors and took all the money."

"May I ask how you knew all this?" Judge Haswell demanded.

"Certainly," Mason said. "My client told me he received those bills from Nesbitt, who took them from the petty-cash drawer in the safe. He also told the sheriff that. I happened to be the only one who believed him. It sometimes pays, Your Honor, to have faith in a man, even if he has made a previous mistake. Assuming my client was innocent, I knew either Bernal or Nesbitt must be guilty. I then realized that only Bernal had custody of the *previous* lists of numbers.

"As an employee, Bernal had been paid on the first of the month. He looked at the numbers on the twenty-dollar bills in his pay envelope and found that they had been listed on page eight of the payroll for the first.

"Bernal only needed to abstract all twenty-dollar bills from the petty-cash drawer, substitute twenty-dollar bills from his own pay envelope, call in Corbin, and fire him. His trap was set.

"I let him know I knew what had been done by bringing Addey into court and proving my point. Then I asked for a recess. That was so Bernal would have a chance to skip out. You see, flight may be received as evidence of guilt. It was a professional courtesy to the district attorney. It will help him when Bernal is arrested."

AUGUST DERLETH

Adventure of the Grice-Paterson Curse

"No, Parker," said my friend Solar Pons suddenly, "you need have no fear that the ants, for all their social organization, are close to taking over mankind."

"The prospect is horrible," I cried—and stopped short. I turned. "But how did you know what I was thinking? Pons, this is uncanny."

"Tut, tut—you are too much given to overstatement. It is only the simplest deduction. You have been reading Mr. H. G. Wells' admirable fantasies. When I observed you just now staring at an ant on the pane with an expression that can only be described as one of horror, it was not too much to conclude that you have at last read *The Empire of the Ants.*"

"How simple it is, after all!"

"As most seemingly complex matters are simple." He gestured toward the windows. "Draw the curtains, will you, Parker?"

I stepped across the room to shut the weather from sight. Rain whispered steadily at the panes, and from the street came now and then the sound of vehicles splashing through the water, for the warm, late summer rain had been falling the better part of the day, bringing a misty fog to shroud London. It was now twilight, and the yellow glow of lights in windows and along the street could be seen dimly.

"Tell me, Parker, does the name Colonel Sir Ronald Grice-Paterson recall anything to your mind?" asked Pons, as I walked back toward him.

"Nothing but that I seem to remember him as Governor-General of some part of the British Empire. Was it not Malaya?"

"It was indeed."

Pons stretched forth a lean arm, took an envelope off the mantel, and held it out to me. I took it, unfolded the paper inside, and glanced at it.

"From a woman, I see," I said. "She uses a highly individual perfume."

"A musk."

" 'Dear Mr. Pons,' " I read. " 'Against the wishes of my family, I am writing to ask that you receive me tomorrow night at eight on a most urgent matter pertaining to the curse of our unhappy family.' " It was signed, "Edith Grice-Paterson." I looked up. "His daughter?"

"I believe the Colonel's daughter pre-deceased him. His granddaughter, perhaps. What do you make of the postmark?"

I looked at the envelope. Though the stamps were British, the postmark was not; it read "Isle of Uffa," and in its geometrical center were stamped the initials "G. P."

"Where in the world is Uffa?" I asked.

"Ah, Parker, I fear my geography is lacking in the information you ask. But I seem to remember that on his retirement from Malaya, Grice-Paterson went to live out his life on an island estate which exists in a state of quasi-independence from Great Britain. If memory serves me rightly, it lies off the coast of Cornwall, east of the Scilly Isles. It has a status similar, I believe, to the almost incredible Isle of Redonda, which has been a separate little kingdom, though allied to Great Britain, for decades. Uffa, however, is close to England, whereas Redonda is in the Leeward Islands, in the British West Indies."

"I'm afraid both are beyond my knowledge."

"You have never chanced to encounter them."

I turned again to the letter. "She writes in an agitated hand."

"That is hardly surprising. The papers carried a brief notice within the week of the finding of the body of Lt. Austen Hanwell, described as her fiancé. Certain mysterious circumstances attended his death. Let me see, I believe I clipped the account."

Pons opened one of his huge scrapbooks which was lying among newspapers on the table. From a group of loose clippings waiting to be added to the storehouse of criminous occurrences between those covers, he selected one.

"Yes, here we are."

I walked to where he bent and looked past him. The story was indeed brief. "Tragic Death," read the short heading. "The body of Lt. Austen Hanwell, 27, was discovered early yesterday in a study at The Creepers, the home of his fiancée, Miss Edith Grice-Paterson, on the Island of Uffa. He appeared to have been asphyxiated or choked to death, though routine inquiries failed to turn up any evidence of foul play. Lt. Hanwell was a native of Brighton. His death is the third in a series of tragedies which have beset the family of the late Col. Sir Ronald Grice-Paterson."

"It is careful to charge no one with murder," I pointed out.

"Is it not, indeed!" agreed Pons. "There is more here than the press is willing to print. Perhaps our client can enlighten us further. I hear a car driving to a stop below, and, since it is just past the hour set in her letter, I daresay it is she."

In a few moments our client stood before us. She was a tall, willowy young lady, a pronounced blonde, with strong blue eyes. Though she gave evidence of some trepidation, there was an air of grim determination about her also. She was dressed entirely in black, and was enveloped in a full cape which served both to keep her dry and to protect her from the wind. Once she had thrown back her cape, she had the bearing of a young woman well on her way to spinsterhood, so somber was her manner.

She ignored the chair Pons stood out for her and burst at once into speech. "Mr. Pons, I have no one else to turn to. The police of Helston have declined jurisdiction, on the ground that Uffa has a separate government and that its status in relation to Great Britain has never been clearly defined. That is all nonsense—we are part of England—but they do have certain valid reasons for their reluctance to act. Nevertheless, I am determined to bring to an end the curse which has hung over our house ever since I can remember." Though she spoke with suppressed feeling, there was no mistaking the firmness of her resolve. She paused dramatically before she added, "Mr. Pons, in the past eleven years three persons have died very strangely under our roof, in circumstances which strongly suggest murder—but, if so, it is murder without meaning and motive, murder which the authorities are reluctant to accept as that."

She strode up and down before the fireplace, clasping and unclasping her fingers in agitation she fought to control.

"Pray compose yourself, my dear lady," said Pons quietly. "You are the granddaughter of the late Colonel Sir Ronald Grice-Paterson?"

"I am. I am the mistress of The Creepers."

"The late Colonel had two sons and a daughter?"

Our client drew in her breath for a moment and clenched her hands. "His two sons were the first and second victims of the curse which has fallen on our family, Mr. Pons. My aunt, my father's sister, died when she was quite young. My mother died in an accident at sea. There are left of our entire family now only my two brothers and myself. Both are younger than I, and for the time being they live with me at The Creepers.

"My grandfather died eleven years ago, and the estate—that is, the Island of Uffa—fell to his three children. My only aunt and one uncle died without heirs; so the estate fell to my father. He in turn died as mysteriously as his brother, and my poor Austen within a year after he came down from London to assume possession of Uffa. All the children had been living away from the house when my grandfather died; he was a solitary man, very introspective by nature, and with a strong streak of misanthropy. He lived alone but for one servant, and discouraged even his children's visits. His sole occupations were the writing of his memoirs, which were never published, and his devotion to horticultural pursuits. While he made or seemed to make an exception in my case, in that he showed a fondness for me on such occasions as we visited Uffa while my father was employed in London, he was rebelliously rude and cantankerous with everyone else."

Pons sat for a moment in silence, his fingers tented before him, an enigmatic smile on his thin lips. "Will you tell us something of the—'the curse,' I believe you called it?" he asked presently.

"Very well, Mr. Pons, I'll do the best I can," said our visitor. "It began—no, let me say rather that the first time I was aware of it was about a year after Grandfather died. I was then seventeen. My grandfather's house had always seemed a very gloomy place to me—for he had surrounded it with all manner of plants and trees, and it was overgrown with creepers, which give the house its name—and we did not visit there often. However, on that occasion—my seventeenth birthday—we journeyed down from London to spend a week with my Uncle Sydney.

"It was at about this time of the year. My uncle was in the best of spirits, though there had never been much love lost among the members of my father's generation, or, for that matter, between my grandfather and his children. On the morning of the second day of our visit with him, my uncle failed to come down to breakfast. When my father and one of the servants went to see what detained him, they found him stretched out on the floor, dead. Mr. Pons, he had been strangled in some remarkable fashion. There were curious bruises around his neck, as well as on his face, his arms, back, and chest. There was the appearance of a violent struggle, but the room was locked, the key was in the lock on the inside, and, while the window was open, there was no mark to show that anyone had climbed into the second storey window either by ladder or by means of the thick creepers along that wall.

"The medical evidence seemed inconclusive; it was not called death by strangulation, but death by misadventure; his doctor believed he had had some kind of seizure, and, while a cursory investigation was made by the only police sergeant on the island, there was nothing at all that might be called evidence turned up. No strange craft had landed on Uffa; no one had any reason to want Uncle Sydney dead; and my father, who inherited my uncle's share of Uffa, had far more wealth of his own through his business interests and his investments in the City."

Our client struggled visibly to control herself. She was clearly still under great strain, and had undoubtedly forced herself to make the journey to consult my companion. "Mr. Pons, I didn't see my uncle lying there—but I did see my father in exactly similar circumstances just seven years later, almost to the day—and now, God help us all!—I've seen my fiancé similarly slain—all without motive, as if it were an act of a vengeful God! Mr. Pons, our family—our house— our Uffa is cursed! Now my brothers are urging me to sell, to give up Uffa, and move to England. I have no wish to do so, for I am senti- mentally attached to our island, but certainly I cannot sell until I can be sure that only the Grice-Patersons and those who are close to us are victims of this dread curse which seems to know no limita- tion of time."

"Do I understand you to say that all these deaths have taken place in the same room, Miss Grice-Paterson?" asked Pons.

"No, Mr. Pons. Two of them occurred in the same room on the second floor—my uncle's and my father's. My fiancé was found on the ground floor, in the study directly below that room. He had been reading late, and had apparently fallen asleep. The circumstances of my father's and uncle's deaths were very much the same—that is, the door was locked, the open windows showed no sign of disturb- ance. In the case of my fiancé, the door was ajar, but nothing had

been disturbed. There were the same strangling lines about his neck . . ."

"Pons!" I cried out suddenly, memory flooding me—"A dacoit!"

Our client flashed a startled glance in my direction, and then gazed wonderingly back toward Pons.

"Pray forgive Dr. Parker, Miss Grice-Paterson. He is addicted to the reading of the exploits of Dr. Fu Manchu, who employs thugs and dacoits to accomplish his lethal work for him."

"You may well make sport of me," I answered hotly, "but it's certainly not beyond the bounds of possibility that the one-time Governor-General of Malaya may have brought back with him some sacred symbol, the recovery of which has brought about these strange deaths."

"Perhaps not beyond the bounds of possibility, but certainly of probability," countered Pons.

Our client fingered a curiously-wrought golden brooch at her throat, a thoughtful expression on her attractive features. "It is true I've heard my grandfather speak often of the mysteries of Malaya—of the strange customs and the unbelievable things one might learn from the ancient native culture—but I'm quite certain he was not the kind of man who would have made off with anything which did not belong to him. He was no doubt a martinet in many ways, and in most ways a typical British colonial administrator, I am convinced—but, Mr. Pons, he was not a thief."

"I should be inclined to agree with you, since I know something of your grandfather's record," said Pons soothingly, his eyes warning me to be silent. "Now tell me, would it be possible for Dr. Parker and myself to examine the body of Lt. Hanwell?"

Our client bit her lip, and an expression of anguish washed into her face. "Mr. Pons, he has been put into his coffin, and we're shipping his body home to Brighton tomorrow. Do you think it necessary?"

"It may be helpful," replied Pons.

"Very well, then, if we were to leave immediately—my car is below, and there will be a boat waiting to take us to Uffa at Penzance—we might be able to accomplish what you ask before the body is sent away."

"Capital! We shall leave at once."

Pons leapt to his feet, threw aside his purple dressing gown, kicked off his slippers, and in a thrice was ready, deerstalker, Inverness and all, having moved with an agility only too typical of him, and managing to chivvy me for my slowness at the same time. He did not speak to our client again until we were comfortably ensconced in her car, a handsome Rolls-Royce, driven by a chauffeur.

"Tell me, Miss Grice-Paterson, has there ever occurred any other untoward incident at The Creepers?"

In the darkness of the car, our client's sensitive face was visible only in the light of passing street lamps. She appeared to ponder Pons' question before she answered.

"Mr. Pons, I cannot say. Perhaps in the light of life in an ordinary suburban villa or semi-detached house, there have been strange events at The Creepers. Our inability to keep dogs, for instance."

"Ah, what of that?"

"They die, Mr. Pons. Despite the fact that our winter temperatures rarely fall below forty-five degrees, and our summer temperatures do not often rise above eighty degrees, our dogs have been unable to weather a year at The Creepers. We have lost no less than seven of them in the course of the past decade. Of all kinds, too. And two cats, I might mention, shared the dogs' inability to live on Uffa."

"Is this a general condition on the island?"

"Well, now that I think of it—it isn't. There is a dog in a tenant house at the other end of the island. An old sheep dog. He doesn't seem to have been troubled by the atmosphere of Uffa. He may be an exception. Then again, it may be the atmosphere of The Creepers, which brings me to another of the incidents you asked about—the night of the perfume—when the entire island seemed to be pervaded with a most bewitching and demoralizing perfume, as cloying as that of heliotrope, and giddying. It came, of course, from one of my late grandfather's rare plants, which had come into blossom after many years of sterility.

"Then there are, I suppose one might add, the strange, whispering sounds of the leaves, which seem to caress one another even on the most windless nights. Oh, Mr. Pons—how can I speak of these things which are so much a part of the house and of life on Uffa, when I am still bowed by the curse of the Grice-Patersons! How shall I ever again survive the month of August! I shall never spend another summer on Uffa."

She spoke with passion and determination.

"You do not live alone at The Creepers?"

"No, Mr. Pons. My brothers Avery and Richard live there with me. Mrs. Flora Brinton is our cook. Aram Malvaides is an old servant who was my grandfather's orderly for many years. He is the gardener, and he has an assistant who comes some days from the mainland. There are certain other minor servants responsible to Mrs. Brinton or to Aram."

"You've not mentioned hearing any outcry in the case of any one of the three unfortunate deaths, Miss Grice-Paterson."

"None was heard. The crimes took place late at night, evidently after the victims were asleep."

"Yet there was evidence of struggle in each case?"

"Yes, Mr. Pons."

"Does it not seem strange to you that none cried out, that no struggle was overheard?"

"No, Mr. Pons. The Creepers is built in the shape of a T with a short stem. The family usually sleep in the west wing, or the left arm of the T, whereas our guest rooms and winter quarters are in the east wing. There is the entire length of the house to separate the one from the other. Even if there had been an outcry, there's no certainty that it would have been heard by any of us. But there was none, for the servants would surely have heard a cry if one had sounded."

Pons flashed a baffling smile at me and lapsed into silence. Once or twice I caught sight of his hawklike face in semi-repose, but soon we were out of London, away from the occasional gleams of light, riding through the dark countryside into the southeast.

At dawn we rode out of Dartmoor into Cornwall, and soon we were catching glimpses of what is surely one of the most beautiful faces of England—the Cornish coast near Truro, and then Camborne, and then at last, Penzance, where there was indeed a boat awaiting us—it was no less than a small yacht. But of Uffa there was no sign from land; our client explained that it lay over the horizon. Her car was quartered in Penzance, since there was little use for it on Uffa, which consisted of but a small settlement in addition to The Creepers and the immediate grounds of the estate, though the entire island was the domain of the Grice-Paterson family, and had been for two centuries.

The morning was free of fog, and presently Uffa rose out of the sea like the embodiment of a dream, like fabled Lyonesse, all green, save for a few rocks along one coast, and for a cluster of white which was the little fishing village on the opposite shore. It was there that we landed. A carriage waited for us there, driven by a dour, dark-skinned old man.

"This is Aram, Mr. Pons," said Miss Grice-Paterson.

Aram gazed at us with the darkest suspicion manifest on his features. His attitude was aloof and unfriendly.

"I don't know what my brothers will say," our client went on, as we got into the carriage. "They may be rude; if so, I hope you will forgive them. It is I who am mistress here, and the decision is mine to make. They've opposed your coming—they fear 'any further scandal'—as they put it."

"We shall see," said Pons imperturbably.

The Grice-Paterson brothers were indeed displeased to the point of rudeness at sight of us. Avery, the older, was but a year younger than his sister; he was a dark-haired brute of a man, as massive as our client was well-proportioned, with the shoulders of a professional athlete. Richard was as fair as his brother was dark, and slight of build against Avery's thickness. Neither was entirely civil at our introduction, and neither was co-operative, being disinclined to answer the few questions Pons put.

We did not linger in their company, however, for Pons was anxious to view the body of Lt. Austen Hanwell before its removal. We therefore followed our client from the house through the heavily overgrown lawns and gardens east of the widespread dwelling, past the abandoned dog kennels, to the old stone family vault, where the coffin containing the body lay waiting to be sealed by the authorities before being taken on shipboard.

"Forgive me," said Miss Grice-Paterson at the great iron door. "I cannot bear to see him again. I'll wait here beside the path."

The coffin stood just inside. Pons left the door ajar, and so we had ample light at the entranceway to the vault, though Pons had brought his pocket flash. He lost no time in raising the coffin lid, exposing to view a handsome, moustached face, that of a man who looked even younger than his years. But face and neck—when his clothing was withdrawn—still showed the livid marks our client had described to us.

"Your department, I think, Parker," said Pons, holding his light close to the dead man's skin.

I examined the marks with the greatest care, though I was at a distinct disadvantage in doing so two days past the event. But there was no mistaking what I saw, and, when I had completed my examination, I said so.

"These are the marks of thin but powerful cords, applied with great pressure."

"Enough to cause death?"

"Enough, in my opinion."

"There are no wounds except the marks of the cords?"

"Only on the marks themselves. Here and there small openings in the flesh, which might have been made by rough spots on the cords. You may laugh at me all you like, Pons, but if this is not the work of dacoits, I shall be very greatly surprised."

For a few moments Pons said nothing. He bent to examine the marks himself. When he straightened up, his aspect was grave as he replied, "I fear it is something far more sinister, my dear fellow, than dacoits. Look again. Are those tears in the flesh not regular punctures?"

I threw up my hands. "It's one and the same thing."

Pons closed the coffin and stood aside for me to pass.

We found our client standing at some little distance from the vault. Beyond her, approaching the place, was a complement of four men from the ship in the harbor, preceded by an official who was clearly a member of the police. Miss Grice-Paterson, however, avoided meeting them by stepping down a side path.

"I will take you around to the room where my fiancé was found," she said. And in a moment she indicated the east wall of the building, a towering mass of creepers. "See, those are the windows—those two there. And directly above them are the windows of the other room in which my uncle and my father died."

The windows were framed in singularly beautiful crimson flowers which adorned the creepers massed upon the stone wall of the house. In the bright morning sunlight, their appearance was remote indeed from the nameless horror which had taken place just beyond them.

Pons paused a moment, crossed over, and smelled a blossom. From the proximity of the windows, where he stood intently examining the earth below, he asked, "Should something happen to you, Miss Grice-Paterson, who will inherit the property?"

"My brother Avery."

"And after him?"

"My brother Richard."

"And then?"

Miss Grice-Paterson looked at Pons, puzzled. "How curious you should ask that, Mr. Pons! Or perhaps you knew of my grandfather's strange will. If some catastrophe were to wipe out our family, the entire estate is to go to old Aram. We have no other close relatives. My grandfather had a brother with him in Malaya, but he was killed in an accident there. His only son succumbed to one of those mysterious East Indian diseases while he too worked as a commissioner on my grandfather's staff. I told you," she concluded grimly, "that there is a horrible curse on our family—I assure you most earnestly I was not exaggerating."

"I believe you," answered Pons. "Tell me, if you know—what were your grandfather's relations with his brother and his nephew?"

She shrugged. "I cannot say, except by what I've heard. Grandfather was a hard man. I understand the change came on him after Grandmother's death."

"Was she, too, a victim of the curse?"

"Oh, it is all of a piece, Mr. Pons," she cried. "Grandmother was accidentally killed at a family birthday party. Grandfather went to pieces. He brooded for days, and never afterward seemed to come out of his shell except as an irascible old man, filled with hatred of mankind."

"I see. Now let us have a look at the room in which Lt. Hanwell met his death."

Once more we braved the scowls of Avery and Richard Grice-Paterson as we passed through the front part of the house on our way to the east wing. The room in which Lt. Hanwell had been found was a spacious one, lined with shelves of books on all but one wall, and handsomely apportioned to be as pleasant as possible for anyone who chose to spend his time in it. Our client indicated a comfortable old leather-covered chair between a table lamp and the near window.

"Austen had apparently been reading there and had fallen asleep. He was found between the chair and the window. The chair had been kicked out of place, and the table moved somewhat out of its usual position. The lamp had fallen over; it was still alight when we found him."

"The window was open?"

"Yes, Mr. Pons. Our windows are unscreened because we are never troubled with insects of any kind."

"So that anyone might have entered that way?"

"There was no sign of such entry."

"Nevertheless, it was open."

"But who would have motive for such an act, Mr. Pons?"

"Ah, Miss Grice-Paterson, I am not so bold as to say. But let us suppose it was to someone's interest to prevent your marriage."

"Why?"

"To prevent any change in the line of succession. Or am I mistaken in that your marriage would alter the provisions of your grandfather's will?"

She colored briefly and looked down. "No, Mr. Pons," she said in a scarcely audible voice. "The property would go to my oldest child."

"As for the absence of signs of entry by way of the windows . . ." began Pons.

"A dacoit could manage it without leaving a trace," I said with asperity.

Pons did not so much as blink an eye in acknowledgment. "Lt. Hanwell slept in the room above?" he asked.

"Oh no, Mr. Pons. Austen slept in the west wing, where we all sleep. We seldom use the east wing, except in winter, when we move out of the west wing for this."

Pons examined the window and its frame. Then he looked over the chair, studying what appeared to be lines of wear, after which he got down on his hands and knees to look about on the rug, having been assured by our client that it had not been cleaned. He seemed to find nothing there but fragments of drying leaves, which he discarded. Then he went back to the window, opening it and leaning out. By bending down, he could almost have touched the ground, which he had scrutinized outside. The sphinx-like expression on his face told me nothing as he drew back into the room and closed the window.

"And now the room upstairs, if you please," he said.

In a few minutes we stood in a gracious, sunlit bedroom which was the very antithesis of a murder chamber. The room contained a large double bed immediately adjacent to the window; if this were the position of the bed at the time of the death of the two Grice-Patersons, I could not help thinking how immoderately convenient it was for any murderous dacoit. Pons must have been thinking along similar lines, for he crossed at once to the window and leaned out to test the strength of the creepers, the heady perfume of the flowers of which wafted into the room as soon as he opened the window.

"They look as if they would bear the weight of a small man," I could not help saying.

"They would bear a two-hundred-pound man," replied Pons.

"My grandfather planted them when he came into the estate, just after Grandmother's death in Malaya. He was on his first visit home," explained our client. "We naturally thought of someone's climbing them to come in through the window, but there was no mark on them, and the creepers would surely carry some sign of having been climbed, Mr. Pons."

"It is reasonable to assume so—in all but an exceptional case. These windows, too, were open on those lethal dates?"

"I believe so, Mr. Pons. I remember the questions that were asked when my uncle was found. I was seventeen then, as I told you."

"And your brothers?"

"They were sixteen and fourteen."

Pons stood looking about, but there was nothing to be seen, for the room was spotlessly clean. Then he appeared to come to a sudden decision. "Can it be arranged for us to spend the night in this room, Miss Grice-Paterson?"

"Why, yes, Mr. Pons. I had expected to put you into the west wing —but perhaps you would have greater privacy here."

"Thank you. We'll try this room for a night or two."

For the next few hours, Pons wandered through The Creepers, questioning the servants and making a vain attempt to inquire about certain events of the Grice-Paterson brothers, who remained patently unwilling to be of any assistance, a circumstance I regarded with the gravest suspicion, though Pons shrugged it off. He walked about the gardens and lawns, marveling at the variety of exotic plants, shrubs and trees which abounded there—the fruit of the late Colonel Sir Ronald Grice-Paterson's industry. Indeed, so overgrown was the estate that it seemed almost as if the one-time Governor-General of Malaya had sought to create here on this island off the coast of Cornwall a home reproducing, as far as the climate permitted, his residence in the Malay States. Nor was Pons content with the environs of the house; he wandered all over the island, pausing in the little harbor village, quite as if he were on holiday instead of busy at an inquiry into as dreadful a crime as either of us had encountered for a long time.

Our lunch we had taken alone. Our dinner was taken with the family. This proved to be an extremely uncomfortable meal for all but Pons, for the Grice-Paterson brothers took no pains to conceal their animosity to us. Pons, however, affected not to notice. Now and then he turned to one or the other of them with a question.

"Tell me," he said to Avery on one occasion, "were you aware of the terms of your late grandfather's will?"

"You're fishing for motive, aren't you, Mr. Pons?" answered Avery hostilely. "You should realize, sir, we've had enough scandal without your meddling."

"The question, Mr. Grice-Paterson," insisted Pons, his enthusiasm for the leg of lamb on his plate not at all diminished by Avery's manner.

"Answer him," said our client angrily.

"I was," said Avery sullenly.

And to Richard, later, Pons said, "I cannot escape the impression
that neither of you cared very much for Lt. Hanwell."

"Oh, we didn't," answered Richard. "We're solitaries, my brother
and I. And you'll find, if you dig deep enough, Mr. Pons, that when
I was a boy I could get up and down those creepers like a monkey.
Without trace," he added with heavy sarcasm.

Pons thanked him gravely, and continued to show no annoyance
when all his other questions were similarly treated by the brothers.

Not until we were once more in the room in the east wing, following that stiff, uncomfortable meal, did Pons relax his insistent casual-
ness.

"Now, then, Parker have you given up that fancy of yours about
the stolen idol and the dacoit?"

"No, Pons, I haven't," I answered firmly. "I can think of no other
theory which fits the facts so well. Yet I concede that there is the
little matter of the succession—I've failed no more than you to notice
that, except for Miss Grice-Paterson's fiancé—and perhaps he, too,
indirectly—each of these deaths has furthered the succession of the
estate."

"Ah, death always furthers something of the kind," said Pons.
"Would that not make the ultimate author of these murders, to your
mind, then, Aram Malvaides?"

"Who else? Mark this—he alone of all the parties who have an
interest in the Grice-Paterson estate was present on the occasion of
each murder. The boys were not."

"Ah, that is well reasoned, Parker," admitted Pons.

Thus encouraged, I went on. "If Miss Grice-Paterson had married,
there might be still more heirs to dispose of."

"You conceive of his wanting to eliminate everyone who stood between him and the inheritance?"

"Would it not have to be all or none?"

"Indeed it would, if your theory were tenable. But why wait so
long between crimes, when he is not growing younger?"

"No one knows the dark mind of the murderer."

"And just how did he manage to gain entry without leaving a
clue?" pressed Pons. "Pray spare me that dacoit, Parker. I find it
inconceivable that a convenient dacoit would be standing by on call
to suit the whims of so reluctant a murderer."

"I have not yet come to any conclusion about his clueless entrance," I was forced to admit.

"I fear that is the flaw in most armchair rationalization—particularly when it is based so largely on romance."

Once again I knew Pons was laughing at me; I was nettled. "No doubt you already know the identity of the murderer?"

"I suspected it before we left London."

"Oh, come, Pons. I am a patient man, but . . ."

"I never knew a more patient one, to tolerate my idiosyncrasies for so many years," replied Pons handsomely. "But there are several salient factors which, I submit, may have some bearing on the matter. I am no lover of coincidence, though I am willing to concede that it takes place far more often in life than could be justified in fiction. It has not occurred to you that it may be significant that all these deaths should have taken place at approximately the same time of the year?"

"Coincidence."

"I feared you would say as much. The family occupies the east wing only in winter. Why? I have made certain enquiries, and understand that this practice was inaugurated by Sir Ronald; the family only followed his custom. This does not seem meaningful to you?"

I confessed that it did not.

"Very well. I may be in error. Yet I suggest that there may be a connection to certain other curious factors. I fancy we are in agreement that ingress was accomplished through the open window in each case?"

With this I agreed unreservedly.

"It does not seem to you curious, if that is so, that there was no mark to be found on any occasion?—no footprint below the ground-floor window, though there is a respectable area where one might be impressed on the ground there;—no abrasion of the creepers to indicate the presence of a climber to this room—nothing?"

"Someone sufficiently light—and trained—could accomplish all that was done without leaving a trace."

"Surely that would be almost insurmountably difficult," protested Pons.

"Richard has admitted that as a boy he did it."

Pons smiled. "Richard was having us."

"You may think so, if you like," I retorted hotly. "But hasn't it occurred to you that these murders may have been started by someone else, and only carried on in this generation by another hand?"

"It has indeed," answered Pons. "Let us for the moment concede that it may be possible for undetected entry to have been made by way of the creepers. Let us look at another aspect of this strange little horror. Why should there be so long an interval from one crime to the next?"

"Obviously to diminish attention."

"If diminishing attention were of importance, surely some less dramatic manner of committing the crime might have been found?"

"Except to one specially trained in the chosen method."

"Ah, we are back once more to the dacoit. I had no conception of the depth of your devotion to the sinister Doctor."

"You're making sport of me, yet I'm in deadly earnest," I said. "Is there any other solution which so admirably fits all the facts?"

"Manifestly."

"What is it?"

"That which was in fact the method and motive for the crimes."

"That is a riddle unworthy of you, Pons."

"Surpassed only by the true solution of the curse of the Grice-Patersons."

"If you're so sure of the solution," I cried, "why are we dawdling here? Why haven't you arrested the murderer?"

"Though I am sure, I want a little more verification than my deduction alone. I am entitled to wait upon events for that verification, just as you are for the dacoit to make a return engagement, for our presence in this room this hot summer night will duplicate the superficial aspects of the situation prior to each of the three crimes which have been committed."

"Except for one," I hastened to point out. "We are not heirs to the estate."

"You have your revolver with you, I notice," Pons went on. "That should be adequate defense against your dacoit. I have asked that the Colonel's old sword be sent up; that, in turn, should serve me long enough to sever any cord which may loop about us."

"Surely you're not expecting another attack!"

"Say, rather, I am hoping for one. We shall hope to catch the murderer in the act."

"Pons, this is absurd. An attack on us would be completely without motive; it would be a basic flaw in our concept of the motive for this sequence of events."

"Pray permit me to correct you—your concept of the motive, not ours."

"If I were to act, I would have Malvaides under arrest without delay."

Pons smiled grimly. "Yet it is no less logical to suppose that somehow our client's late father slew his brother; that she herself slew her father; that her brother, Avery, likewise developed enough agility to make away with Lt. Hanwell—they, too, were directly or indirectly in line to inherit.

"And now, Parker, it's past the dinner hour; night will soon be upon us. In hot latitudes, people take siestas after lunch; we did not. It is almost hot enough here for the torrid zone, and I for one am going to take a little rest before what I hope will be a strenuous night."

A strenuous night, indeed!

How often since that time have I recalled the singular events of that night spent in the twice fatal room of The Creepers on the Island of Uffa! We retired together at a late hour, despite our tiredness, but I was soon drowsily aware that Pons had left our bed and had gone to sit instead in a large, old-fashioned rocking chair which stood opposite the open window, so that he could face outward and still keep an eye on the bed.

Behind him, the door to the room was locked. We had prepared, as he put it, the identical situation which had maintained on the occasions of the two previous murders which had taken place in this room. Had I not been so exhausted after our long night ride and the difficulty of following Pons about during the day, I would not have slept, for the room and the night were cloyingly hot and humid; but the distant roar of the surf was lulling, and I was soon asleep. My last memory was of Pons sitting grimly on guard, the late Sir Ronald's sword ready to hand, even as my revolver lay beneath my pillow, ready for instant firing.

I do not know how many hours I slept before I was awakened, gasping for air, trying to call out, in the grip of a deadly menace. Before I could reach for my revolver—before I was sufficiently awake to grasp what was taking place—I felt myself being drawn bodily from my bed.

I had a horrified glimpse of Pons whipping away with the sword, even as the life was being squeezed out of me, and I felt a dozen pinpoints of pain upon my throat, my wrists, my face. Briefly, I was aware of a distorted picture, inexplicably terrible, filled with the imminence of death, of Pons' desperation against an enemy I could not see but only feel, of the tightening cords wound so insidiously about me . . .

Then I swooned.

When I came to, Pons was bending above me, chafing my brow.

"Thank God, Parker!" he cried. "I would never have forgiven myself if anything had happened to you in my anxiety to satisfy my suspicions!"

I struggled dazedly to a sitting position. "The murderer?" I gasped, looking vainly for him.

"The murderer—if murderer there was—has been dead these twelve years," answered Pons. "Colonel Sir Ronald Grice-Paterson. Only his unique weapon remains."

Then I saw all around me on the floor the severed, fleshy creepers from the plant with the crimson flowers that covered the east wall of the house, and knew what it was that had sought to clasp me in its lethal embrace, even as it had taken the Grice-Patersons and Lt. Austen Hanwell in their sleep.

"I believe it to be an experience without par," said Pons, helping me to my feet. "I had slipped into a doze and woke to a sound from the bed. The creepers had come through the window seeking the prey they sensed lay there—indeed, the entire opening was filled with the waving tendrils and limbs. I shall never forget the sight!"

In the morning, in our compartment of the train making its way from Penzance to London—for Pons would not permit our client to have us driven home, remaining only long enough to assist in the destruction of Sir Ronald's deadly creeper—Pons spoke reflectively of our strange adventure.

"The limiting circumstances of the deaths suggested a limited agent from the beginning," he said. "Each death had taken place in a room on the east side of the house—the same side on which the dogs and cats were found dead at various times of summer mornings —and each at the height of summer. 'How shall I ever again survive the month of August!' cried Miss Grice-Paterson. Furthermore, each had taken place at night, while the victims slept, thus enabling an insidious and silent slayer to transfix its victims in a fatal embrace which a waking man would readily have escaped.

"The creeper was unquestionably a mutation developed by Sir Ronald himself, a relative of the upas tree, and, like certain other plants, was carnivorous, becoming especially active at the height of its growth, which was its time of flowering—midsummer. An importation from Malaya, beyond question. Curiously, no one seems to have thought of examining the dead men or animals for loss of blood, for the creeper was, quite literally, vampiric.

"Sir Ronald knew its properties, there can be no doubt. He knew very well why he avoided the east wing in summer, and only the family's habit of following his custom explains their survival. Otherwise they might all have died long before this.

"Sir Ronald's motive in planting and cultivating the creeper on Uffa is obscured by time. Did his misanthropy indeed compel him to lay so effective and mortal a trap for those who succeeded him in the ironic intention that his one-time orderly should come into the estate? Or did his hatred of mankind unbalance him? We have had repeated reference to the old man's dislike of the human race, which included his own family. Perhaps in that lay the root of the evil that was the curse of the Grice-Patersons. It makes an interesting speculation, though we shall never know."

MICHAEL GILBERT

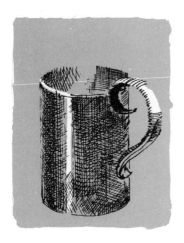

The Headmaster

The master spies at work in this country numbered, last year, four. They were known to Intelligence as the Language Master, the Science Master, the Games Master, and, in some undefined position of authority of all of them, the Headmaster.

Since the Portsmouth affair there have been but two. The Language Master was behind bars, and the Games Master had retired to Switzerland. The Science Master was still at his shadowy work in the Midlands, and the Headmaster was in the London area.

When it is said that Intelligence knew about these men, it must be understood that it was a matter of analysis and deduction rather than knowledge. A lot of confidential information was reaching the other side, much of it unimportant, but some of it highly important. Most of such items could be traced to their sources. And the lines drawn from these sources pointed inward and came together somewhere in the center of the metropolis.

"If I had to create the Headmaster," said Mr. Fortescue, "in the way that a scientist creates a megalosaurus from small fragments of tooth and bone, I should have to construct someone with the combined knowledge of a cabinet minister, a senior civil servant, and a don."

"An all-round man," said Mr. Calder. "Have we any hopeful line at all?"

"We have a line," said Mr. Fortescue. "I'm not sure if it's hopeful or not. Craven has disappeared."

"John Craven? I've seen nothing in the papers—"

"It will be there. Somewhat prominently, I'm afraid."

Since John Craven was a Queen's Counsel and Recorder of a Kentish borough, this seemed only too probable.

"He went down from his chambers by car on Saturday morning to his house at Charing. He was planning to return to town on Sunday night. The first time we knew anything was wrong was when he failed to turn up for a conference on Monday morning."

"Yesterday."

"Yes. We got busy at once, of course."

"Of course," said Mr. Calder. John Craven was one of his oldest friends. He was perfectly aware that he had another occupation besides his legal one.

"His car was still in the garage of his Charing house. The daily woman who cooks for him and cleans the house saw him start out for a walk after lunch on Sunday."

"He was a great walker," said Mr. Calder. He thought of his old friend, striding along a woodland path, red-cheeked, white-topped, head bent forward, stick swinging. "Have you any reason to connect it with the Headmaster?"

"Two reasons," said Mr. Fortescue. "First, Craven was one of three men who had been specially assigned to locating him. He had had, so far, absolutely no apparent success. Had he found out anything, he would of course have reported it at once."

"Of course," said Mr. Calder.

"However, the path that he was treading must have taken him unknowingly very close to the man. Too close for his comfort."

"You mentioned two reasons."

"It has the feel of a professional job," said Mr. Fortescue. "Carefully arranged, perfectly executed."

"I expect you're right," said Mr. Calder. He had never known Fortescue to be wrong in any important matter. "Just what would you like me to do?"

"The first thing must be to find Craven. I'd like it done, if possible, before the news is made public. I have informed our friends in the Special Branch. They can control ordinary police inquiry for a reasonable period. But I don't think we can keep the papers off it for more than forty-eight hours."

"I'll see what I can do," said Mr. Calder. "There was a sister, wasn't there? A widow. What was her name?"

"Mrs. Gordon. I have written down her address and telephone number. A very sensible woman. You should find her a great help."

So Mr. Calder and Mrs. Gordon traveled down to Charing together, and on Charing platform they found reinforcements.

"This is my friend, Mr. Behrens. He is a keen naturalist. I felt that four pairs of eyes would be better than two."

"It's very good of you to take so much trouble," said Mrs. Gordon. "Did you say four—?" She turned and found that a great dog had moved up silently behind her. Its head came nearly up to her waist.

"Oh," she said. "He's beautiful."

Rasselas eyed her coldly. For Mr. Calder, who talked to him in his own tongue, he would do anything. He had become accustomed to Mr. Behrens, and even allowed himself to be taken by him in his car when he understood from Mr. Behrens' manner that the matter was urgent. But this was the limit of his tolerance.

"I spent a little time on the way down," said Mr. Calder, "working out, with Mrs. Gordon's help, the sort of walks her brother might have taken in the time available. Ah, you've got the maps—good."

Mrs. Gordon said, "Truscott, his head clerk, told me that he planned to be back in London well before dinner. He had some papers to read, and he hated reading after dinner. That would have meant leaving Charing at five at the latest—and he liked to get his own tea before starting back."

"Two hours, almost exactly," said Mr. Calder. "Less, if he wanted, but not more."

"He'd go as far as he could in the time. There were two walks I've taken with him which would have fitted in almost exactly. There's not much to choose between them."

They spent a long morning, without result. What had taken the quick-striding barrister two hours to cover cost them nearly four. There were parts of it—along used roads and past houses—which they could ignore. But the rest had to be studied carefully.

After a quick lunch at a pub, they started on the second round. The path rose almost at once on a long slant, climbing the downs toward a wood.

"They could have watched him from up there—Mrs. Gordon, by the way, knows what we fear may have happened."

"I knew John did secret work. He didn't talk about it, of course."

"Of course not," said Mr. Calder. The path plunged into the wood—it turned out to be a mere screen of trees—then out again onto the downland.

Rasselas ran free ahead of them, his tail feathering in the breeze. Occasionally his nose dipped to the ground and rose again as he ran. He was like a great golden galleon answering to the first chops of the open sea.

"We won't waste much time here," said Mr. Calder. "It's lonely enough, but it's a lot too open. John had his wits about him. And he carried a gun."

The path turned now, and ran along the ridgeway. There were small coppices which were promising, and which they searched carefully but without success. Rasselas watched them, and from time to time Mr. Calder talked to him.

"He's not a bloodhound," he explained. "And there's no question of him acting as a tracker. What he's been trained to do is to notice when things are wrong—when they've been moved or altered. Anyone hiding in the bushes there, for instance, would have upset the pattern of the branches when he came out. If something which had been standing in the same place for some time had been shifted, it would leave a mark. That's the sort of thing he notices."

Rasselas sat on his haunches, grinning quietly as he watched Mr. Calder talking.

"He hasn't shown much interest yet," said Mr. Behrens.

"He'll tell us as soon as he sees anything."

They had already covered nearly fifteen miles that day, and were getting tired by the time they came to the deserted farm. The path skirted the farmyard. Under the collapsed Dutch barn there still lay a few trusses of gray and moldy hay. The tiles were off the roof, daylight showed through the walls. The nettle was in command of the garden and yard.

Rasselas padded quietly round the back of the house, and when he did not reappear Mr. Calder went to look for him. He was sitting on his haunches, still as stone, looking at a rusty rain-water tank propped on its side against the broken brick wall.

In the tank, his knees to his chin, was John Craven.

"There were three men involved," said Mr. Calder to Mr. Fortescue. "And you were right. The planning was meticulous. As John reached the corner of the farm, one man directly ahead of him attracted his attention and made him stop. There were two other men, one on each side behind him and hidden. One hit him to stun him, the other caught his arms as he fell and held him while the first one hit him again, this time hard enough to break his neck."

"How do you know all this?"

"Rasselas worked it out for me," said Mr. Calder. And, after a pause, "What next?"

"The finding of the body will be given to the press. In the public version the body will be found by hikers, *behind* the tank, not in it. Craven's walking habits will be mentioned. It will be strongly suggested that Craven felt faint, sat down to rest and died of heart failure. There will be an inquest, of course. But the only evidence will be of identity. And an adjournment for—how long will you require?"

"It depends on what I have to do," said Mr. Calder cautiously.

"The Headmaster took a grave risk in acting as he did. He must have felt that Craven represented a very real danger. And yet, curiously, Craven didn't know it. If he had suspected anything, he would have reported at once."

"Yes," said Mr. Calder.

"What you will have to do is to trace Craven's movements, his professional and social contacts, and try to discover why he should have become so dangerous without realizing it. Would a month be enough?"

Mr. Calder said, "I ought to know by the end of a month if there is any chance of success. . . ."

The first person he called on was Truscott. Craven's head clerk Truscott, and his sister Mrs. Gordon, were the only two people who knew that John Craven was more than a very successful barrister; and of the two, Truscott had been deeper in his confidence.

Mr. Calder sat in the barrister's neat room in Crown Office Row, overlooking the lawn of Middle Temple Gardens. It was a room walled with books. There were other books, marked with slips of paper, on a side table; a pile of briefs which would now have to be returned; a book diary with professional appointments; a flat desk diary with private engagements; and a locked cabinet of personal papers.

"He was a very methodical man," said Truscott.

"I hope it will make our job a bit easier," said Mr. Calder. He had explained to Truscott what he planned to do. "We'll start by listing everyone he saw privately in the last six months. The names will be in his private engagement book."

"I think this will help us, too," said Truscott. He produced, from the cabinet, a folder marked PERSONAL. "He kept all private letters here, and carbons of his replies. If he answered them by hand, he often made a spare copy."

"We'll use one as a check on the other. As a further cross-check, would you get your telephonist to give us a note of any numbers he called. If she doesn't keep a record, the post office could at least give us the toll calls."

"She keeps a record," said Truscott. "I'm not sure if it goes back six months, but I'll find out."

There followed a fortnight of work as hard and demanding as any that Mr. Calder could remember. He sat at John Craven's desk from nine o'clock in the morning until seven o'clock at night. He was introduced to the other members of the chambers as Craven's literary executor; Craven had been a considerable contributor to all sorts of journals, on legal and nonlegal topics, and had published two books of essays and reminiscences. Many of the friends whom Mr. Calder so patiently checked came from Fleet Street and New Fetter Lane.

The professional contacts caused little trouble. With Truscott's assistance he was able, in the first two days, to identify and put on one side the various solicitors who consulted Craven professionally.

This left a clutter of personal friends, relations, literary contacts, people he had met in the course of his political work, tradesmen, club acquaintances, and odd members of the public who will write to anyone whose name is known and who is foolish enough to have his address in the telephone book. A Christmas card list, with notes on some of the recipients, proved invaluable.

After a week of such work Mr. Calder felt so limp that he thought he might be in for a bout of flu. But he was not dissatisfied with his results.

"There are three people," he said, "that I'd like to concentrate on. Any one of them could have access to secret information. And all three are new acquaintances."

Truscott looked over his shoulder at the names he had jotted down.

"Sir George Gould," he said. "He's something in the Treasury, I believe. Mr Craven met him over his work with the Inns of Court Conservative Association. They were both concerned in the drafting of a new Rating Bill. General Hamish Fairside. He works in the War Office."

"Military Intelligence," said Mr. Calder.

"Freddie Lake. The name is familiar, but I don't think I ever met him."

"You're lucky," said Mr. Calder. "I have."

In the course of a long career, Sir Frederick Lake had held every conceivable post in the Foreign Service, had visited every known country in the world, and had developed into the most compulsive bore of his generation.

"I'd better start with General Fairside," said Mr. Calder. "I have a nodding acquaintance with him. Let's have a look at *Who's Who*.

"Clubs. United Services, Naval and Military, and the Hambone." He turned the pages until he came to *Gould. George Anstruther, educated Winchester and New College, Oxford.* His clubs were the United University Club—and the Hambone.

"This is too good to be true," said Mr. Calder. With fumbling fingers he turned to the letter L.

Sir Frederick Lake belonged to no fewer than six clubs. The Hambone was fourth on the list.

Mr. Calder sat turning this odd coincidence over in his mind. A further thought struck him.

"Did Mr. Craven belong to any clubs?"

"He was a member of the Travelers', sir."

"No other ones?"

"Fairly recently, I remember, he was talking about joining the Hambone. But you know what these clubs are like, sir. There was some opposition, somewhere, so of course he withdrew his candidature."

"I wonder," said Mr. Calder. "I wonder."

The Hambone Club in Carver Street is the offspring of that eccentric aristocrat, Sir Rawnsley Clayton. Having been turned out of the Athenæum for giving dinner there to a troupe of clowns, he had founded it as a place where he could meet his more Bohemian acquaintances. It was still much used by actors and writers, but had acquired a solid addition of politicians who found the Carlton too stuffy and of soldiers who found the Senior too exclusive.

It was to the Hambone Club that Mr. Calder was now making his way. Three weeks had passed since the death of John Craven. Mr. Calder had not hurried. The quarry he was hunting, if it existed at all, would await his coming.

He was conscious, as he walked through the misty lamplit streets, of a feeling close to guilt. He was breaking one of the oldest rules of the game. For so slight, so intangible, so elusive had been the clue upon which he had stumbled that he had not yet dared to record his suspicions. Possibly "suspicions" was too concrete a word altogether. It was a breath, a whisper, the first faint stirring of apprehension.

Yet when General Fairside, their acquaintanceship skillfully renewed, had invited him to dinner at the Hambone, and had mentioned casually that George Gould might be joining them for a drink afterward, he had paused to consider matters very carefully. In the end, he had slipped into the special pocket of his coat an automatic pistol. It had—like its owner—a short stout body; and it was equipped with a most efficient silencer. The moment he had put it into his pocket, he had felt the extravagance of the action. But he had allowed it to remain.

Mr. Calder found his host warming himself in front of a hospitable fire of logs.

"Nice of you to come out on a night like this," he boomed. "What are you drinking? Nonsense. Must have something before we start eating. Take away the taste of the food."

Over an excellent dinner they talked about the Service charity in which Mr. Calder was interested and which was the ostensible reason for their meeting; and about old friends, in the Army and out of it. The General had been a subaltern in a rifle regiment which had shared a particularly unpleasant section of the line with Mr. Calder's regiment in 1918.

"Sensible of you not to stay on in the Army," said the General. "No future in it."

"I wouldn't say that," said Mr. Calder.

"Oh, it suited someone like me. I meant for a brainy chap like you. By the way, what *did* you go in for?"

"Import and export," said Mr. Calder promptly. "What excellent Burgundy this is."

"I'm glad you like it. They know how to buy wine in this club. *And* how to look after it. Barlow! My guest likes the Corton."

Barlow, who was the doyen of the Hambone staff, smiled politely.

"I am glad you enjoyed it, sir," he said. "I had half a bottle with my own dinner." He sailed off down the room to attend to a black-haired man who had just come in.

"That's Sir George Gould, isn't it?" asked Mr. Calder.

"That's him. Doesn't look like a senior Treasury official, does he?"

"To be absolutely candid, I think he looks like a retired boxer."

"Not bad. Not bad at all. I fought him myself, in the first inter-regimental tournament after the war. He was in the Sixtieth. A dirty fighter. We'll lure him along with a glass of brandy after dinner."

No lure was needed. Sir George came over as if drawn by a magnet, was introduced to Mr. Calder and was given a large brandy. Mr. Calder settled himself in one of the large leather armchairs which make the coffee room of the Hambone one of the best sitting-out places in London. Sir George, he reflected, would be a very difficult man to fool. His had been a lifetime of committees and desk work, a lifetime of watching the wheels go round, and occasionally of making them turn.

He was in an unbuttoned mood now, telling stories of under-secretaries and their ways, of experiences at the bar of the House of Commons, of the foibles of his own master. Another brandy, thought Mr. Calder, and he might become thunderingly indiscreet. Or would he? There was an inner wall of cold reserve in those gray eyes which were turned upon Mr. Calder from time to time.

It was quite late when the General said, "Hullo, Freddie, come and join us," and Mr. Calder looked up and saw the tall, spare figure of Sir Frederick Lake bearing down on them.

A sense of completion seized Mr. Calder. It was the feeling which assails a scientist when, at the end of a long and difficult series of calculations full of imponderables and unknown quantities, he feels the shifting ground hardening under his feet at last. It was a sense of satisfaction, but mingled with alarm.

He had known that Sir Frederick would come. His arrival had been part of a ritual. How often, he wondered, had these three men met together in this way, in this place, at this hour of night?

Mr. Calder shifted in his seat, and felt the weight of the silenced automatic pressing against his stomach.

"I think we could all do with another drink," said Sir Frederick. "What would you like? Port or brandy? George? General? And you, sir?"

"It's too late for formal introductions," said the General. "But this is Mr. Calder. He's an old friend of mine. And he knew John Craven very well indeed."

The diplomat bowed very slightly toward Mr. Calder and said, "A sad business. All the same, when it happens, it's not a bad way out, is it?"

Mr. Calder felt three pairs of eyes upon him, and his lips were dry. He said, "I suppose not, no."

"In the open air," said the General. "On a Sunday afternoon walk. Quite suddenly. I'd settle for that myself, eh?"

"If I am destined to die quite suddenly," said Sir George, "I think I should like it to be when I was in the box of the House of Commons at question time. Imagine the look on the Minister's face—"

The three men laughed.

Sir Frederick, still standing, said, "May I have your orders, gentlemen?"

Sir George and the General said, "Brandy," in perfect unison.

Mr. Calder said, "At this time of night, I'm very fond of a half pint of bitter."

"An excellent choice," said Sir Frederick, and rang the bell. "In certain circumstances, the grain and the grape go very well together. I can only suggest one amendment. You should have a pint, not a half pint."

"I will fall in with your suggestion," said Mr. Calder.

The benign figure of Barlow appeared out of the gloom. Sir Frederick gave the order.

"I sometimes wonder," said the General, "if Barlow ever goes to bed. If you want a drink at any time between ten o'clock and four in the morning, he always brings it himself."

"He sends the younger waiters home," said Sir George, "and sits, in solitary splendor, in a great padded chair in a sort of pantry next to the kitchen. On one occasion, when the electric bell was out of order, I penetrated to his lair."

"I picture him," said the General, "as leading a Regency life, going to bed at six in the morning and getting up at lunchtime—"

This speculation was cut short by the reappearance of Barlow. He was bearing, on a silver salver, three glasses of brandy and a half-pint tankard of beer.

"Barlow," said Sir Frederick, "that's the first time in twenty years I have known you to make a mistake. I said a pint."

Even in the gloom Mr. Calder could see the man flush. He said hastily, "That's quite all right. Don't think of changing it. It'll do me very nicely."

In truth, he had only one idea now—to get the three men out of the club. Patience, patience and still more patience. Mr. Calder, who had played many waiting games in his life, had rarely been tried higher than he was that night.

But all things must have an end, even Sir Frederick Lake's anecdotes. Two o'clock was striking as Mr. Calder followed his three hosts down the steps of the Hambone Club, past the empty porter's hutch, through the great doors and out into the street.

There were three cars there. Mr. Calder said, "I won't trouble any of you for a lift. My flat is only ten minutes away, and I'd welcome the walk. And thank you, General, once more, for a most enjoyable evening."

As soon as he had turned the corner he paused, drew into a doorway and waited. He could hear the three voices; a laugh, a shouted good night; the slamming of car doors; three separate cars starting and driving away. Then silence returned.

While they had been sitting in the club, the mist had thickened. Since he had to move, and more quickly now, mist might be a useful ally.

He turned about and walked back the way he had come. The porter's hutch was still empty. One of Barlow's self-imposed duties would be locking up when the last member had taken himself home to bed.

The lights in the inner hall had been reduced to one reading lamp. From the walls the pictures of actors and actresses looked down from their heavy gold frames. Their incurious eyes followed Mr. Calder as he tiptoed across the floor.

A melodrama, thought Mr. Calder. In three acts. Act one, a deserted farmstead. Act two, a barrister's chambers. Act three, a London club.

He pulled on a pair of cotton gloves before opening the baize-covered door. His rubbersoled shoes hissed softly on the flagstones.

The club kitchen lay at the end of the passage. The door was open, and from a room leading off it a light showed. Mr. Calder drifted across, breath held, silent as thistledown. He pushed the door open with his gun.

Barlow was not sitting in the great padded chair which the General had described. He was standing beside it, working at the leather upholstery.

"Good evening, Headmaster," said Mr. Calder.

"I recognized you when you came here this evening." The voice was harsh. The tones of the well-bred club servant had disappeared with the deferential smile. The face was grinning. But it was the grin of a death mask. "I should have taken steps at once. First Craven, then you."

"I suppose it's no use me telling you that Craven suspected nothing. That you killed him to no purpose."

"I could not afford to take a chance."

Mr. Calder said, "I imagine there is some sort of concealed microphone in the coffee room, behind where the eminent gossips sit over their brandies? And a listening apparatus in this room?"

"You imagine correctly. The microphone and receiver are removable. Only the wiring is permanent."

"And the receiver is somewhere in that chair?"

"It was. I have removed it. In ten minutes I should have had the whole apparatus dismantled."

"It is interesting to reflect," said Mr. Calder, "that had Sir Frederick Lake indulged in one more reminiscence, you would have got away with all this."

"I should like to know how you found out."

"Oh, it was a stupid thing," said Mr. Calder. "You brought me the half pint of beer which you *overheard* me asking for, instead of the pint which Sir Frederick actually told you to bring. An incredible mistake for an experienced club servant."

"Ah!" said the man. He raised his hand, without haste, to his mouth. The stench of cyanide filled the room. As Mr. Calder watched, the body arched, clung for a moment with hands braced to the chairback, then emptied itself into a black pool on the floor.

Before he left, Mr. Calder removed the microphone and the headset. The wiring he left. It would attract no notice. London clubs are full of aged and inexplicable wiring.

He was in bed by three, and asleep ten minutes later. His influenza seemed to be better.

The Adventure of the Seven Black Cats

The tinkley bell quavered over the door of Miss Curleigh's Pet Shoppe on Amsterdam Avenue, and Mr. Ellery Queen wrinkled his nose and went in. The instant he crossed the threshold he was thankful it was not a large nose, and that he had taken the elementary precaution of wrinkling it. The extent and variety of the little shop's odors would not have shamed the New York Zoological Park itself. And yet it housed only creatures, he was amazed to find, of the puniest proportions; who, upon the micrometrically split second of his entrance, set up such a chorus of howls, yelps, snarls, yawps, grunts, squeaks, caterwauls, croaks, screeches, chirrups, hisses, and growls that it was a miracle the roof did not come down.

"Good afternoon," said a crisp voice. "I'm Miss Curleigh. What can I do for you, please?"

In the midst of bedlam Mr. Queen found himself gazing into a pair of mercurial eyes. There were other details—she was a trim young piece, for example, with masses of titian hair and curves and at least one dimple—but for the moment her eyes engaged his earnest attention. Miss Curleigh, blushing, repeated herself.

"I beg your pardon," said Ellery hastily, returning to the matter at hand. "Apparently in the animal kingdom there is no decent ratio between lung-power and—ah—aroma on the one hand and size on the other. We live and learn. Miss Curleigh, would it be possible to purchase a comparatively noiseless and sweet-smelling canine with frizzy brown hair, inquisitive ears at the half-cock, and crooked hind legs?"

Miss Curleigh frowned. Unfortunately, she was out of Irish terriers. The last litter had been gobbled up. Perhaps a Scottie——?

No, he had been specifically enjoined by Djuna, the martinet, to procure an Irish terrier; no doleful-looking, sawed-off substitute, he was sure, would do.

"I expect," said Miss Curleigh professionally, "to hear from our Long Island kennels tomorrow. If you'll leave your name and address?"

As Miss Curleigh read what he had written the mask of business fell away. "You're not *Ellery* Queen!" she exclaimed with animation. "Well, I declare. I've heard *so* much about you, Mr. Queen. And you live practically around the corner, on Eighty-seventh Street! This is really thrilling. I never expected to meet——"

"Nor I," murmured Mr. Queen. "Nor I."

Miss Curleigh automatically prodded her hair. "One of my best customers lives right across the street from you, Mr. Queen. I should say one of my most *frequent* customers. Perhaps you know her? A Miss Tarkle—Euphemia Tarkle? She's in that large apartment house, you know."

"I've never had the pleasure," said Mr. Queen absently. "What extraordinary eyes you have! I mean—Euphemia Tarkle? This is a world of sudden wonders. Is she as improbable as her name?"

"That's unkind," said Miss Curleigh severely, "although she *is* something of a character, the poor creature. A squirrelly-faced old lady, *and* an invalid. Paralytic, you know. The queerest, frailest, tiniest little thing. Really, she's quite mad."

"Somebody's grandmother, no doubt," said Mr. Queen, picking up his stick from the counter. "Cats?"

"Why, however did you guess?"

"It always is."

"*You'd* find her interesting, I'm sure," said Miss Curleigh.

"And why I, Diana?"

"The name," said Miss Curleigh shyly, "is Marie. Well, she's *so* strange, Mr. Queen. And I've always understood that strange people interest you."

"At present," said Mr. Queen hurriedly, taking a firmer grip on his stick, "I am enjoying the fruits of idleness."

"But do you know what Miss Tarkle's been doing, the mad thing?"

"I haven't the ghost of a notion."

"She's been buying cats from me at the rate of about one a week for weeks now!"

Mr. Queen sighed. "I see no special cause for suspicion. An ancient and invalid lady, a passion for cats—they go together, I assure you. I once had an aunt like that."

"That's what's so strange about it," said Miss Curleigh triumphantly. "She doesn't *like* cats!"

Mr. Queen blinked twice. He looked at Miss Curleigh's pleasant little nose. Then he rather absently set his stick on the counter again. "And how do you know that?"

"Her sister told me. Hush, Ginger! You see, Miss Tarkle is absolutely helpless with her paralysis and all, and her sister Sarah-Ann keeps house for her; they're both of an age, I should say, and they look so much alike. Dried-up little apples of old ladies, with the same tiny features and faces like squirrels. Well, Mr. Queen, about a year ago Miss Sarah-Ann came into my shop and bought a black male cat—she hadn't much money, she said, couldn't buy a really expensive one; so I got just a—well, just a cat for her, you see."

"Did she ask for a black tomcat?" asked Mr. Queen intently.

"No. Any kind at all, she said; she liked them all. Then only a few days later she came back. She wanted to know if she could return him and get her money back. Because, she said, her sister Euphemia couldn't stand having a cat about her; Euphemia just *detested* cats, she said with a sigh, and since she was more or less living off Euphemia's bounty she couldn't very well cross her, you see. I felt a little sorry for her and told her I'd take the cat back; but I suppose she changed her mind, or else her ister changed *her* mind, because Sarah-Ann Tarkle never came back. Anyway, that's how I know Miss Euphemia doesn't like cats."

Mr. Queen gnawed a fingernail. "Odd," he muttered. "A veritable saga of oddness. You say this Euphemia creature has been buying 'em at the rate of one a week? What kind of cats, Miss Curleigh?"

Miss Curleigh sighed. "Not very good ones. Of course, since she has pots of money—that's what her sister Sarah-Ann said, anyway—I tried to sell her an Angora—I had a beauty—and a Maltese that took a ribbon at one of the shows. But she wanted just cats, she said, like the one I sold her sister. Black ones."

"Black. . . . It's possible that——"

"Oh, she's not at all superstitious, Mr. Queen. In some ways she's a very weird old lady. Black tomcats with green eyes, all the same size. I thought it very queer."

Mr. Ellery Queen's nostrils quivered a little, and not from the racy odor in Miss Curleigh's Pet Shoppe, either. An old invalid lady named Tarkle who bought a black tomcat with green eyes every week!

"Very queer indeed," he murmured; and his gray eyes narrowed. "And how long has this remarkable business been going on?"

"You *are* interested! Five weeks now, Mr. Queen. I delivered the sixth one myself only the other day."

"Yourself? Is she totally paralyzed?"

"Oh, yes. She never leaves her bed; can't walk a step. It's been that way, she told me, for ten years now. She and Sarah-Ann hadn't lived together up to the time she had her stroke. Now she's absolutely dependent on her sister for everything—meals, baths, bedp . . . all sorts of attention."

"Then why," demanded Ellery, "hasn't she sent her sister for the cats?"

Miss Curleigh's mercurial eyes wavered. "I don't know," she said slowly. "Sometimes I get the shivers. You see, she's always telephoned me—she has a 'phone by her bed and can use her arms sufficiently to reach for it—the day she wanted the cat. It would always be the same order—black, male, green eyes, the same size as before, and as cheap as possible." Miss Curleigh's pleasant features hardened. "She's something of a haggler, Miss Euphemia Tarkle is."

"Fantastic," said Ellery thoughtfully. "Utterly fantastic. Tell me: how has her sister acted on the occasions when you've delivered the cats?"

"*Hush*, Ginger! I can't tell you, Mr. Queen, because she hasn't been there."

Ellery started. "Hasn't been there! What do you mean? I thought you said the Euphemia woman is helpless——"

"She is, but Sarah-Ann goes out every afternoon for some air, I suppose, or to a movie, and her sister is left alone for a few hours. It's been at such times, I think, that she's called me. Then, too, she always warned me to come at a certain time, and since I've never seen Sarah-Ann when I made the delivery, I imagine she's planned to keep her purchases a secret from her sister. I've been able to get in because Sarah-Ann leaves the door unlocked when she goes out. Euphemia has told me time and time again not to breathe a word about the cats to anyone."

Ellery pulled his nose—an unfailing sign of emotion. "More and more muddled," he muttered. "Miss Curleigh, you've stumbled on something—well, morbid."

Miss Curleigh blanched. "You don't think——"

"I *do* think; and that's why I'm disturbed. For instance, how on earth could she have hoped to keep knowledge of the cats she's bought from her sister? Sarah-Ann isn't blind, is she?"

"Blind? Why, of course not. And Euphemia's sight is all right, too."

"I was only joking. It doesn't make sense, Miss Curleigh."

"Well," said Miss Curleigh brightly, "at least I've given the great Mr. Queen something to think about. . . . I'll call you the moment an Ir——"

Ellery threw back his shoulders and picked up the stick again. "Miss Curleigh, I'm an incurable meddler in the affairs of others. How would you like to help me meddle in the affairs of the mysterious Tarkle sisters?"

Scarlet spots appeared in Miss Curleigh's cheeks. "You're not serious?" she cried.

"Quite."

"I'd love to! What am I to do?"

"Suppose you take me up to the Tarkle apartment and introduce me as a customer. Let's say that the cat you sold Miss Tarkle the other day had really been promised to me, that as a stubborn fancier of felines I won't take any other, and that you'll have to have hers back and give her another. Anything to permit me to see and talk to her. It's mid-afternoon, so Sarah-Ann is probably in a movie theater somewhere. What do you say?"

Miss Curleigh flung him a ravishing smile. "I say it's—it's too magnificent for words. One minute while I powder my nose and get someone to tend the shop, Mr. Queen. I wouldn't miss this for *anything*!"

Ten minutes later they stood before the front door to Apartment 5-C of the "Amsterdam Arms," a rather faded building, gazing in silence at two full quart-bottles of milk on the floor. Miss Curleigh looked troubled, and Mr. Queen stooped. When he straightened he looked troubled, too.

"Yesterday's and today's," he muttered, and he put his hand on the doorknob and turned. The door was locked. "I thought you said her sister leaves the door unlocked when she goes out?"

"Perhaps she's in," said Miss Curleigh uncertainly. "Or, if she's out, she's forgotten to take the latch off."

Ellery pressed the bell button. There was no reply. He rang again. Then he called loudly: "Miss Tarkle, are you there?"

"I can't understand it," said Miss Curleigh with a nervous laugh. "She really should hear you. It's only a three-room apartment, and both the bedroom and the living room are directly off the sides of a little foyer on the other side of the door. The kitchen's straight ahead."

Ellery called again, shouting. After a while he put his ear to the door. The rather dilapidated hall, the ill-painted door . . .

Miss Curleigh's extraordinary eyes were frightened silver lamps. She said in the queerest voice: "Oh, Mr. Queen. Something dreadful's happened."

"Let's hunt up the superintendent," said Ellery quietly.

They found "Potter, Sup't" in a metal frame before a door on the ground floor. Miss Curleigh was breathing in little gusts. Ellery rang the bell.

A short fat woman with enormous forearms flecked with suds opened the door. She wiped her red hands on a dirty apron and brushed a strand of bedraggled gray hair from her sagging face. "Well?" she demanded.

"Mrs. Potter?"

"That's right. We ain't got no empty apartments. The doorman could 'a' told you——"

Miss Curleigh reddened. Ellery said hastily: "Oh, we're not apartment-hunting, Mrs. Potter. Is the superintendent in?"

"No, he's not. He's got a part-time job at the chemical works in Long Island City, and he never gets home till ha' past three. What you want?"

"I'm sure you'll do nicely, Mrs. Potter. This young lady and I can't seem to get an answer from Apartment 5-C."

The fat woman scowled. "Ain't the door open? Generally is this time o' day. The spry one's out, but the paralyzed one——"

"It's locked, Mrs. Potter."

"Now ain't that funny," shrilled the fat woman, staring at Miss Curleigh. "I can't see—— Miss Euphemia's a cripple; she *never* goes out. Maybe the poor thing's threw a fit!"

"I hope not. When did you see Sarah-Ann last?"

"The spry one? Let's see, now. Why, two days ago. And, come to think of it, I ain't seen the cripple for two days, neither."

"Heavens," whispered Miss Curleigh, thinking of the two milk-bottles. "Two days!"

"Oh, you do see Miss Euphemia occasionally?" asked Ellery grimly.

"Yes, sir." Mrs. Potter began to wring her red hands as if she were still over the tub. "Every once in a while she calls me up in the afternoon if her sister's out to take somethin' out to the incinerator, or do somethin' for her. The other day it was to mail a letter for her. She—she gives me somethin' once in a while. But it's been two days now. . . ."

Ellery pulled something out of his pocket and cupped it in his palm before the fat woman's tired eyes. "Mrs. Potter," he said sternly, "I want to get into that apartment. There's something wrong. Give me your master-key."

She stared at the shield. Then she fluttered off and returned to thrust a key into Ellery's hand. "Oh, I wish Mr. Potter was home!" she wailed. "You won't——"

"Not a word about this to anyone, Mrs. Potter."

They left the woman gaping and took the self-service elevator back to the fifth floor. Miss Curleigh looked a little sick.

"Perhaps," said Ellery kindly, inserting the key into the lock, "you had better not come in with me, Miss Curleigh. It might be unpleasant. I——" He stopped abruptly.

Somebody was on the other side of the door.

There was the unmistakable sound of running feet, accompanied by an uneven scraping, as if something were being dragged. Ellery twisted the key and turned the knob in a flash, Miss Curleigh panting at his shoulder. The door moved a half-inch and stuck. The feet retreated.

"Barricaded the door," growled Ellery. "Stand back, Miss Curleigh." He flung himself sidewise at the door. There was a splintering crash and the door shot inward, a broken chair toppling over backward. "Too late——"

"The fire-escape!" screamed Miss Curleigh. "In the bedroom. To the left!"

He darted into a large narrow room with twin beds and an air of disorder and made for an open window. But there was no one to be seen on the fire-escape. He looked up: an iron ladder curved and vanished a few feet overhead.

"Whoever it is got away by the roof, I'm afraid," he muttered, lighting a cigaret. "Smoke? Now then. No bloodshed, apparently. This may be a pig-in-the-poke after all. See anything interesting?"

Miss Curleigh pointed a shaking finger. "That's her—her bed. The messy one. But where is she?"

The other bed was neatly made up, its lace spread undisturbed. But Miss Euphemia Tarkle's was in a state of turmoil. The sheets had been ripped away and its mattress slashed open; some of the ticking was on the floor. The pillows had been torn to pieces. A depression in the center of the mattress indicated where the missing invalid had lain.

Ellery stood still, studying the bed. Then he made the rounds of the closets, opening doors, poking about, and closing them again. Followed closely by Miss Curleigh, who had developed an alarming habit of looking over her right shoulder, he glanced briefly into the living room, the kitchen and the bathroom. But there was no one in the apartment. And, except for Miss Tarkle's bed, nothing apparently had been disturbed. The place was ghastly, somehow. It was as if violence had visited it in the midst of a cloistered silence; a tray full of dishes, cutlery, and half-finished food lay on the floor, almost under the bed.

Miss Curleigh edged closer to Ellery. "It's so—so deserted here," she said, moistening her lips. "Where's Miss Euphemia? And her sister? And who was that—that creature who barred the door?"

"What's more to the point," murmured Ellery, gazing at the tray of food, "where are the seven black cats?"

"Sev——"

"Sarah-Ann's lone beauty, and Euphemia's six. Where are they?"

"Perhaps," said Miss Curleigh hopefully, "they jumped out the window when that man——"

"Perhaps. And don't say 'man.' We just don't know." He looked irritably about. "If they did, it was a moment ago, because the catch on the window has been forced, indicating that the window has been closed and consequently that the cats might have——" He stopped short. "Who's there?" he called sharply, whirling.

"It's me," said a timid voice, and Mrs. Potter appeared hesitantly in the foyer. Her tired eyes were luminous with fear and curiosity. "Where's——"

"Gone." He stared at the slovenly woman. "You're sure you didn't see Miss Euphemia or her sister today?"

"Nor yesterday. I——"

"There was no ambulance in this neighborhood within the past two days?"

Mrs. Potter went chalky. "Oh, no, sir! I can't understand how she got *out*. She couldn't walk a step. If she'd been carried, *someone* would have noticed. The doorman, sure. I just asked him. But nobody did. I know everythin' goes on——"

"Is it possible your husband may have seen one or both of them within the past two days?"

"Not Potter. He saw 'em night before last. Harry's been makin' a little side-money, sort of, see. Miss Euphemia wanted the landlord to do some decoratin' and paperin', and a little carpentry, and they wouldn't do it. So, more'n a month ago, she asked Harry if he wouldn't do it on the sly, and she said she'd pay him, although less than if a reg'lar decorator did it. So he's been doin' it spare time, mostly late afternoons and nights—he's handy, Potter is. He's most done with the job. It's pretty paper, ain't it? So he saw Miss Euphemia night before last." A calamitous thought struck her, apparently, for her eyes rolled and she uttered a faint shriek. "I just thought if—if anythin's happened to the cripple, we won't get paid! All that work . . . And the landlord——"

"Yes, yes," said Ellery impatiently. "Mrs. Potter, are there mice or rats in this house?"

Both women looked blank. "Why, not a one of 'em," began Mrs. Potter slowly. "The exterminator comes——" when they all spun about at a sound from the foyer. Someone was opening the door.

"Come in," snapped Ellery, and strode forward; only to halt in his tracks as an anxious face poked timidly into the bedroom.

"Excuse me," said the newcomer nervously, starting at sight of Ellery and the two women. "I guess I must be in the wrong apartment. Does Miss Euphemia Tarkle live here?" He was a tall needle-thin young man with a scared, horsey face and stiff tan hair. He wore a rather rusty suit of old-fashioned cut and carried a small handbag.

"Yes, indeed," said Ellery with a friendly smile. "Come in, come in. May I ask who you are?"

The young man blinked. "But where's Aunt Euphemia? I'm Elias Morton, Junior. Isn't she here?" His reddish little eyes blinked from Ellery to Miss Curleigh in a puzzled, worried way.

"Did you say 'Aunt' Euphemia, Mr. Morton?"

"I'm her nephew. I come from out of town—Albany. Where——"

Ellery murmured: "An unexpected visit, Mr. Morton?"

The young man blinked again; he was still holding his bag. Then he dumped it on the floor and eagerly fumbled in his pockets until he produced a much-soiled and wrinkled letter. "I got this only a few days ago. I'd have come sooner, only my father went off somewhere on a—— I don't understand this."

Ellery snatched the letter from his lax fingers. It was scrawled painfully on a piece of ordinary brown wrapping paper; the envelope

was a cheap one. The pencilled scribble, in the crabbed hand of age,
said:

DEAR ELIAS,—You have not heard from your Auntie for so
many years, but now I need you, Elias, for you are my only blood
kin to whom I can turn in my Dire Distress! I am in great danger,
my dear boy. You must help your poor Invalid Aunt who is so
helpless. *Come at once.* Do not tell your Father or anyone, Elias!
When you get here make believe you have come just for a Visit.
Remember. Please, please do not fail me. Help me, please! Your
Loving Aunt—EUPHEMIA.

"Remarkable," frowned Ellery. "Written under stress, Miss Curleigh. Genuine enough. Don't tell anyone, eh? Well, Mr. Morton,
I'm afraid you're too late."

"Too———" The young man's horse-face whitened. "I tried to
come right off, but my father had gone off somewhere on one of his
drunken spells, and I couldn't find him. I didn't know what to do.
Then I came. To think———" His buck teeth were chattering.

"This *is* your aunt's handwriting?"

"Oh, yes. Oh, yes."

"Your father, I gather, is not a brother of the Tarkle sisters?"

"No, sir. My mother was their sister, God rest her." Morton
groped for a chair-back. "Is Aunt Euphemia—dead? And where's
Aunt Sarah?"

"They're both gone." Ellery related tersely what he had found.
The young visitor from Albany looked as if he might faint. "I'm—
er—unofficially investigating this business, Mr. Morton. Tell me all
you know about your two aunts."

"I don't know much," mumbled Morton. "Haven't seen them for
about fifteen years, since I was a kid. I heard from my Aunt Sarah-
Ann once in a while, and only twice from Aunt Euphemia. They
never—— I never expected—— I do know that Aunt Euphemia
since her stroke became . . . funny. Aunt Sarah wrote me that. She
had some money—I don't know how much—left her by my grandfather, and Aunt Sarah said she was a real miser about it. Aunt
Sarah didn't have anything; she had to live with Aunt Euphemia
and take care of her. She wouldn't trust banks, Aunt Sarah said,
and had hidden the money somewhere about her, Aunt Sarah didn't
know where. She wouldn't even have doctors after her stroke, she
was—is so stingy. They didn't get along; they were always fighting,
Aunt Sarah wrote me, and Aunt Euphemia was always accusing her

of trying to steal her money, and she didn't know how she stood it. That's about all I know."

"The poor things," murmured Miss Curleigh with moist eyes. "What a wretched existence! Miss Tarkle can't be responsible for——"

"Tell me, Mr. Morton," said Ellery. "It's true that your Aunt Euphemia detested cats?"

"Why, how'd you know? She hates them. Aunt Sarah wrote me that many times. It hurt her a lot, because *she's* so crazy about them she treats her own like a child, you see, and that makes Aunt Euphemia jealous, or angry, or something. I guess they just didn't— don't get along."

"We seem to be having difficulty with our tenses," said Ellery. "After all, Mr. Morton, there's no evidence to show that your aunts aren't merely off somewhere on a vacation, or a visit." But the glint in his eyes remained. "Why don't you stop at a hotel somewhere near by? I'll keep you informed." He scribbled the name and address of a hotel in the Seventies on the page of a notebook, and thrust it into Morton's damp palm. "Don't worry. You'll hear from me." And he hustled the bewildered young man out of the apartment. They heard the click of the elevator door a moment later.

Ellery said slowly: "The country cousin in full panoply. Miss Curleigh, let me look at your loveliness. People with faces like that should be legislated against." He patted her cheek with a frown, hesitated, and then made for the bathroom. Miss Curleigh blushed once more and followed him quickly, casting another apprehensive glance over her shoulder.

"What's this?" she heard Ellery say sharply. "Mrs. Potter, come out of that—— By George!"

"What's the matter now?" cried Miss Curleigh, dashing into the bathroom behind him.

Mrs. Potter, her powerful forearms crawling with goose pimples, was glaring with open mouth into the tub. The woman made a few inarticulate sounds and fled from the apartment.

Miss Curleigh said: "Oh, my God!" and put her hand to her breast. "Isn't that *horrible*!"

"Horrible," said Ellery grimly and slowly, "and illuminating. I overlooked it when I glanced in here before, I think . . ." He stopped and bent over the tub. There was no humor in his eyes or voice now; only a sick watchfulness.

A black tomcat stiff and boneless, lay in a welter of blood in the tub. He was large, glossy black, green-eyed, and very dead. His head was smashed in; his body seemed broken in several places. His blood had clotted in splashes on the porcelain sides of the tub. The weapon lay beside him: a blood-splattered bathbrush with a heavy handle.

"That solves the mystery of the disappearance of at least one of the seven," murmured Ellery, straightening. "Battered to death with the brush. He hasn't been dead more than a day or so, either, from the looks of him."

Miss Curleigh, her first horror swept away by rage, was crying: "Anyone who would kill a puss so brutally is a monster!" Her silvery eyes were blazing. "That terrible old woman——"

"Don't forget," sighed Ellery, "she can't walk."

"Now this," said Mr. Queen some time later, putting away his cunning and compact little pocket kit, "is growing more and more curious, Miss Curleigh. Have you any notion what I've found here?"

They were back in the bedroom again, stooped over the bed tray which he had picked up from the floor and deposited on the night table between the missing sisters' beds. Miss Curleigh had recalled that on all her previous visits she had found the tray on Miss Tarkle's bed or on the table, the invalid explaining with a tightening of her pale lips that she had taken to eating alone of late, implying that she and the long-suffering Sarah-Ann had reached a parting of the ways.

"I saw you mess about with powder and things, but——"

Ellery stared enigmatically down at the knife, fork, and spoon lying awry in the tray. "My kit's a handy gadget at times. You saw me test this cutlery, Miss Curleigh. You would say that these implements had been used by Euphemia in the process of eating her last meal here?"

"Why, of course," frowned Miss Curleigh. "You can still see the dried food clinging to the knife and fork."

"Exactly. The handles of knife, fork, and spoon are not engraved, as you see—simple silver surfaces. They should bear fingerprints." He shrugged. "But they don't."

"What do you mean, Mr. Queen? How is that possible?"

"I mean that someone has wiped this cutlery free of prints. Odd, eh?" Ellery lit a cigaret absently. "Examine it, however. This is Euphemia Tarkle's bed tray, her food, her dishes, her cutlery. She is known to eat in bed, and alone. But if only Euphemia handled the cutlery, who wiped off the prints? She? Why should she? Someone else? But surely there would be no sense in someone else's wiping off *Euphemia's* prints. Her fingerprints have a right to be there. Then, while Euphemia's prints were probably on these implements, someone else's prints were also on them. Someone else, therefore, handled

Euphemia's cutlery. Why? I begin," said Ellery in the grimmest of voices, "to see daylight. Miss Curleigh, would you like to serve as handmaiden to Justice?" Miss Curleigh, overwhelmed, could only nod. Ellery began to wrap the cold food leftovers from the invalid's tray. "Take this truck down to Dr. Samuel Prouty—here's his address—and ask him to analyze it for me. Wait there, get his report, and meet me back here. Try to get in here without being observed."

"The *food?*"

"The food."

"Then you think it's been——"

"The time for thinking," said Ellery evenly, "is almost over."

When Miss Curleigh had gone, he took a final look around, even to the extent of examining some empty cupboards which had a look of newness about them, set his lips firmly, locked the front door behind him—pocketing the master-key which Mrs. Potter had given him—took the elevator to the ground floor, and rang the bell of the Potter apartment.

A short thickset man with heavy, coarse features opened the door; his hat was pushed back on his head. Ellery saw the agitated figure of Mrs. Potter hovering in the background.

"That's the policeman!" shrilled Mrs. Potter. "Harry, don't get mixed up in——"

"Oh, so you're the dick," growled the thickset man, ignoring the fat woman. "I'm the super here—Harry Potter. I just get home from the plant and my wife tells me there's somethin' wrong up in the Tarkle flat. What's up, for God's sake?"

"Now, now, there's no cause for panic, Potter," said Ellery. "Glad you're home, though; I'm in need of information which you can probably provide. Has either of you found, anywhere on the premises recently, any dead cats?"

Potter's jaw dropped, and his wife gurgled with surprise. "Now that's damn' funny. We sure have. Mrs. Potter says one of 'em's dead up in 5-C now—I never thought *those* two old dames might be the ones——"

"Where did you find them, and how many?" snapped Ellery.

"Why, down in the incinerator."

Ellery smacked his thigh. "Of course! I see it now. The incinerator, eh? There were six, Potter, weren't there?"

"How'd you know that?"

"Incinerator," muttered Ellery, sucking his lip. "The bones, I suppose—the skulls?"

"That's right," exclaimed Potter; he seemed distressed. "I found

'em myself. Empty out the incinerator every morning for ash removal. Six cats' skulls and a mess o' little bones. I raised the devil
around here with the tenants lookin' for the numbskull who threw
'em down the chute, but they all played dumb. Didn't all come down
the same time. It's been goin' on now maybe four-five weeks. One a
week, almost. I'd like to get my paws on——"

"You're certain you found six?"

"Sure."

"And nothing else of a suspicious nature?"

"No."

"Thanks. I don't believe there will be any more trouble. Just forget the whole business." And Ellery pressed a bill into the man's
hand and strolled out of the lobby.

He did not stroll far. He strolled, in fact, only to the sidewalk steps
leading down into the basement and cellar. Five minutes later he
quietly let himself into Apartment 5-C again.

When Miss Curleigh stopped before the door to Apartment 5-C
in late afternoon, she found it locked. She could hear Ellery's voice
murmuring inside and a moment later the click of a telephone receiver. Reassured, she pressed the bell; he appeared instantly, pulled
her inside, noiselessly shut the door again, and led her to the bedroom, where she slumped into a rosewood chair, an expression of
bitter disappointment on her pleasant little face.

"Back from the wars, I see. Well, sister, what luck?"

"You'll be dreadfully put out," said Miss Curleigh with a scowl.
"I'm sorry I haven't been more helpful——"

"What did Dr. Prouty say?"

"Nothing encouraging. I like your Dr. Prouty, even if he *is* the
Medical Examiner or something and wears a horrible little peaked
hat; but I can't say I'm keen about his reports. He says there's not a
thing wrong with that food you sent by me! It's a little putrefied from
standing, but otherwise it's pure enough."

"Now isn't that too bad?" said Ellery cheerfully. "Come, come,
Diana, perk up. It's the best news you could have brought me."

"Best n——" began Miss Curleigh with a gasp.

"It substitutes fact for theory very nicely. We have," and he pulled
over a chair and sat down facing her, "arrived. By the way, did anyone see you enter this apartment?"

"I slipped in by the basement and took the elevator from there.
No one saw me, I'm sure."

"Commendable; I believe we have some time. I've had an hour

or so here alone for thought, and it's been a satisfactory if morbid business." Ellery lit a cigaret and crossed his legs lazily. "Miss Curleigh, tell me: Why should a wealthy old lady who is almost completely paralyzed stealthily purchase six cats within a period of five weeks?"

Miss Curleigh shrugged. "I told you I couldn't make it out. It's a deep, dark mystery to me."

"It can't be as baffling as all that. Very well, I'll give you a rough idea. For example, so many cats purchased by an eccentric in so short a period suggests vivisection. But neither of the Tarkle ladies is anything like a scientist. So that's out. You see?"

"Oh, yes," said Miss Curleigh breathlessly. "I see now what you mean. Euphemia couldn't have wanted them for companionship, either, because she hates cats!"

"Precisely. Let's wander. For extermination of mice? No, this is from Mrs. Potter's report a pest-free building. For mating? Scarcely; Sarah-Ann's cat was a male, and Euphemia also bought only males. Besides, they were nondescript tabbies, and people don't play Cupid to nameless animals."

"She might have bought them for gifts," said Miss Curleigh with a frown. "That's possible."

"Possible, but I think not," said Ellery dryly. "Not when you know the facts. The superintendent found the skeletal remains of six cats in the ashes of the incinerator downstairs, and the other one lies, a very dead pussy, in the bathtub yonder." Miss Curleigh stared at him, speechless. "We seem to have covered the more plausible theories. Can you think of some wilder ones?"

Miss Curleigh paled. "Not—not for their *fur?*"

"*Brava!*" said Ellery with a laugh. "There's a wild one among wild ones. No, not for their fur; I haven't found any fur in the apartment. And besides, no matter who killed Master Tom in the tub, he remains bloody but unskinned. I think, too, that we can discard the even wilder food theory; to civilized people killing cats for food smacks of cannibalism. To frighten Sister Sarah-Ann? Hardly; Sarah is used to cats and loves them. To scratch Sister Sarah to death? That suggests poisoned claws. But in that case there would be as much danger to Euphemia as to Sarah-Ann; and why *six* cats? As guides? But Euphemia is not blind, and besides she never leaves her bed. Can you think of any others?"

"But those things are *ridiculous!*"

"Don't call my meanderings names. Ridiculous, perhaps, but you can't ignore even apparent nonsense in an elimination."

"Well, I've got one that isn't nonsense," said Miss Curleigh suddenly. "Pure hatred. Euphemia loathed cats. So, since she's cracked, I suppose, she's bought them just for the pleasure of exterminating them."

"All black tomcats with green eyes and identical dimensions?" Ellery shook his head. "Her mania could scarcely have been so exclusive. Besides, she loathed cats even before Sarah-Ann bought her distinctive tom from you. No, there's only one left that I can think of, Miss Curleigh." He sprang from the chair and began to pace the floor. "It's not only the sole remaining possibility, but it's confirmed by several things. . . . *Protection.*"

"Protection!" Miss Curleigh's devastating eyes widened. "Why, Mr. Queen. How could that be? People buy dogs for protection, not cats."

"I don't mean that kind of protection," said Ellery impatiently. "I'm referring to a compound of desire to remain alive and an incidental hatred for felines that makes them the ideal instrument toward that end. This is a truly horrifying business. From every angle. Euphemia Tarkle was afraid. Of what? Of being murdered for her money. That's borne out amply by the letter she wrote to Morton, her nephew; and it's bolstered by her reputed miserliness, her distrust of banks, and her dislike for her own sister. How would a cat be protection against intended murder?"

"Poison!" cried Miss Curleigh.

"Exactly. *As a food-taster.* There's a reversion to mediævalism for you! Are there confirming data? Plenty. Euphemia had taken to eating alone of late; that suggests some secret activity. Then she re-ordered cats five times within a short period. Why? Obviously, because each time her cat, purchased from you, had acted in his official capacity, tasted her food, and gone the way of all enslaved flesh. The cats were poisoned, poisoned by food intended for Euphemia. So she had to re-order. Final confirmation: the six feline skeletons in the incinerator."

"But she can't walk," protested Miss Curleigh. "So how could she dispose of the bodies?"

"I fancy Mrs. Potter innocently disposed of them for her. You'll recall that Mrs. Potter said she was often called here to take garbage to the incinerator for Euphemia when Sarah-Ann was out. The 'garbage,' wrapped up, I suppose, was a cat's dead body."

"But why all the black, green-eyed tomcats of the same size?"

"Self-evident. Why? Obviously, again, *to fool Sarah-Ann.* Because

Sarah-Ann had a black tom of a certain size with green eyes, Euphemia purchased from you identical animals. Her only reason for this could have been, then, to fool Sarah-Ann into believing that the black tom she saw about the apartment at any given time was her own, the original one. That suggests, of course, that Euphemia used Sarah-Ann's cat to foil the first attempt, and Sarah-Ann's cat was the first poison-victim. When he died, Euphemia bought another from you—without her sister's knowledge.

"How Euphemia suspected she was slated to be poisoned, of course, at the very time in which the poisoner got busy, we'll never know. It was probably the merest coincidence, something psychic— you never know about slightly mad old ladies."

"But if she was trying to fool Sarah-Ann about the cats," whispered Miss Curleigh, aghast, "then she suspected——"

"Precisely. She suspected her sister of trying to poison her."

Miss Curleigh bit her lip. "Would you mind giving me a cigaret?" Ellery complied. "It's the most terrible thing I've ever heard of. Two old women, sisters, practically alone in the world, one dependent on the other for attention, the other for subsistence, living at cross-purposes—the invalid helpless to defend herself against attacks. . . ." She shuddered. "What's *happened* to those poor creatures, Mr. Queen?"

"Well, let's see. Euphemia is missing. We know that there were at least six attempts to poison her, all unsuccessful. It's logical to assume that there was a seventh attempt, then, and that—since Euphemia is gone under mysterious circumstances—*the seventh attempt was successful.*"

"But how can you *know* she's dead?"

"Where is she?" asked Ellery dryly. "The only other possibility is that she fled. But she's helpless, can't walk, can't stir from bed without assistance. Who can assist her? Only Sarah-Ann, the very one she suspects of trying to poison her. The letter to her nephew shows that she wouldn't turn to Sarah-Ann. So flight is out, and, since she's missing, she must be dead. Now, follow. Euphemia knew she was the target of poisoning attacks via her food and took precautions against them; then how did the poisoner finally penetrate her defenses—the seventh cat? Well, we may assume that Euphemia made the seventh cat taste the food we found on the tray. We know that food was not poisoned, from Dr. Prouty's report. The cat, then, didn't die of poisoning from the food itself—confirmed by the fact that he was beaten to death. But if the cat didn't die of poisoned *food,* neither did Euphemia. Yet all the indications are that she must have died of poisoning. Then there's only one answer: she died of poisoning not in eating but *in the process of* eating."

"I don't understand," said Miss Curleigh intently.

"The cutlery!" cried Ellery. "I showed you earlier this afternoon that someone other than Euphemia had handled her knife, spoon, and fork. Doesn't this suggest that the poisoner had *poisoned the cutlery* on his seventh attempt? If, for example, the fork had been coated with a colorless odorless poison which dried, Euphemia would have been fooled. The cat, flung bits of food by hand—for no one feeds an animal with cutlery—would live; Euphemia, eating the food with the poisoned cutlery, would die. Psychologically, too, it rings true. It stood to reason that the poisoner, after six unsuccessful attempts one way, should in desperation try a seventh with a variation. The variation worked and Euphemia, my dear, is dead."

"But her body—— Where——"

Ellery's face changed as he whirled noiselessly toward the door. He stood in an attitude of tense attention for an instant and then, without a word, laid violent hands upon the petrified person of Miss Curleigh and thrust her rudely into one of the bedroom closets, shutting the door behind her. Miss Curleigh, half-smothered by a sea of musty-smelling feminine garments, held her breath. She had heard that faint scratching of metal upon metal at the front door. It must be—if Mr. Queen acted so quickly—the poisoner. Why had he come back? she thought wildly. The key he was using—easy—a duplicate. Earlier when they had surprised him and he had barricaded the door, he must have entered the apartment by the roof and fire-escape window because he couldn't use the key . . . someone may have been standing in the hall. . . .

Her thoughts snapped off. A hoarse voice—the sounds of a struggle —a crash . . . they were fighting!

Miss Curleigh saw red. She flung open the door of the closet and plunged out. Ellery was on the floor in a tangle of threshing arms and legs. A hand came up with a knife. . . . Miss Curleigh sprang and kicked in an instantaneous reflex action. Something snapped sharply, and she fell back, sickened, as the knife dropped from a broken hand.

"The door!" panted Ellery, pressing his knee viciously downward. Through a roaring in her ears Miss Curleigh heard pounding on the door, and tottered toward it. The last thing she remembered before she fainted was a weird boiling of blue-clad bodies as police poured past her to fall upon the struggling figures.

"It's all right now," said a faraway voice, and Miss Curleigh opened her eyes to find Mr. Queen, cool and immaculate, stooping over her. She moved her head dazedly. The fireplace, the crossed swords on the wall. . . . "Don't be alarmed," grinned Ellery; "this isn't an abduction. You have achieved Valhalla. It's all over, and you're on the divan in my apartment."

"Oh," said Miss Curleigh, and she swung her feet unsteadily to the floor. "I—I must look a sight. What happened?"

"We caught the bad one. Now you rest, young lady, while I rustle a dish of tea——"

"Nonsense!" said Miss Curleigh with asperity. "Come on, now."

"Just what do you want to know?"

"Did you *know* that creature was coming back?"

Ellery shrugged. "It was a likely possibility. Euphemia had been poisoned, patently for her hidden money. She must have been murdered at the very latest yesterday—you recall yesterday's milk-bottle —perhaps the night before last. Had the murderer found the money after killing her? Then who was the prowler whom we surprised this afternoon and who made his escape out the window after barricading the door? It must have been the murderer. But if he came back *after* the crime, then he had not found the money when he committed the crime. Perhaps he had so much to do immediately after the commission of the crime that he had no time to search. At any rate, on his return we surprised him—probably just after he had made a mess of the bed. It was quite possible that he had still not found the money. If he had not, I knew he would come back—after all, he had committed the crime for it. So I took the chance that he would return when he thought the coast was clear, and he did. I 'phoned for police assistance while you were out seeing Dr. Prouty."

"Did you *know* who it was?"

"Oh, yes. It was demonstrable. The first qualification of the poisoner was availability; that is, in order to make those repeated poisoning attempts, the poisoner had to be near Euphemia or near her food at least since the attempts began, which was presumably five weeks ago. The obvious suspect was her sister. Sarah-Ann had motive—hatred and possibly cupidity; and certainly opportunity, since she prepared the food herself. But Sarah-Ann I eliminated on the soundest basis in the world.

"For who had brutally beaten to death the seventh black tomcat? Palpably, either the victim or the murderer in a general sense. But it couldn't have been Euphemia, since the cat was killed in the bathroom and Euphemia lay paralyzed in the bedroom, unable to walk. Then it must have been the murderer who killed the cat. But if

Sarah-Ann were the murderer, would she have clubbed to death a cat—she, who loved cats? Inconceivable. Therefore Sarah-Ann was not the murderer."

"Then——"

"I know. What happened to Sarah-Ann?" Ellery grimaced. "Sarah-Ann, I'm afraid, went the way of the cat and her sister. It must have been the poisoner's plan to kill Euphemia and have it appear that Sarah-Ann had killed her—the obvious suspect. Sarah-Ann, then, should be on the scene. But she isn't. Well, her disappearance tends to show—I think the confession will bear me out—that she was accidentally a witness to the murder and was killed by the poisoner on the spot to eliminate a witness to the crime. He wouldn't have killed her under any other circumstances."

"Did you find the money?"

"Yes. Lying quite obviously between the pages of a Bible Euphemia kept within reach." He shrugged. "The Poe touch."

"And the bodies . . . ?"

"Surely," smiled Ellery, "the incinerator? It would have been the logical means of disposal. What bones there were . . . Well, no need to get too literal."

"But that means . . . Who was that fiend on the floor? I never saw him before. It couldn't have been Mr. Morton's father——?"

"No, no, Miss Curleigh," said Ellery. "No one but Sarah-Ann and Euphemia lived in the apartment, yet the poisoner had access to the invalid's food for over a month, apparently unsuspected. Who could have had such access? Only one person: the man who'd been decorating the apartment in late afternoons and evenings—around dinner time—for weeks; the man who worked in a chemical plant and so, better than anyone, had knowledge of and access to poisonous substances; the man who tended the incinerator and therefore could dispose of his human victims—and their ashes—without danger to himself. In a word," Ellery said, "the superintendent of the building, Harry Potter."

LESLIE CHARTERIS

The Wicked Cousin

When Simon Templar arrived in Los Angeles there was a leaden ceiling of cloud over the sky and a cool wind blowing. A few drops of unenthusiastic rain moistened the pavements and speckled the shoulders of his coat. The porter who was loading his bags into a taxi assured him that it was most unusual weather, and he felt instantly at home.

Later on, comfortably stretched out on a divan in the sitting room of his suite at the hotel in Hollywood upon which he had chosen to confer the somewhat debatable honor of his tenancy, with a highball at his elbow and a freshly lighted cigarette smoldering contentedly between his lips, he turned the pages of the address book on his knee and considered what his next steps should be to improve that first feeling of a welcome return.

He was not there on business. To be quite accurate, none of the stages of the last few months of carefree wandering which had just completed their vague object of leading him across America from coast to coast had been undertaken with a view to business. If business had materialized on more than one occasion, it was because there was something about Simon Templar which attracted adventure by the same kind of mysterious but inescapable cosmic law which compels a magnet to attract steel or a politician to attract attention; and if much of that business was not looked upon favorably by the Law—or would not have been favorably looked upon if the Law had known all that there was to know about it—this was because Simon Templar's business had an unfortunate habit of falling into categories which gave many people good reason to wonder what right he had to the nickname of the Saint by which he was far more widely known than he was by his baptismal titles. Is it true that these buccaneering raids of his which had earned him the subtitle of "The Robin Hood of Modern Crime" were invariably undertaken against the property, and occasionally the persons, of citizens who by no stretch of the imagination could have been called desirable; but the Law took no official cognizance of such small details. The Law, in the Saint's opinion, was a stodgy and elephantine institution which was chiefly justified in its existence by the pleasantly musical explosive noises which it made when he broke it.

Certainly he was not thinking of business. In Hollywood he had many genuine friends, few of whom gave much consideration to the sensational legends that were associated with his name in less unsophisticated circles, and his only immediate problem was to which one of them he should first break the dazzling news of his arrival. He paused at one name after another, recalling its personality: movie executives, directors, writers, actors and actresses both great and small and a certain number of ordinary human beings. He wanted— what did he want? A touch of excitement, preferably feminine, beauty, a little of the glamor and gay unreality with which the very name of Hollywood is inseparably linked in imagination if not in fact. He wanted some of these things very much. His last stop had been made in the state of Utah.

There was a girl called Jacqueline Laine whom Simon remembered suddenly, as one does sometimes remember people, with a sense of startling familiarity and a kind of guilty amazement that he should have allowed her to slip out of his mind for so long. Once she was remembered, he had no more hesitation. No one else could have been so obviously the one person in the world whom he had to call up at that moment.

He picked up the telephone.

"Hello, Jacqueline," he said when she answered. "Do you know who this is?"

"I know," she said. "It's Franklin D. Roosevelt."

"You have a marvelous memory. Do you still eat?"

"Whenever I'm thirsty. Do you?"

"I nibble a crumb now and then. Come out with me tonight and see if we can still take it."

"Simon, I'd love to; but I'm in the most frantic muddle——"

"So is the rest of the world, darling. But it's two years since I've seen you, and that's about seven hundred and thirty days too long. Don't you realize that I've come halfway around the world, surviving all manner of perils and slaying large numbers of ferocious dragons, just to get here in time to take you out to dinner tonight?"

"I know, but—— Oh well. It would be thrilling to see you. Come around about seven and I'll try to get a bit straightened out before then."

"I'll be there," said the Saint.

He spent some of the intervening time in making himself the owner of a car, and shortly after half-past six he turned it westward into the stream of studio traffic homing toward Beverly Hills. Somewhere along Sunset Boulevard he turned off to the right and began to climb one of the winding roads that led up into the hills. The street lights were just beginning to trace their twinkling geometrical network over the vast panorama of cities spread out beneath him, as the car soared smoothly higher into the luminous blue-grey twilight.

He found his way with the certainty of vivid remembrance; and he was fully ten minutes early when he pulled the car into a bay by the roadside before the gate of Jacqueline Laine's house. He climbed out and started toward the gate, lighting a cigarette as he went, and as he approached it he perceived that somebody else was approaching the same gate from the opposite side. Changing his course a little to the left so that the departing guest would have room to pass him, the Saint observed that he was a small and elderly gent arrayed in clothes so shapeless and ill fitting that they gave his figure a comical air of having been loosely and inaccurately strung together from a selection of stuffed bags of cloth. He wore a discolored Panama hat of weird and wonderful architecture, and carried an incongruous green umbrella furled, but still flapping in a bedraggled and forlorn sort of way, under his left arm; his face was rubicund and bulbous like his body, looking as if it had been carelessly slapped together out of a few odd lumps of pink plasticine.

As Simon moved to the left, the elderly gent duplicated the manœuvre. Simon turned his feet and swerved politely to the right. The elderly gent did exactly the same, as if he were Simon's own reflection in a distorting mirror. Simon stopped altogether and decided to economize energy by letting the elderly gent make the next move in the ballet on his own.

Whereupon he discovered that the game of undignified dodging in which he had just prepared to surrender his part was caused by some dimly discernible ambition of the elderly gent's to hold converse with him. Standing in front of him and blinking shortsightedly upward from his lower altitude to the Saint's six foot two, with his mouth hanging vacantly open like an inverted "U" and three long yellow teeth hanging down like stalactites from the top, the elderly gent tapped him on the chest and said, very earnestly and distinctly: "Hig fwmgn glugl phnihklu hgrm skhlglgl?"

"I beg your pardon?" said the Saint vaguely.

"Hig fwmgn," repeated the elderly gent, "glugl phnihklu hgrm skhlglgl?"

Simon considered the point.

"If you ask me," he replied at length, "I should say sixteen."

The elderly gent's knobbly face seemed to take on a brighter shade of pink. He clutched the lapels of the Saint's coat, shaking him slightly in a positive passion of anguish.

"Flogh ghoglu sk," he pleaded, "klngnt hu ughlgstghnd?"

Simon shook his head.

"No," he said judiciously, "you're thinking of weevils."

The little man bounced about like a rubber doll. His eyes squinted with a kind of frantic despair.

"Ogmighogho," he almost screamed, "klngt hu ughglstghnd? Ik ghln ngmnpp sktlghko! Klugt hu hgr? *Ik wgnt hlg phnihklu hgrm skhlglgl!*"

The Saint sighed. He was by nature a kindly man to those whom the gods had afflicted, but time was passing and he was thinking of Jacqueline Laine.

"I'm afraid not, dear old bird," he murmured regretfully. "There used to be one, but it died. Sorry, I'm sure."

He patted the elderly gent apologetically upon the shoulder, steered his way around him, and passed on out of earshot of the frenzied sputtering noises that continued to honk despairingly through the dusk behind him. Two minutes later he was with Jacqueline.

Jacqueline Laine was twenty-three; she was tall and slender; she had grey eyes that twinkled and a demoralizing mouth. Both of these temptations were in play as she came towards him; but he was still slightly shaken by his recent encounter.

"Have you got any more village idiots hidden around?" he asked warily, as he took her hands; and she was puzzled.

"We used to have several, but they've all got into Congress. Did you want one to take home?"

"My God, no," said the Saint fervently. "The one I met at the gate was bad enough. Is he your latest boy friend?"

Her brow cleared.

"Oh, you mean the old boy with the cleft palate? Isn't he marvelous? I think he's got a screw loose or something. He's been hanging around all day—he keeps ringing the bell and bleating at me. I'd just sent him away for the third time. Did he try to talk to you?"

"He did sort of wag his adenoids at me," Simon admitted, "but I don't think we actually got on to common ground. I felt quite jealous of him for a bit, until I realized that he couldn't possibly kiss you nearly as well as I can, with that set of teeth."

He proceeded to demonstrate this.

"I'm still in a hopeless muddle," she said presently. "But I'll be ready in five minutes. You can be fixing a cocktail while I finish myself off."

In the living room there was an open trunk in one corner and a half-filled packing case in the middle of the floor. There were scattered heaps of paper around it, and a few partially wrapped and unidentifiable objects on the table. The room had that curiously naked and inhospitable look which a room has when it has been stripped of all those intimately personal odds and ends of junk which make it a home, and only the bare furniture is left.

The Saint raised his eyebrows.

"Hullo," he said. "Are you moving?"

"Sort of." She shrugged. "Moving out, anyway."

"Where to?"

"I don't know."

He realized then that there should have been someone else there, in that room.

"Isn't your grandmother here any more?"

"She died four weeks ago."

"I'm sorry."

"She was a good soul. But she was terribly old. Do you know she was just ninety-seven?" She held his hand for a moment. "I'll tell you all about it when I come down. Do you remember where to find the bottles?"

"Templars and elephants never forget."

He blended bourbon, applejack, vermouth and bitters, skilfully and with the zeal of an artist, while he waited for her, remembering the old lady whom he had seen so often in that room. Also, he remembered the affectionate service that Jacqueline had always lavished on her, cheerfully limiting her own enjoyment of life to meet the demands of an unconscious tyrant who would allow no one else to look after her, and wondered if there was any realistic reason to regret the ending of such a long life. She had, he knew, looked after Jacqueline herself in her time, and had brought her up as her own child since she was left an orphan at the age of three; but life must always belong to the young. . . . He thought that for Jacqueline it must be a supreme escape, but he knew that she would never say so.

She came down punctually in the five minutes which she had promised. She had changed her dress and put a comb through her hair, and with that seemed to have achieved more than any other woman could have shown for an hour's fiddling in front of a mirror.

"You should have been in pictures," said the Saint, and he meant it.

"Maybe I shall," she said. "I'll have to do something to earn a living now."

"Is it as bad as that?"

She nodded.

"But I can't complain. I never had to work for anything before. Why shouldn't I start? Other people have to."

"Is that why you're moving out?"

"The house isn't mine."

"But didn't the old girl leave you anything?"

"She left me some letters."

The Saint almost spilt his drink. He sat down heavily on the edge of the table.

"She left you some *letters*? After you'd practically been a slave to her ever since you came out of finishing school? What did she do with the rest of her property—leave it to a home for stray cats?"

"No, she left it to Harry."

"Who?"

"Her grandson."

"I didn't know you had any brothers."

"I haven't. Harry Westler is my cousin. He's—well, as a matter of fact he's a sort of black sheep. He's a gambler, and he was in prison once for forging a check. Nobody else in the family would have anything to do with him, and if you believe what they used to say about him they were probably quite right; but Granny always had a soft spot for him. She never believed he could do anything wrong—he was just a mischievous boy to her. Well, you know how old she was . . ."

"And she left everything to him?"

"Practically everything. I'll show you."

She went to a drawer of the writing table and brought him a type-written sheet. He saw that it was a copy of a will, and turned to the details of the bequests.

To my dear granddaughter Jacqueline Laine, who has taken care of me so thoughtfully and unselfishly for four years, One Hundred Dollars and my letters from Sidney Farlance, knowing that she will find them of more value than anything else I could leave her.

To my cook, Eliza Jefferson, and my chauffeur, Albert Gordon, One Hundred Dollars each, for their loyal service.

The remainder of my estate, after these deductions, including my house and other personal belongings, to my dear grandson Harry Westler, hoping it will help him to make the success of life of which I have always believed him capable.

Simon folded the sheet and dropped it on the table from his finger tips as if it were infected.

"Suffering Judas," he said helplessly. "After all you did for her—to pension you off on the same scale as the cook and the chauffeur! And what about Harry—doesn't he propose to do anything about it?"

"Why should he? The will's perfectly clear."

"Why shouldn't he? Just because the old crow went off her rocker in the last days of senile decay is no reason why he shouldn't do something to put it right. There must have been enough for both of you."

"Not so much. They found that Granny had been living on her capital for years. There was only about twenty thousand dollars left —and the house."

"What of it? He could spare half."

Jacqueline smiled—a rather tired little smile.

"You haven't met Harry. He's—difficult . . . He's been here, of course. The agents already have his instructions to sell the house and the furniture. He gave me a week to get out, and the week is up the day after tomorrow. . . . I couldn't possibly ask him for anything."

Simon lighted a cigarette as if it tasted of bad eggs and scowled malevolently about the room.

"The skunk! And so you get chucked out into the wide world with nothing but a hundred dollars."

"And the letters," she added ruefully.

"What the hell are these letters?"

"They're love letters," she said; and the Saint looked as if he would explode.

"*Love letters?*" he repeated in an awful voice.

"Yes. Granny had a great romance when she was a girl. Her parents wouldn't let her get any further with it because the boy hadn't any money and his family wasn't good enough. He went abroad with one of these heroic young ideas of making a fortune in South America and coming back in a gold-plated carriage to claim her. He died of fever somewhere in Brazil very soon after, but he wrote her three letters—two from British Guiana and one from Colombia. Oh, I know them by heart—I used to have to read them aloud to Granny almost every night, after her eyes got too bad for her to be able to read them herself. They're just the ordinary simple sort of thing that you'd expect in the circumstances, but to Granny they were the most precious thing she had. I suppose she had some funny old idea in her head that they'd be just as precious to me."

"She must have been screwy," said the Saint.

Jacqueline came up and put a hand over his mouth.

"She was very good to me when I was a kid," she said.

"I know, but——" Simon flung up his arms hopelessly. And then, almost reluctantly, he began to laugh. "But it does mean that I've just come back in time. And we'll have so much fun tonight that you won't even think about it for a minute."

Probably he made good his boast, for Simon Templar brought to the solemn business of enjoying himself the same gay zest and inspired impetuosity which he brought to his battles with the technicalities of the law. But if he made her forget, he himself remembered; and when he followed her into the living room of the house again much later, for a goodnight drink, the desolate scene of interrupted packing, and the copy of the will still lying on the table where he had put it down, brought the thoughts with which he had been subconsciously playing throughout the evening back into the forefront of his mind.

"Are you going to let Harry get away with it?" he asked her, with a sudden characteristic directness.

The girl shrugged.

"What else can I do?"

"I have an idea," said the Saint; and his blue eyes danced with an unholy delight which she had never seen in them before.

Mr. Westler was not a man whose contacts with the Law had conspired to make him particularly happy about any of its workings; and therefore when he saw that the card which was brought to him

in his hotel bore in its bottom left-hand corner the name of a firm
with the words "Attorneys at Law" underneath it, he suffered an
immediate hollow twinge in the base of his stomach for which he
could scarcely be blamed. A moment's reflection, however, reminded
him that another card with a similar inscription had recently been
the forerunner of an extremely welcome windfall, and with this reassuring thought he told the bellboy to bring the visitor into his
presence.

Mr. Tombs, of Tombs, Tombs, and Tombs, as the card introduced
him, was a tall lean man with neatly brushed white hair, bushy white
eyebrows, a pair of gold-rimmed and drooping pince-nez on the end
of a broad black ribbon and an engagingly avuncular manner which
rapidly completed the task of restoring Harry Westler's momentarily
shaken confidence. He came to the point with professional efficiency
combined with professional pomposity,

"I have come to see you in connection with the estate of the—ah—
late Mrs. Laine. I understand that you are her heir."

"That's right," said Mr. Westler.

He was a dark, flashily dressed man with small greedy eyes and a
face rather reminiscent of that of a sick horse.

"Splendid." The lawyer placed his finger tips on his knees and
leaned forward, peering benevolently over the rims of his glasses.
"Now I for my part am representing the Sesame Mining Develop-
ment Corporation."

He said this more or less as if he were announcing himself as the
personal herald of Jehovah, but Mr. Westler's mind ran in practical
channels.

"Did my grandmother have shares in the company?" he asked
quickly.

"Ah—ah—no. That is—ah—no. Not exactly. But I understand
that she was in possession of a letter or document which my clients
regard as extremely valuable."

"A letter?"

"Exactly. But perhaps I had better give you an outline of the situation. Your grandmother was in her youth greatly—ah—enamoured
of a certain Sidney Farlance. Perhaps at some time or other you have
heard her speak of him."

"Yes."

"For various reasons her parents refused to give their consent to
the alliance; but the young people for their part refused to take no
for an answer, and Farlance went abroad with the intention of making his fortune in foreign parts and returning in due course to claim

his bride. In this ambition he was unhappily frustrated by his—ah—premature decease in Brazil. But it appears that during his travels in British Guiana he did become the owner of a mining concession in a certain very inaccessible area of territory. British Guiana, as you are doubtless aware," continued Mr. Tombs in his dry pedagogic voice, "is traditionally reputed to be the source of the legend of El Dorado, the Gilded King, who was said to cover himself with pure gold and to wash it from him in the waters of a sacred lake called Manoa———"

"Never mind all that baloney," said Harry Westler, who was not interested in history or mythology. "Tell me about this concession."

Mr. Tombs pressed his lips with a pained expression but he went on.

"At the time it did not appear that gold could be profitably obtained from this district and the claim was abandoned and forgotten. Modern engineering methods, however, have recently revealed deposits of almost fabulous value in the district, and my clients have obtained a concession to work it over a very large area of ground. Subsequent investigations into their title, meanwhile, have brought out the existence of this small—ah—prior concession granted to Sidney Farlance, which is situated almost in the center of my client's territory and in a position which—ah—exploratory drillings have shown to be one of the richest areas in the district."

Mr. Westler digested the information, and in place of the first sinking vacuum which had afflicted his stomach when he saw the word Law on his visitor's card, a sudden and ecstatic awe localized itself in the same place and began to cramp his lungs as if he had accidentally swallowed a rubber balloon with his breakfast and it was being rapidly inflated by some supernatural agency.

"You mean my grandmother owned this concession?"

"That is what—ah—my clients are endeavouring to discover. Farlance himself, of course, left no heirs, and we have been unable to trace any surviving members of his family. In the course of our inquiries, however, we did learn of his—ah—romantic interest in your grandmother, and we have every reason to believe that in the circumstances he would naturally have made her the beneficiary of any such asset, however problematical its value may have seemed at the time."

"And you want to buy it out—is that it?"

"Ah—yes. That is—ah—provided that our deductions are correct and the title can be established. I may say that my clients would be prepared to pay very liberally———"

"They'd have to," said Mr. Westler briskly. "How much are they good for?"

The lawyer raised his hands deprecatingly.

"You need have no alarm, my dear Mr. Westler. The actual figure would, of course, be a matter for negotiation but it would doubtless run into a number of millions. But first of all, you understand, we must trace the actual concession papers which will be sufficient to establish your right to negotiate. Now it seems that in view of the relationship between Farlance and your grandmother, she would probably have treasured his letters as women do even though she later married someone else, particularly if there was a document of that sort among them. People don't usually throw things like that away. In that case you will doubtless have inherited these letters along with her other personal property. Possibly you have not yet had an occasion to peruse them, but if you would do so as soon as possible——"

One of Harry Westler's few Napoleonic qualities was a remarkable capacity for quick and constructive thinking.

"Certainly I have the letters," he said, "but I haven't gone through them yet. My lawyer has them at present and he's in San Francisco today. He'll be back tomorrow morning, and I'll get hold of them at once. Come and see me again tomorrow afternoon and I expect I'll have some news for you."

"Tomorrow afternoon, Mr. Westler? Certainly. I think that will be convenient. Ah—certainly." The lawyer stood up, took off his pince-nez, polished them and revolved them like a windmill on the end of their ribbon. "This has indeed been a most happy meeting, my dear sir. And may I say that I hope that tomorrow afternoon it will be even happier?"

"You can go on saying that right up till the time we start talking prices," said Harry.

The door had scarcely closed behind Mr. Tombs when he was on the telephone to his cousin. He suppressed a sigh of relief when he heard her voice and announced as casually as he could his intention of coming around to see her.

"I think we ought to have another talk—I was terribly upset by the shock of Granny's death when I saw you the other day and I'm afraid I wasn't quite myself, but I'll make all the apologies you like when I get there," he said in an unfamiliarly gentle voice which cost him a great effort to achieve, and was grabbing his hat before the telephone was properly back on its bracket.

He made a call at the bank on his way, and sat in the taxi which carried him up into the hills as if its cushions had been upholstered with hot spikes. The exact words of that portion of the will which referred to the letters drummed through his memory with a staggering significance. *"My letters from Sidney Farlance, knowing that she will find them of more value than anything else I could leave her."* The visit of Mr. Tombs had made him understand them perfectly. His grandmother had known what was in them; but did Jacqueline know? His heart almost stopped beating with anxiety.

As he leaped out of the taxi and dashed toward the house he cannoned into a small and weirdly apparelled elderly gent who was apparently emerging from the gate at the same time. Mr. Westler checked himself involuntarily, and the elderly gent, sent flying by the impact, bounced off a gatepost and tottered back at him. He clutched Harry by the sleeve and peered up at him pathetically.

"Glhwf hngwglgl," he said pleadingly, "kngnduk glu bwtlhjp mnyihgli?"

"Oh, go climb a tree," snarled Mr. Westler impatiently.

He pushed the little man roughly aside and went on.

Jacqueline opened the door to him, and Mr. Westler steeled himself to kiss her on the forehead with cousinly affection.

"I was an awful swine the other day, Jackie. I don't know what could have been the matter with me. I've always been terribly selfish," he said with an effort, "and at the time I didn't really see how badly Granny had treated you. She didn't leave you anything except those letters, did she?"

"She left me a hundred dollars," said Jacqueline calmly.

"A hundred dollars!" said Harry indignantly. "After you'd given up everything else to take care of her. And she left me more than twenty thousand dollars and the house and everything else in it. It's—disgusting! But I don't have to take advantage of it, do I? I've been thinking a lot about it lately——"

Jacqueline lighted a cigarette and regarded him stonily.

"Thanks," she said briefly. "But I haven't asked you for any charity."

"It isn't charity," protested Mr. Westler virtuously. "It's just a matter of doing the decent thing. The lawyers have done their share —handed everything over to me and seen that the will was carried out. Now we can start again. We could pool everything again and divide it the way we think it ought to be divided."

"As far as I'm concerned, that's been done already."

"But I'm not happy about it. I've got all the money, and you know what I'm like. I'll probably gamble it all away in a few months."

"That's your affair."

"Oh, don't be like that, Jackie. I've apologized, haven't I? Besides, what Granny left you is worth a lot more than money. I mean those letters of hers. I'd willingly give up five thousand dollars of my share if I could have had those. They're the one thing of the old lady's which really means a great deal to me."

"You're becoming very sentimental all of a sudden, aren't you?" asked the girl curiously.

"Maybe I am. I suppose you can't really believe that a rotter like me could feel that way about anything, but Granny was the only person in the world who ever really believed any good of me and liked me in spite of everything. If I gave you five thousand dollars for those letters, it wouldn't be charity—I'd be paying less than I think they're worth. Let's put it that way if you'd rather, Jackie. An ordinary business deal. If I had them," said Mr. Westler, with something like a sob in his voice, "they'd always be a reminder to me of the old lady and how good she was. They might help me to go straight . . ."

His emotion was so touching that even Jacqueline's cynical incredulity lost some of its assurance. Harry Westler was playing his part with every technical trick that he knew, and he had a mastery of these emotional devices which victims far more hard-boiled than Jacqueline had experienced to their cost.

"I'm thoroughly ashamed of myself and I want to put things right in any way I can. Don't make me feel any worse than I do already. Look here, I'll give you ten thousand dollars for the letters and I won't regret a penny of it. You won't regret it either, will you, if they help me to keep out of trouble in future?"

Jacqueline smiled in spite of herself. It was not in her nature to bear malice, and it was very hard for her to resist an appeal that was made in those terms. Also, with the practical side of her mind, she was honest enough to realize that her grandmother's letters had no sentimental value for her whatever, and that ten thousand dollars was a sum of money which she could not afford to refuse unless her pride was compelled to forbid it; her night out with the Saint had helped her to forget her problems for the moment, but she had awakened that morning with a very sober realization of the position in which she was going to find herself within the next forty-eight hours.

"If you put it like that I can't very well refuse, can I?" she said, and Harry jumped up and clasped her fervently by the hand.

"You'll really do it, Jackie? You don't know how much I appreciate it."

She disengaged herself quietly.

"It doesn't do me any harm," she told him truthfully. "Would you like to have the letters now?"

"If they're anywhere handy. I brought some money along with me, so we can fix it all up right away."

She went upstairs and fetched the letters from the dressing table in her grandmother's room. Mr. Westler took them and tore off the faded ribbon with which they were tied together with slightly trembling fingers which she attributed to an unexpected depth of emotion. One by one he took them out of their envelopes and read rapidly through them. The last sheet of the third letter was a different kind of paper from the rest. The paper was brown and discolored and cracked in the folds, and the ink had the rust-brown hue of great age; but he saw the heavy official seal in one corner and strained his eyes to decipher the stiff old-fashioned script.

We, Philip Edmond Wodehouse, Commander of the Most Noble Order of the Bath, Governor in the name of His Britannic Majesty of the Colony of British Guiana, ·by virtue of the powers conferred upon us by His Majesty's Privy Council, do hereby proclaim and declare to all whom it may concern that we have this day granted to Sidney Farlance, a subject of His Majesty the King, and to his heirs and assigns being determined by the possession of this authority, the sole right to prospect and mine for minerals of any kind whatsoever in the territory indicated and described in the sketch map at the foot of this authority, for the term of nine hundred and ninety-nine years from the date of these presents.

Given under our hand and seal this third day of January Eighteen Hundred and Fifty-Six.

At the bottom of the sheet below the map and description was scrawled in a different hand: *"This is all for you. S.F."*

Harry Westler stuffed the letters into his pocket and took out his wallet. His heart was beating in a delirious rhythm of ecstasy and sending the blood roaring through his ears like the crashing crescendo of a symphony. The Gates of Paradise seemed to have opened up and deluged him with all their reservoirs of bliss. The whole world was his sweetheart. If the elderly gent whose strange nasal garglings he had dismissed so discourteously a short time ago had cannoned into him again at that moment, it is almost certain that

Mr. Westler would not have told him to go and climb a tree. He would probably have kissed him on both cheeks and given him a nickel.

For the first time in his life, Harry Westler counted out ten thousand-dollar bills as cheerfully as he would have counted them in.

"There you are, Jackie. And I'm not kidding—it takes a load off my mind. If you think of anything else I can do for you, just let me know."

"I think you've done more than anyone could have asked," she said generously. "Won't you stay and have a drink?"

Mr. Westler declined the offer firmly. He had no moral prejudice against drinking, and in fact he wanted a drink very badly, but more particularly he wanted to have it in a place where he would not have to place any more restraint on the shouting rhapsodies that were seething through his system like bubbles through champagne.

Some two hours later, when Simon Templar drifted into the house, he found Jacqueline still looking slightly dazed. She flung her arms around his neck and kissed him.

"Simon!" she gasped. "You must be a mascot or something. You'll never guess what's happened."

"I'll tell you exactly what's happened," said the Saint calmly. "Cousin Harry has been here, told you that he'd rather have dear old Granny's love letters than all the money in the world and paid you a hell of a good price for them. At least I hope he paid you a hell of a good price."

Jacqueline gaped at him weakly.

"He paid me ten thousand dollars. But how on earth did you know? Why did he do it?"

"He did it because a lawyer called on him this morning and told him that Sidney Farlance had collared an absolutely priceless mining concession when he was in British Guiana, and that there was probably something about it in the letters which would be worth millions to whoever had them to prove his claim."

She looked at him aghast.

"A mining concession? I don't remember anything about it——"

"You wouldn't," said the Saint kindly. "It wasn't there until I slipped it in when I got you to show me the letters at breakfast time this morning. I sat up for the other half of the night faking the best imitation I could of what I thought a concession ought to look like, and apparently it was good enough for Harry. Of course I was the lawyer who told him all about it, and I think I fed him the oil pretty smoothly, so perhaps there was some excuse for him. I take it that he was quite excited about it—I see he didn't even bother to take the envelopes."

Jacqueline opened her mouth again, but what she was going to say with it remained a permanently unsolved question, for at that moment the unnecessarily vigorous ringing of a bell stopped her short. The Saint cocked his ears speculatively at the sound and a rather pleased and seraphic smile worked itself into his face.

"I expect this is Harry coming back," he said. "He wasn't supposed to see me again until tomorrow but I suppose he couldn't wait. He's probably tried to ring me up at the address I had printed on my card and discovered that there ain't no such lawyers as I was supposed to represent. It will be rather interesting to hear what he has to say."

For once, however, Simon's guess was wrong. Instead of the indignant equine features of Harry Westler, he confronted the pink imploring features of the small and shapeless elderly gent with whom he had danced prettily around the gateposts the day before. The little man's face lighted up and he bounced over the doorstep and seized the Saint joyfully by both lapels of his coat.

"Mnyng hlfwgl!" he crowed triumphantly. "Ahkgmp glglgl hndiuphwmp!"

Simon recoiled slightly.

"Yes. I know," he said soothingly. "But it's five o'clock on Fridays. Two dollars every other yard."

"Ogh hmbals!" said the little man.

He let go of the Saint's coat, ducked under his arms and scuttled on into the living room.

"Oi!" said the Saint feebly.

"May I explain, sir?"

Another voice spoke from the doorway, and Simon perceived that the little man had not come alone. Someone else had taken his place on the threshold—a thin and mournful-looking individual whom the Saint somewhat pardonably took to be the little man's keeper.

"Are you looking after that?" he inquired resignedly. "And why don't you keep it on a lead?"

The mournful-looking individual shook his head.

"That is Mr. Horatio Ive, sir—he is a very rich man, but he suffers from an unfortunate impediment in his speech. Very few people can understand him. I go about with him as his interpreter, but I have been in bed for the last three days with a chill——"

A shrill war whoop from the other room interrupted the explanation.

"We'd better go and see how he's getting on," said the Saint.

"Mr. Ive is very impulsive, sir," went on the sad-looking interpreter. "He was most anxious to see somebody here, and even though I was unable to accompany him he has called here several times alone. I understand that he found it impossible to make himself understood. He practically dragged me out of bed to come with him now."

"What's he so excited about?" asked the Saint, as they walked towards the living room.

"He's interested in some letters, sir, belonging to the late Mrs. Laine. She happened to show them to him when they met once several years ago, and he wanted to buy them. She refused to sell them for sentimental reasons, but as soon as he read of her death he decided to approach her heirs."

"Are you talking about her love letters from a bird called Sidney Farlance?" Simon asked hollowly.

"Yes sir. The gentleman who worked in British Guiana. Mr. Ive is prepared to pay something like fifty thousand dollars—— Is anything the matter, sir?"

Simon Templar swallowed.

"Oh, nothing," he said faintly. "Nothing at all."

They entered the living room to interrupt a scene of considerable excitement. Backing towards the wall, with a blank expression of alarm widening her eyes, Jacqueline Laine was staring dumbly at the small elderly gent, who was capering about in front of her like a frenzied redskin, spluttering yard after yard of his incomprehensible adenoidal honks interspersed with wild piercing squeaks apparently expressive of intolerable joy. In each hand he held an envelope aloft like a banner.

As his interpreter came in, he turned and rushed towards him, loosing off a fresh stream of noises like those of a hysterical duck.

"Mr. Ive is saying, sir," explained the interpreter, raising his voice harmoniously above the din, "that each of those envelopes bears a perfect example of the British Guiana one-cent magenta stamp of 1856, of which only one specimen was previously believed to exist. Mr. Ive is an ardent philatelist, sir, and these envelopes——"

Simon Templar blinked hazily at the small crudely printed stamp in the corner of the envelope which the little man was waving under his nose.

"You mean," he said cautiously, "that Mr. Ive is really only interested in the envelopes?"

"Yes, sir."

"Not the letters themselves?"

"Not the letters."

"And he's been flapping around the house all this time trying to tell somebody about it?"

"Yes, sir."

Simon Templar drew a deep breath. The foundations of the world were spinning giddily around his ears but his natural resilience was unconquerable. He took out a handkerchief and mopped his brow.

"In that case," he said contentedly, "I'm sure we can do business. What do you say, Jacqueline?"

Jacqueline clutched his arm and nodded breathlessly.

"Hlgagtsk sweghlemlgl," beamed Mr. Ive.

JOHN DICKSON CARR

The Footprint in the Sky

She awoke out of confused dreams; awoke with a start, and lay staring at the white ceiling of her bedroom for a minute or two before she could convince herself it was anything but a dream.

But it was a dream.

The cold, brittle sunlight poured in at the open window. The cold, brittle air, blowing the curtains, stirred a light coating of snow on the window sill. It stirred briskly in that little, bare room; it should have set the blood racing, and Dorothy Brant breathed it deeply.

Everything was all right. She was at the country cottage, where she and Dad and Harry had come down for the skating on the frozen lake; possibly even a little mild skiing, if the snow came on according to the weather forecast. And the snow had fallen. She should have been glad of that, though for some reason the sight of it on the window sill struck her with a kind of terror.

Shivering in the warm bed, the clothes pulled up about her chin, she looked at the little clock on her bedside. Twenty minutes past nine. She had overslept; Dad and Harry would be wanting their breakfast. Again she told herself that everything was all right: though now, fully awake, she knew it was not. The unpleasantness of yesterday returned. Mrs. Topham next door—that old shrew and thief as well . . .

It was the only thing which could have marred this week end. They had looked forward to the skating: the crisp blades thudding and ringing on the ice, the flight, the long scratching drag as you turned, the elm trees black against a clear cold sky. But there was Mrs. Topham with her stolen watch and her malicious good manners, huddled up in the cottage next door and spoiling everything.

Put it out of your mind! No good brooding over it: put it out of your mind!

Dorothy Brant braced herself and got out of bed, reaching for her dressing gown and slippers. But it was not her dressing gown she found draped across the chair; it was her heavy fur coat. And there were a pair of soft-leather slippers. They were a pair of soft-leather moccasins, ornamented with beadwork, which Harry had brought back from the States; but now the undersides were cold, damp, and stiff, almost frozen. That was when a subconscious fear struck at her, took possession, and would not leave.

Closing the window, she padded out to the bathroom. The small cottage, with its crisp white curtains and smell of old wood, was so quiet that she could hear voices talking downstairs. It was a mumble in which no words were distinguishable: Harry's quick tenor, her father's slower and heavier voice, and another she could not identify, but which was slowest and heaviest of all.

What was wrong? She hurried through her bath and through her dressing. Not only were they up but they must be getting their own breakfast, for she could smell coffee boiling. And she was very slow; in spite of nine hours' sleep she felt as edgy and washed-out as though she had been up all night.

Giving a last jerk of the comb through her brown bobbed hair, putting on no powder or lipstick, she ran downstairs. At the door of the living room she stopped abruptly. Inside were her father, her cousin Harry, and the local Superintendent of Police.

"Good morning, miss," said the Superintendent.

She never forgot the look of that little room or the look on the faces of those in it. Sunlight poured into it, touching the bright-colored rough-woven rugs, the rough stone fireplace. Through side windows she could see out across the snow-covered lawn to where—twenty yards away and separated from them only by a tall laurel hedge, with a gateway—was Mrs. Topham's white weather-boarded cottage.

But what struck her with a shock of alarm as she came into the room was the sense of a conversation suddenly cut off; the look she surprised on their faces when they glanced around, quick and sallow, as a camera might have surprised it.

"Good morning, miss," repeated Superintendent Mason saluting.

Harry Ventnor intervened, in a kind of agony. His naturally high color was higher still; even his large feet and bulky shoulders, his small sinewy hands, looked agitated.

"Don't say anything, Dolly!" he urged. "Don't say anything! They can't make you say anything. Wait until——"

"I certainly think——" began her father slowly. He looked down his nose, and then along the side of his pipe, everywhere except at Dorothy. "I certainly think," he went on, clearing his throat, "that it would be as well not to speak hastily until——"

"*If* you please, sir," said Superintendent Mason, clearing his own throat. "Now, miss, I'm afraid I must ask you some questions. But it is my duty to tell you that you need not answer my questions until you have seen your solicitor."

"Solicitor? But I don't want a solicitor. What on earth should I want with a solicitor?"

Superintendent Mason looked meaningly at her father and Harry Ventnor, as though bidding them to mark that.

"It's about Mrs. Topham, miss."

"Oh!"

"Why do you say 'Oh'?"

"Go on, please. What is it?"

"I understand, miss, that you and Mrs. Topham had 'words' yesterday? A bit of a dust-up, like?"

"Yes, you could certainly call it that."

"May I ask what about?"

"I'm sorry," said Dorothy; "I can't tell you that. It would only give the old cat an opportunity to say I had been slandering her. So that's it! What has she been telling you?"

"Why, miss," said Superintendent Mason, taking out a pencil and scratching the side of his jaw with it, "I'm afraid she's not exactly in a condition to tell us anything. She's in a nursing home at Guildford, rather badly smashed up round the head. Just between ourselves, it's touch and go whether she'll recover."

First Dorothy could not feel her heart beating at all, and then it seemed to pound with enormous rhythm. The Superintendent was looking at her steadily. She forced herself to say:

"You mean she's had an accident?"

"Not exactly, miss. The doctor says she was hit three or four times with that big glass paperweight you may have seen on the table at her cottage. Eh?"

"You don't mean—you don't mean somebody *did* it? Deliberately? But who did it?"

"Well, miss," said Superintendent Mason, looking at her still harder until he became a huge Puritan face with a small mole beside his nose. "I'm bound to tell you that by everything we can see so far, it looks as though you did it."

This wasn't happening. It couldn't be. Afterward she remembered, in a detached kind of way, studying all of them: the little lines around Harry's eyes in the sunlight, the hastily brushed light hair, the loose leather wind-jacket whose zip fastener was half undone. She remembered thinking that despite his athletic prowess he looked ineffectual and a little foolish. But then her own father was not of much use now.

She heard her own voice. "But that's absurd!"

"I hope so, miss. I honestly hope so. Now tell me: were you out of this house last night?"

"When?"

"At any time."

"Yes. No. I don't know. Yes, I think I was."

"For God's sake, Dolly," said her father, "don't say anything more until we've got a lawyer here. I've telephoned to town; I didn't want to alarm you; I didn't even wake you—there's some explanation for this. There must be!"

It was not her own emotion; it was the wretchedness of his face which held her. Bulky, semi-bald, worried about business, worried about everything else in this world—that was John Brant. His crippled left arm and black glove were pressed against his side. He stood in the bright pool of sunlight, a face of misery.

"I've—seen her," he explained. "It wasn't pretty. Not that I haven't seen worse. In the war." He touched his arm. "But you're a little girl, Dolly; you're only a little girl. You couldn't have done that."

His plaintive tone asked for confirmation.

"Just one moment, sir," interposed Superintendent Mason. "Now, miss! You tell me you *were* outside the house last night?"

"Yes."

"In the snow?"

"Yes, yes!"

"Do you remember the time?"

"No, I don't think so."

"Tell me, miss: what size shoes do you wear?"

"Four."

"That's a rather small size, isn't it?" When she nodded dumbly, Superintendent Mason shut up his notebook. "Now, if you'll just come with me?"

The cottage had a side door. Without putting his fingers on the knob, Mason twisted the spindle around and opened it. The overhang of the eaves had kept clear the two steps leading down; but beyond, a thin coating of snow lay like a plaster over the world between here and the shuttered cottage across the way.

There were two strings of footprints in that snow. Dorothy knew whose they were. Hardened and sharp-printed, one set of prints moved out snakily from the steps, passed under the arch of the powdered laurel hedge, and stopped at the steps to the side door of Mrs. Topham's house. Another set of the same tracks—a little blurred, spaced at longer intervals where the person had evidently been running desperately—came back from the cottage to these steps.

That mute sign of panic stirred Dorothy's memory. It wasn't a dream. She had done it. Subconsciously she had known it all the time. She could remember other things: the fur coat clasped around her pajamas, the sting of the snow to wet slippers, the blind rush in the dark.

"Yours, miss?" inquired Superintendent Mason.

"Yes. Oh, yes, they're mine."

"Easy, miss," muttered the Superintendent. "You're looking a bit white around the gills. Come in here and sit down; I won't hurt you." Then his own tone grew petulant. Or perhaps something in the heavy simplicity of the girl's manner penetrated his official bearing. "But why did you do it, miss? Lord, why did you do it? That's to say, breaking open that desk of hers to get a handful of trinkets not worth ten quid for the lot? And then not even taking the trouble to mess up your footprints afterward!" He coughed, checking himself abruptly.

John Brant's voice was acid. "Good, my friend. Very good. The first sign of intelligence so far. I presume you don't suggest my daughter is insane?"

"No, sir. But they were her mother's trinkets, I hear."

"Where did you hear that? You, I suppose, Harry?"

Harry Ventnor pulled up the zip fastener of his wind-jacket as though girding himself. He seemed to suggest that he was the good fellow whom everybody was persecuting; that he wanted to be friends with the world, if they would only let him. Yet such sincerity blazed in his small features that it was difficult to doubt his good intentions.

"Now look here, old boy. I *had* to tell them, didn't I? It's no good trying to hide things like that. I know that, just from reading those stories——"

"Stories!"

"All right: say what you like. They always find out, and then they make it worse than it really was." He let this sink in. "I tell you, you're going about it in the wrong way. Suppose Dolly did have a row with the Topham about that jewelry? Suppose she *did* go over there last night? Suppose those are her footprints? Does that prove she bashed the Topham? Not that a public service wasn't done; but why couldn't it have been a burglar just as well?"

Superintendent Mason shook his head. "Because it couldn't, sir."

"But why? I'm asking you, why?"

"There's no harm in telling you that, sir, if you'll just listen. You probably remember that it began to snow last night at a little past eleven o'clock."

"No, I don't. We were all in bed by then."

"Well, you can take my word for it," Mason told him patiently. "I was up half the night at the police station; and it did. It stopped snowing about midnight. You'll have to take my word for that too, but we can easily prove it. You see, sir, Mrs. Topham was alive and in very good health at well after midnight. I know that too, because she rang up the police station and said she was awake and nervous and thought there were burglars in the neighborhood. Since the lady does that same thing," he explained with a certain grimness, "on the average of about three times a month, I don't stress *that*. What I am telling you is that her call came in at 12:10, at least ten minutes after the snow had stopped."

Harry hesitated, and the Superintendent went on with the same patient air: "Don't you see it, sir? Mrs. Topham wasn't attacked until after the snow stopped. Round her cottage now there's twenty yards of clean, clear, unmarked snow in every direction. The only marks in that snow, the only marks of any kind at all, are the footprints Miss Brant admits she made herself."

Then he looked at them in exasperation.

" 'Tisn't as though anybody else could have made the tracks. Even if Miss Brant didn't admit it herself, I'm absolutely certain nobody else did. You, Mr. Ventnor, wear size ten shoes. Mr. Brant wears size nine. Walk in size four tracks? Ayagh! And yet somebody did get into that cottage with a key, bashed the old lady pretty murderously, robbed her desk, and got away again. If there are no other tracks or marks of any kind in the snow, who did it? Who must have done it?"

Dorothy could consider it, now, in almost a detached way. She remembered the paperweight with which Mrs. Topham had been struck. It lay on the table in Mrs. Topham's stuffy parlor, a heavy glass globe with a tiny landscape inside. When you shook the glass globe, a miniature snowstorm rose within—which seemed to make the attack all the more horrible.

She wondered if she had left any fingerprints on it. But over everything rose Renée Topham's face, Renée Topham, her mother's bosom friend.

"I hated her," said Dorothy; and, unexpectedly, she began to cry.

Dennis Jameson, of the law firm of Morris, Farnsworth & Jameson, Lincoln's Inn Fields, shut up his brief case with a snap. He was putting on his hat and coat when Billy Farnsworth looked into the office.

"Hullo!" said Farnsworth. "You off to Surrey over that Brant business?"

"Yes."

"H'm. Believe in miracles, do you?"

"No."

"That girl's guilty, my lad. You ought to know that."

"It's our business," said Jameson, "to do what we can for our clients."

Farnsworth looked at him shrewdly. "I see in your ruddy cheek that quixotry is alive again. Young idealist storms to relief of good-looker in distress, swearing to———"

"I've met her twice," said Jameson. "I like her, yes. But, merely using a small amount of intelligence on this, I can't see that they've got such a thundering good case against her."

"Oh, my lad!"

"Well, look at it. What do they say the girl did? This Mrs. Topham was struck several times with a glass paperweight. There are no fingerprints on the paperweight, which shows signs of having been wiped. But, after having the forethought to wipe her fingerprints carefully off the paperweight, Dorothy Brant then walks back to her cottage and leaves behind two sets of footprints which could be seen by aerial observation a mile up. Is that reasonable?"

Farnsworth looked thoughtful. "Maybe they would say she isn't reasonable," he pointed out. "Never mind the psychology. What you've got to get around are the physical facts. Here is the mysterious widow Topham entirely alone in the house; the only servant comes in by day. Here are one person's footprints. Only that girl could have made the tracks; and, in fact, admits she did. It's a physical impossibility for anybody else to have entered or left the house. How do you propose to get around that?"

"I don't know," said Jameson rather hopelessly. "But I want to hear her side of it first. The only thing nobody seems to have heard, or even to be curious about, is what she thinks herself."

Yet, when he met her at the cottage late that afternoon, she cut the ground from under his feet.

Twilight was coming down when he turned in at the gate, a bluish twilight in which the snow looked gray. Jameson stopped a moment at the gate, and stared across at the thin laurel hedge dividing this property from Mrs. Topham's. There was nothing remarkable about this hedge, which was some six feet high and cut through by a gateway like a Gothic arch. But in front of the arch, peering up at the snow-coated side of the hedge just above it, stood a large figure in cap and waterproof. Somehow he looked familiar. At his elbow another man, evidently the local Superintendent of Police, was holding up a camera; and a flash-bulb glared against the sky. Though he was too far away to hear anything, Jameson had a queer impression that the large man was laughing uproariously.

Harry Ventnor, whom he knew slightly, met Jameson at the door.

"She's in there," Harry explained, nodding toward the front room. "Er—don't upset her, will you? Here, what the devil are they doing with that hedge?"

He stared across the lawn.

"Upset her?" said Jameson with some asperity. "I'm here, if possible, to help her. Won't you or Mr. Brant give some assistance? Do you honestly think that Miss Brant in her rational senses could have done what they say she did?"

"In her rational senses?" repeated Harry. After looking at Jameson in a curious way, he said no more; he turned abruptly and hurried off across the lawn.

Yet Dorothy, when Jameson met her, gave no impression of being out of her rational senses. It was her straightforwardness he had always liked, the straightforwardness which warmed him now. They sat in the homely, firelit room, by the fireplace over which were the silver cups to denote Harry's athletic and gymnastic prowess, and the trophies of John Brant's earlier days at St. Moritz. Dorothy herself was an outdoor girl.

"To advise me?" she said. "You mean, to advise me what to say when they arrest me?"

"Well, they haven't arrested you yet, Miss Brant."

She smiled at him. "And yet I'll bet that surprises you, doesn't it? Oh, I know how deeply I'm in! I suppose they're only poking about to get more evidence. And then there's a new man here, a man named March, from Scotland Yard. I feel almost flattered."

Jameson sat up. He knew now why that immense figure by the hedge had seemed familiar. "Not Colonel March?"

"Yes. Rather a nice person, really," answered Dorothy, shading her eyes with her hand. Under her light tone he felt that her nerves were raw. "Then again, they've been all through my room. And they can't find the watch and the brooch and the rings I'm supposed to have stolen from Aunt Renée Topham. Aunt Renée!"

"So I've heard. But that's the point—what are they getting at? A watch and a brooch and a couple of rings! Why should you steal that from anybody, let alone from her?"

"Because they weren't hers," said Dorothy, suddenly looking up with a white face, and speaking very fast. "They belonged to my mother."

"Steady."

"My mother is dead," said Dorothy. "I suppose it wasn't just the watch and the rings, really. That was the excuse, the breaking point, the thing that brought it on. My mother was a great friend of Mrs. Topham. It was 'Aunt Renée' this and 'Aunt Renée,' that, while my mother was alive to pamper her. But my mother wanted me to have those trinkets, such as they were. Dear Aunt Renée Topham coolly appropriated them, as she appropriates everything else she can. I never knew what had happened to them until yesterday.

"Do you know that kind of woman? Mrs. Topham is really charming, aristocratic and charming, with the cool charm that takes all it can get and expects to go on getting it. I know for a fact that she's really got a lot of money, though what she does with it I can't imagine: and the real reason why she buries herself in the country is that she's too mean to risk spending it in town. I never could endure her. Then, when my mother died and I didn't go on pampering Aunt Renée as she thought I should, it was a very different thing. How that woman loves to talk about us! Harry's debts and my father's shaky business. And *me*."

She checked herself again, smiling at him. "I'm sorry to inflict all this on you."

"You're not inflicting anything on me."

"But it's rather ridiculous, isn't it?"

" 'Ridiculous,' " said Jameson grimly, "is not the word I should apply to it. So you had a row with her?"

"Oh, a glorious row. A beautiful row. The grandmother of all rows."

"When?"

"Yesterday. When I saw her wearing my mother's watch."

She looked at the fire, over which the silver cups glimmered.

"Maybe I said more than I should have," she went on. "But I got no support from my father or Harry. I don't blame Dad: he's so worried about business, and that bad arm of his troubles him so much sometimes that all he wants is peace and quiet. As for Harry, *he* doesn't really like her; but she took rather a fancy to him, and that flatters him. He's a kind of male counterpart of Aunt Renée. Out of a job?—well, depend on somebody else. And I'm in the middle of all this. It's 'Dolly, do this,' and 'Dolly, do that,' and 'Good old Dolly; she won't mind.' But I do mind. When I saw that woman standing there wearing my mother's watch, and saying commiserating things about the fact that we couldn't afford a servant, I felt that something ought to be done about it. So I suppose I must have done something about it."

Jameson reached out and took her hands. "All right," he said. "What did you do?"

"I don't know! That's just the trouble."

"But surely——"

"No. That was one of the things Mrs. Topham always had such sport with. You don't know much when you walk in your sleep.

"Ridiculous, isn't it?" she went on, after another pause. "Utterly ludicrous. But not to me! Not a bit. Ever since I was a child, when I've been overtired or nervously exhausted, it's happened. Once I came downstairs and built and lit a fire in the dining room, and set the table for a meal. I admit it doesn't happen often, and never before with results like this." She tried to laugh. "But why do you think my father and Harry looked at me like that? That's the worst of it. I really don't know whether I'm a near-murderer or not."

This was bad.

Jameson admitted that to himself, even as his reason argued against it. He got up to prowl around the room, and her brown eyes never left him. He could not look away; he saw the tensity of her face in every corner.

"Look here," he said quietly, "this is nonsense."

"Oh, please. Don't you say that. It's not very original."

"But do you seriously think you went for that woman and still don't know anything about it now?"

"Would it be more difficult than building a fire?"

"I didn't ask you that. *Do* you think you did it?"

"No," said Dorothy.

That question did it. She trusted him now. There was understanding and sympathy between them, a mental force and communication that could be felt as palpably as the body gives out heat.

"Deep down inside me, no, I don't believe it. I think I should have waked up. And there was no—well, no blood on me, you know. But how are you going to get around the evidence?"

The evidence. Always the evidence.

"I did go across there. I can't deny that. I remember half waking up as I was coming back. I was standing in the middle of the lawn in the snow. I had on my fur coat over my pajamas; I remember feeling snow on my face and my wet slippers under me. I was shivering. And I remember running back. That's all. If I didn't do it, how could anybody else have done it?"

"I beg your pardon," interposed a new voice. "Do you mind if, both figuratively and literally, I turn on the light?"

Dennis Jameson knew the owner of that voice. There was the noise of someone fumbling after an electric switch; then, in homely light, Colonel March beamed and basked. Colonel March's seventeen stone was swathed around in a waterproof as big as a tent. He wore a large tweed cap. Under this his speckled face glowed in the cold; and he was smoking, with gurgling relish, the large-bowled pipe which threatened to singe his sandy mustache.

"Ah, Jameson!" he said. He took the pipe out of his mouth and made a gesture with it. "So it *was* you. I thought I saw you come in. I don't want to intrude; but I think there are at least two things that Miss Brant ought to know."

Dorothy turned around quickly.

."First," pursued Colonel March, "that Mrs. Topham is out of danger. She is at least able, like an after-dinner speaker, to say a few words; though with about as much coherence. Second, that out on your lawn there is one of the queerest objects I ever saw in my life."

Jameson whistled. "You've met this fellow?" he said to Dorothy. "He is the head of the Department of Queer Complaints. When they come across something outlandish, which may be a hoax or a joke but, on the other hand, may be a serious crime, they shout for him. His mind is so obvious that he hits it every time. To my certain knowledge he has investigated a disappearing room, chased a walking corpse, and found an invisible piece of furniture. If he goes so far as to admit that a thing is a bit unusual, you can look out for squalls."

Colonel March nodded quite seriously. "Yes," he said. "That is why I am here, you see. They thought we might be interested in that footprint."

"That footprint?" cried Dorothy. "You mean——?"

"No, no; not your footprint, Miss Brant. Another one. Let me explain. I want you, both of you, to look out of the window; I want you to take a look at the laurel hedge between this cottage and the other. The light is almost gone, but study it."

Jameson went to the window and peered out.

"Well?" he demanded. "What about it? It's a hedge."

"As you so shrewdly note, it is a hedge. Now let me ask you a question. Do you think a person could walk along the top of that hedge?"

"Good lord, no!"

"No? Why not?"

"I don't see the joke," said Jameson, "but I'll make the proper replies. Because the hedge is only an inch or two thick. It wouldn't support a cat. If you tried to stand on it, you'd come through like a ton of bricks."

"Quite true. Then what would you say if I told you that someone weighing at least twelve stone must have climbed up the side of it?"

Nobody answered him; the thing was so obviously unreasonable that nobody could answer.

Dorothy Brant and Dennis Jameson looked at each other.

"For," said Colonel March, "it would seem that somebody at least climbed up there. Look at the hedge again. You see the arch cut in for a gate? Just above that, in the snow along the side of the hedge, there are traces of a footprint. It is a large footprint. I think it can be identified by the heel, though most of it is blurred and sketchy."

Walking quickly and heavily, Dorothy's father came into the room. He started to speak, but seemed to change his mind at the sight of Colonel March. He went over to Dorothy, who took his arm.

"Then," insisted Jameson, "somebody did climb up on the hedge?"

"I doubt it," said Colonel March. "How could he?"

Jameson pulled himself together. "Look here, sir," he said quietly. " 'How could he?' is correct. I never knew you to go on like this without good reason. I know it must have some bearing on the case. But I don't care if somebody climbed up on the hedge. I don't care if he danced the tango on it. The hedge leads nowhere. It doesn't lead to Mrs. Topham's; it only divides the two properties. The point is, how did somebody manage to get from here to that other cottage —across sixty feet of unbroken snow—without leaving a trace on it?

I ask you that because I'm certain you don't think Miss Brant is guilty."

Colonel March looked apologetic. "I know she isn't," he answered.

In Dorothy Brant's mind was again that vision of the heavy paperweight inside which, as you shook it, a miniature snowstorm arose. She felt that her own wits were being shaken and clouded in the same way.

"I knew Dolly didn't do it," said John Brant, suddenly putting his arm around his daughter's shoulder. "I knew that. I told them so. But——"

Colonel March silenced him. "The real thief, Miss Brant, did not want your mother's watch and brooch and chain and rings. It may interest you to know what he did want. He wanted about fifteen hundred pounds in notes and gold sovereigns, tucked away in that same shabby desk. You seem to have wondered what Mrs. Topham did with her money. That is what she did with it. Mrs. Topham, by the first words she could get out in semi-consciousness, was merely a common or garden variety of miser. That dull-looking desk in her parlor was the last place any burglar would look for a hoard. Any burglar, that is, except one."

"Except one?" repeated John Brant, and his eyes seemed to turn inward.

A sudden ugly suspicion came to Jameson.

"Except one who knew, yes. You, Miss Brant, had the blame deliberately put on you. There was no malice in it. It was simply the easiest way to avoid pain and trouble to the gentleman who did it.

"Now hear what you really did, Miss Brant," said Colonel March, his face darkening. "You did go out into the snow last night. But you did not go over to Mrs. Topham's; and you did not make those two artistic sets of footprints in the snow. When you tell us in your own story that you felt snow sting on your face as well as underfoot, it requires no vast concentration, surely, to realize that the snow was still falling. You went out into it, like many sleepwalkers; you were shocked into semi-consciousness by the snow and the cold air; and you returned long before the end of the snowfall, which covered any real prints you may have made.

"The real thief—who was very much awake—heard you come back and tumble into bed. He saw a heaven-sent opportunity to blame you for a crime you might even think you had committed. He slipped in and took the slippers out of your room. And, when the snow had stopped, he went across to Mrs. Topham's. He did not mean to attack her. But she was awake and surprised him; and so, of course, Harry Ventnor struck her down."

"Harry———" The word, which Dorothy had said almost at a scream, was checked. She looked around quickly at her father; then she stared straight ahead; then she began to laugh.

"Of course," said Colonel March. "As usual, he was letting his—what is it?—his 'good old Dolly' take the blame."

A great cloud seemed to have left John Brant; but the fussed and worried look had not left him. He blinked at Colonel March.

"Sir," he said, "I would give my good arm to prove what you say. That boy has caused me half the trouble I ever had. But are you raving mad?"

"No."

"I tell you he couldn't have done it! He's Emily's son, my sister's son. He may be a bad lot; but he's not a magician."

"You are forgetting," said Colonel March, "a certain size-ten footprint. You are forgetting that interesting sight, a smeared and blurred size-ten foot print on the side of a hedge which would not have held up a cat. A remarkable footprint. A disembodied footprint."

"But that's the whole trouble," roared the other. "The two lines of tracks in the snow were made by a size four shoe! Harry couldn't have made them, any more than I could. It's a physical impossibility. Harry wears size ten. You don't say he could get his feet into flat leather moccasins which would fit my daughter?"

"No," said Colonel March. "But he could get his hands into them."

There was a silence. The Colonel wore a dreamy look, almost a pleased look.

"And in this unusual but highly practical pair of gloves," the Colonel went on, "Harry Ventnor simply walked across to the other cottage on his hands. No more than that. For a trained gymnast—as those silver cups will indicate—it was nothing. For a rattle-brained gentleman who needed money it was ideal. He crossed in a thin coating of snow, which would show no difference in weight. Doorsteps, cleared of snow by the overhanging roof, protected him at either end when he stood upright. He had endless opportunities to get a key to the side door. Unfortunately, there was that rather low archway in the hedge. Carrying himself on his hands, his feet were curved up and back over the arch of his body to balance him; he blundered, and smeared that disembodied footprint on the side of the hedge. To be quite frank, I am delighted with the device. It is crime upside down; it is leaving a footprint in the sky; it is———"

"A fair cop, sir," concluded Superintendent Mason, sticking his head in at the door. "They got him on the other side of Guildford. He must have smelled something wrong when he saw us taking photographs. But he had the stuff on him."

Dorothy Brant stood looking for a long time at the large, untidy blimp of a man who was still chuckling with pleasure.

Then she joined in.

"I trust," observed Dennis Jameson politely, "that everybody is having a good time. For myself, I've had a couple of unpleasant shocks today; and just for a moment I was afraid I should have another one. For a moment I honestly thought you were going to pitch on Mr. Brant."

"So did I," agreed Dorothy, and beamed at her father. "That's why it's so funny now."

John Brant looked startled—but not half so startled as Colonel March.

"Now there," the Colonel said, "I honestly do not understand you. I am the Department of Queer Complaints. If you have a ghost in your attic or a footprint on top of your hedge, ring me up. But a certain success has blessed us because, as Mr. Jameson says, I look for the obvious. And Lord love us!—if you have decided that a crime was committed by a gentleman who could walk on his hands, I will hold under torture that you are not likely to succeed by suspecting the one person in the house who has a crippled arm."